UNANIMOUS PRAISE FOR LYNN S. HIGHTOWER'S ELAKI NOVELS...

"ONE OF THE BEST NEW SERIES IN THE GENRE!"
—*Science Fiction Chronicle*

ALIEN BLUES

The smash debut novel—introducing homicide detective David Silver and String, the partner from another planet...

"A GRITTILY REALISTIC AND DOWN-AND-DIRTY SERIAL KILLER NOVEL...IMPRESSIVE!"
—*Locus*

ALIEN EYES

The exciting return of homicide detective David Silver and his Elaki partner, String—a shocking case of interstellar violence brought to a new battleground: Earth...

"COMPLEX...SNAPPY...ORIGINAL!"
—*Asimov's Science Fiction*

ALIEN HEAT

Silver and String are back, investigating arsonists and interstellar real estate investors who may well be part of a massive, bizarre cult...

"AN INTRIGUING WORLD!"
—*Analog*

Ace Books by Lynn S. Hightower

ALIEN BLUES
ALIEN EYES
ALIEN HEAT

Alien Eyes

Lynn S. Hightower

ACE BOOKS, NEW YORK

If you purchased this book without a cover you should be aware that this book is stolen property. It was reported as "unsold and destroyed" to the publisher and neither the author nor the publisher has received any payment for this "stripped book."

This book is an Ace original edition,
and has never been previously published.

ALIEN EYES

An Ace Book / published by arrangement with
the author

PRINTING HISTORY
Ace edition / February 1993

All rights reserved.
Copyright © 1993 by Lynn S. Hightower.
Cover art by Michael Herring.
This book may not be reproduced in whole or in part,
by mimeograph or any other means, without permission.
For information address: The Berkley Publishing Group,
200 Madison Avenue, New York, NY 10016.

ISBN: 0-441-01688-X

Ace Books are published by The Berkley Publishing Group,
200 Madison Avenue, New York, New York 10016.
The name "ACE" and the "A" logo
are trademarks belonging to Charter Communications, Inc.

PRINTED IN THE UNITED STATES OF AMERICA

10 9 8 7 6 5 4 3 2

This one is for Scott

The light that lies
In women's eyes,
Has been my heart's undoing.
—Thomas Moore, *The Time I've Lost in Wooing*

Each man kills the thing he loves.
—Oscar Wilde, *The Ballad of Reading Gaol*

ONE

IT WAS GOING TO BE A HEARTBREAKER. IN A NICE NEIGHBORHOOD, where things like this didn't happen.

David moved across the ivy ground cover, plants tearing underfoot. The SWAT team was supposed to be on call only, but they'd already taken positions around the house. An ambulance stood by, red lights pulsing. People and Elaki pressed against the barriers. If the Mother-One inside hadn't freaked already, she was going to.

"Yo, David."

A shrill whistle caught his attention, and he narrowed his eyes, searching through the noise and bright lights for his partner, Mel Burnett.

Mel stood under the eaves of the small front porch. The late-afternoon sun sent rainbows of color through the scalelike shingles on the side of the house. The Elaki shockee was tall and narrow.

Mel handed David a vest. "Captain said wear it."

"She armed?"

Mel blew air through his nose. "Six millimeter Glock with ablative sheath bullets."

"So much for that." David tossed the vest behind a bush. "What's she saying? Got any background?"

"Captain sent String in before you got here. Figured Elaki to Elaki, right? Ever see an Elaki Mother-One have a shit fit? She thinks we're all Izicho secret police."

"Izicho not a secret. Elaki enforcement, all aboveboard."

David turned, saw String, raised a hand.

"All aboveboard unless they decide to cho you off in the night," Mel said.

"You all right?" David asked.

String rippled, shedding scales. He was tall, as were most Elaki, roughly seven and a half feet. His inner pink coloring had a yellow tint, and there was a certain rigidity in his normally fluid stance.

He teetered back and forth on his bottom fringe.

"I want only to help," String said. "Is most distressing. She must know Izicho not hurt the Mother-One."

"Not what she said." Mel scratched his left armpit.

"Kids inside?" David felt sweat in the small of his back. It was hot out.

"Pouchlings, yes," String said. "Four of them."

"Four?"

"Big litter," Mel said.

String's eye stalks swiveled toward Mel. "Large birthing."

A helicopter passed overhead, blades thudding.

"Aw shit," Mel said. "Press is here. It's official; we're a circus."

"Media blackout," David said.

"You'll get reamed for it."

"Blackout." David looked over Mel's shoulder. "Della? Good. See the techs. Media blackout."

Della was compactly built, her hair done in cornrows. She put a hand on her hip. "David, don't we got trouble enough?"

He ignored her. "Mikes in place? Cameras?"

She nodded and handed him a headset. "Captain's got a command post a mile up the road. Want to ask him about the . . . okay, no you don't. He'll be feeding me info whenever he gets it, and I'll be watching all the monitors and feeding it to you. Soon as I'm in the truck you go."

"Do it," David said. He handed his gun to Mel. "I want you right behind me. I don't want to scare her, so I'm going in raw. If we have to kill her to save the kids, I want you to do the snipe."

Mel frowned, chewed his lip. Nodded.

"Trust me to call it?" David said.

"Be right behind you."

David put the set in his ears, and Della's voice came through immediately.

" . . . ready for takeoff. David?"

"Yeah, Della, I'm here."

"Okay, good, you're coming through. Wait a sec." Her voice was muffled. "Okay. I got you on the screen."

David looked at String. "Any advice?"

String's belly slits flared. The Elaki was an unattractive specimen, his scales patchy, his left eye prong drooping.

"She is badly alone," String said. "Neighbors say no visits from chemaki. This is Elaki—"

"Family?"

String teetered on his fringe. "Something like. Sex group—"

"Dance partners," Mel said.

"Not sex the human relationship. Elaki responsibility and friendship and procreation connections."

"Where'd she get the gun?" Mel asked.

"Not known, and very odd," String said. "*Please* to see to the pouchlings."

"What's her name?" David asked. A fly buzzed his ear and he batted it away.

"Packer."

"Her *Elaki* name."

"Dahmi."

David nodded. "Going in."

The front door was ajar. David pushed it open. His hand shook, just a little. The door hinge groaned softly.

It was dark inside, the temperature over ninety. Sweat coated David's cheeks and slid down his back. The ceiling was high, the hallway so narrow David could touch both walls without stretching.

"Dahmi?"

The heels of his shoes were loud on the ochre-colored clay tiles that Elaki favored. Mel was silent behind him.

"She's close," Della said. "Kitchen on the right, some kind of little room on the left. The hall turns a little to the left, yeah, the left, and opens into the living room. She's in there."

"The kids?"

"Not sure. Pouchlings are hard to pick up, but we get bursts of something in back. No window in the living room, but there's a small one in the bedroom. We got a snipe set up from there."

"Lose it."

"Captain's orders, Silver."

Noise came from the living room, a one-note, whispery whistle that made him stop and listen.

"Dahmi?" David said. He swallowed.

The noise stopped.

David paused where the hall turned to the left, looked at Mel, mouthed the word "stay." Mel nodded once, his back to the wall. The whistling noise started again.

David moved down the short, dark hallway into the living room.

The Elaki Mother-One was backed into a corner. Her eye stalks were rigid, the pistol held snugly in extruded sections of her right fin. The whistling noise came from the oxygen slits in her belly. She was pressed against the wall, like a boneless, beached fish. Scales littered the floor around her, iridescent, catching the light that came from slits in the walls.

"Izzzzzicho," the Elaki whispered.

David looked over his shoulder, hoping for a glimpse of the pouchlings. He could barely breathe in here. Why had she turned off the air conditioning?

"Dahmi?" He kept his voice gentle. "My name is David. I thought maybe you could use some help. The Elaki Mother-One next door called me in. She wanted me to check and see if you needed anything. She said she hasn't seen you in a couple of days, hasn't seen your little ones running around. She said you wouldn't come to the door."

"Izzzicho."

"No, Dahmi, I'm not Izicho. I'm David. David Silver. I'm a detective with the Saigo City PD."

"Izicho *coming.*"

"No. Nobody's coming. Just you and me, Dahmi. Just to talk." Just to keep you from killing your children, he thought.

David glanced over his shoulder. There was a familiar feeling here, one he didn't like. His mind brought the memory of the woman who had drowned her baby in the toilet and kept the body in the living room for six weeks. Paranoid delusional, the experts had said. David remembered the small efficiency apartment, and the woman crying and talking about getting pregnant again.

David smiled gently. "Dahmi, how many kids . . . how many pouchlings do you have?"

A wonder, how friendly and conversational he sounded.

The Elaki watched him. "My little baby ones."

"I've got three kids myself," David said. He moved closer, watching from the corner of his eye. Another few steps and he'd be able to see into the bedroom. "All girls. It must be hard for you, taking care of four pouchlings all alone."

"Alone," Dahmi said. "Little baby ones." Her voice was young and tired.

David moved closer. "I bet you spoil them, don't you?"

"Four."

"Four?" David said. "You have four pouchlings?"

"Four."

"You must be proud of them."

"Little baby ones. Proud?"

"Love them, feel good about them, like to show them off."

"Proud," Dahmi said. "So proud of little baby ones."

"Why don't you let me take the pouchlings next door for a while? Then you and I can talk. I think you need somebody just to talk to." David glanced over his shoulder. "Are the little ones in the bedroom? They back that way?"

"Little baby ones."

The light in the bedroom was off. No noise. Dim gloom. The pouchlings might be very quiet if they were afraid. They could well be all right, just frightened.

David wiped his palms on the sides of his jeans. The hair on his arms felt prickly. "Dahmi, I'm going to check on the kids, okay?"

She surged forward, the pistol pointed at his neck. "No one hurt my pouchlings."

"No." He took a breath, held his hands up. His heart was beating—faster, faster. "No one's going to hurt your pouchlings."

"Cannot hurt the pouchlings. No more cannot hurt the pouchlings."

He didn't like the sound of it.

"Do you, David Silver, you must . . ."

"I must what, Dahmi? Go on, sweetheart."

"The right . . . the . . . is it too much love, or not enough? How is it for the human?"

"It's hard for the human, Dahmi. It's hard for any parent. I know you're a good Mother-One, I know you love your pouchlings, but you need to let me go in and check on them. Put the gun down, Dahmi, okay? Want to set it down . . . okay, that's all right, just don't point it at me. You stay there, and I'll just look in on them."

"Wait," she said. "I come."

He waited, watching her belly plates ripple beneath her fringe, watching her move slowly across the tiles, her body tilting sideways in some odd manifestation of Elaki distress.

David glanced out the small square window. No sign of the cop who was there, waiting to kill.

He went in first, staying clear of Dahmi and the window. Elaki slept standing up. No bed in the room, no mattress. The room was dark, thick with odor. A white chenille cloth, lumpy underneath, was spread over something on the floor.

David's left fist clenched and unclenched.

"Cannot take them next door, David Silver."

"No," he said, and cleared his throat.

The Mother-One raised the Glock pistol, waving it from side to side. David knew that she meant him no harm. He also knew that Mel, and the cops outside, would see it another way.

It might be kindest to let her die.

Mel's voice echoed in his mind. Ablative sheath bullets.

The weapon came full circle, and the Elaki Mother-One aimed it at the delicate juncture of brain and nerve in her midsection. David leaped forward and grabbed her just as the fusillade broke out.

The thin, whippy body was easy to bring down. There were tinging noises as scales broke from the Elaki and showered the floor. The gun went off and David's shoulder burned. He covered Dahmi's fragile body with his. The window shattered, someone fired through the walls, and glass, wood splinters, and shingles rained upon his head. The Elaki mother trembled beneath him.

"Hold your fire," David yelled. The gunshots drowned him out. "Hold fire!"

No chance. The bullets stayed fast and furious. No one was going to quit shooting till the clips were spent. The walls shredded, and splinters showered the floor, in jagged, glistening fragments.

Silence suddenly, tense and expectant. David waved a hand in the air, and no one shot it. He lifted his head. A knot of cops in flak jackets peered in the window like juvenile delinquents.

"David?" Mel ran through the doorway. "You okay?"

The Glock pistol was too close to Dahmi. David snatched the weapon and took a deep breath.

"You were supposed to wait for my signal."

"Hell, David. I made a habit of waiting, you'd of been dead years ago."

There were more footsteps, pounding in the hall, and lights shining in the window. David reached for the white spread that was covered now, with bits of wood and glass. He peeled back the edge and looked, because he had to see for sure what he already knew.

He let the spread drop, and moved to shield Dahmi from the cops who crammed through the narrow doorway.

"Mel," he said. "Clear us a way. She's shocky; she may be hurt."

It was wrong to pick her up, but he couldn't leave her on the floor, the cops milling in the room, heavy with weapons, flak jackets, and attitude. He carried her out of the bedroom, and dodged the techs who were already filling the living room, setting up the nano machines that would sweep through the scene.

"C'mon," Mel said. "C'mon, let him through. Yeah, I mean you, asshole, we can go through you, just not around."

David went sideways, trying not to bump the rigid Elaki into the walls. Sweat poured off his forehead.

And then he was out, out of the small, dark house that dredged up black claustrophobic memories. It was cooler outside, dusk now. The glare of lights hit his face like a blow.

He blinked and looked around. Crime scene tape kept the crowd back, but the numbers had swelled, and they pressed close, taking in the details of his torn, sweaty shirt, his worn Levi's with the hole in the knee, the rigid Mother-One in his arms.

There were Elaki in the crowd. Knots of them. As one, they turned their backs, too polite to witness the shame of the Elaki Mother-One. A chopper boomed overhead, and a camera recorded every detail.

"Della!" David took a breath, hating the press of people. "I ordered blackout."

"And I overrode."

The voice was familiar and welcome, for all that it brought bad news. Captain Halliday looked tired, but not annoyed.

"Get that ambulance crew here!" Halliday shouted.

Three men wheeled a stretcher.

"Della, you ride shotgun," Halliday said. "Take care of things on our end. She may still be dangerous—"

"She's not dangerous," David said.

"Put her on the stretcher, David."

David set her down gently, grateful, for once, to be told what to do. She trembled. The attendant tightened a strap across her chest.

"You don't need it," David said. He glanced at Della and she nodded.

"Please," Dahmi said.

David crouched beside her. "Please what?"

"Please . . . nobody to hurt my pouchlings?"

David swallowed and nodded. "Nobody to hurt your pouchlings."

TWO

IT WAS A GENTLE KILLING.

The pouchlings were very small, very young; the size of puppies. Even from the doorway, David could see that they were clean, comfortably laid out on the floor, a small white cloth cushioning the eye stalks that had glazed in death approximately three days ago.

"You going to the hospital?"

David turned, saw Captain Halliday. The captain had put on a few pounds, but his face was still thin and pointed. His black silk tie, slightly askew, was so narrow it looked like a stripe down his midsection. He pushed his reading glasses up on his head and rubbed his eyes.

"While you're there," Halliday said, "better have your shoulder looked at."

"Shoulder?" David frowned at the balloon of blood that had soaked his shirt. "Aw, *hell*."

The coroner's tech, Miriam Kellog, looked up from the pouchlings. Her reddish-brown hair was tied back in a French braid.

"Is it bad?" she said. "Want me to look at it?"

"No, it's the *shirt*. Rose is going to kill me, she told me not to wear it to work. I forgot I had it on." He looked at Halliday. "You got anybody on the neighbors?"

"Mel and String doing either side of the house. Uniforms everywhere else. Just hope they get there before the media. They're like Japanese beetles out there."

David nodded. He squatted beside Miriam.

"Della's already back at the office with Pete," Halliday said. "Pounding the keyboard. They'll have background for you in a couple hours."

David cocked his head sideways, studying the faded pouchlings. "They look peaceful." He looked around the room, harsh now with spotlights, trying to remember it as it was before gunfire had torn it apart. He looked back at the pouchlings, all roughly the same size,

8

lying side by side, fins touching, bottom fringe tucked neatly. He frowned. "They been washed? Did she clean them up after she killed them?"

Miriam Kellog nodded. "Looks like. I'll get you a prelim in a few hours."

"Any ideas?"

"Maybe drowned them, maybe poison. Hard to tell."

David shook his head. "Unlikely. Elaki have odd hangups about water. And poison hurts."

"What do you think she did?" Miriam pushed a piece of hair out of her eyes. It stayed back for about a second, then drifted over her cheek.

David chewed his lip. His shoulder was starting to burn just a little, irritating, like a paper cut.

"My guess would be suffocation. She would wait until they were asleep, then hold a pillow over the belly slits. They would never know."

Miriam took a magnifying light and small forceps and pried open the belly slit of the pouchling on the end.

"Um." She moved to the next pouchling, and pried open another slit. A thin, yellowish fluid seeped out, emitting a faint, sour odor. Miriam held the slit open with the forceps, and, one-handed, selected a tweezer from her kit. She plucked something from the side of the slit and held it up. "Look at this."

"Fiber?"

Miriam nodded. "With a little luck, this'll tell us what she used to smother them. If that's what she did." She put the fiber in a specimen bag and muttered into her mike, then looked at David. "How'd you know?"

"She didn't want to hurt them," he said. "She just wanted to kill them."

Miriam turned back to her kit. "I wonder what made her snap."

David cocked his head to one side. "I'm not sure she did."

Miriam looked at him.

"Something scared her. I just wonder if it was real or in her head."

The emergency room at Bellmini General Hospital was clean, bright, and quiet. The waiting room smelled like flowers, with a tinge of the lime scent David associated with Elaki. One Elaki stood in the corner of the waiting room and looked out a window. David paused, and the glass double doors shushed behind him. He was hit with the aroma of rich, cinnamon-spicy coffee. Elaki made great coffee.

Trays of fruit, cheese, and taifu, an Elaki pastry, were positioned on a mahogany side table. David sighed. He was hungry.

A security guard rushed him before he got to the receiving desk.

"Sir, I think you made a mistake. The hospital you want is Euclid Central. Can I call a car for you?"

David flashed his badge. The guard, an old man with a burr haircut, blushed.

"Oh, my," he said. His eyes were tired. "I'm sorry."

"It's okay."

The old man nodded and moved away. He glanced over his shoulder. "Can I get you some coffee, Detective?"

"Please. Cream, no sugar."

The receptionist was human, a skinny blonde, her lips a thin, tight slash. She frowned at the blood on his shirt.

"Sir, we can't treat you here."

David walked past without a second look. He stepped off the thick black carpet, onto a white tile floor, and passed through double swing doors labeled EMERGENCY.

The staff was a mix, Elaki and human. An Elaki glided toward him, stethoscope wrapped around its waist.

"You need medical aid?" the Elaki said. The voice was feminine, warm. Her side slits were tight.

No Mother-One, David thought.

"Detective Silver." David flashed his badge. "I need to see—"

"Ah. You are the policeman. You wish to interrogate my patient?"

"Talk to her," David said.

"Did she . . ." the Elaki doctor hesitated. "Did she in real effect kill her pouchlings? I understand she cut them in half?"

David's voice was gentle. "Where is she?"

"Please to follow." The Elaki moved toward a white-curtained cubicle. The emergency-room doors opened and David heard a familiar voice.

"Hey, lady, do they pay you extra to be nasty, or do you do it free of charge?"

David turned around. String came into the ER, followed by Mel, who was cramming an Elaki pastry into his mouth.

"My associates," David said.

Mel waved and held up a foam cup. "Old guy out there told me to give this to you."

David waved it away. "Later," he said. "What did you find out?"

"She is ideal Mother-One," String said.

David looked at Mel, who shrugged. "He's right, David. Everybody says how great she was. She sounds perfect, other than the one thing."

"One thing?"

"You know. Killing the kids."

"String," David said. "I hate to say it, but—"

"I will stay here. She is most afraid the Izicho." His left eye prong drooped.

"See if you can get anything from the doctors," David said. "Mel, wipe the crumbs off your mouth."

Mel gulped down the last of the coffee. "Cinnamon." He grimaced. "Next time, David, you don't drink your coffee, order it black." He crumpled the cup and handed it to the Elaki doctor. "Take care of this for me, will you, sweetheart?"

David tried not to smile.

THREE

WIRES RAN FROM DAHMI'S MIDSECTION TO AN IVORY MACHINE on the table nearby. The S-curved hospital bed made David's back ache.

"Dahmi?" David said softly.

The Mother-One rustled in the bed. Heavy restraints had been buckled across her body, and thin strips of webbing ran from thick leather bands.

"I see they made you comfortable." Mel pulled up a chair and straddled it. "Jesus. David, surely all this ain't necessary."

David sat down on the other side of the bed. "Dahmi?"

The Elaki was rigid. Her eye stalks twitched.

"Izicho coming." Her voice dragged.

"She drugged?" Mel said. "This won't hold up, if she's drugged."

"It won't hold up anyway," David said. "Dahmi? All the pouch-lings are dead."

"Yes," Dahmi said. "All the little baby ones are safe now."

"Safe from what?" David said.

"Cho invasion."

David and Mel looked at each other. David felt a chill.

"Uh-oh," Mel said.

David scooted his chair closer. The Elaki tried to turn and shift, but the webbing held her tight.

"Please," she said. "I will not hurt them. Go home. Please to go home."

"Is there somebody we can call?" Mel said. "A friend. A . . ." He looked at David. "Somebody from your chemooki?"

"Chemaki," David said.

"Yeah," said Mel. "Chemaki."

"No one. All gone. All gone. *Guardians.*"

"The Guardians? What about the Guardians?" David asked.

The Elaki stilled and said nothing.

"Dahmi, what happened with the pouchlings?"

"Izicho."

"The Izicho killed them?"

"I kill them."

David kept his gaze steady. "You killed them, Dahmi? You killed your pouchlings?"

"I kill them."

"Why?" Mel asked.

"To keep them safe." Dahmi shifted, and the restraint buckles rattled. "Mikiki did not stay asleep." Her voice was raw, hoarse. *"Mikiki open him eyes."*

Outside Dahmi's cubicle, the noise level was rising. David stepped outside the curtains. Not exactly business as usual. There were few patients, but a profusion of personnel, many of them grouped around a small TV on the counter. There was an almost electric feel of excitement, and Elaki stood off together in groups, murmuring. David watched for belly ripples. Sure enough, he decided, looking around. Something they thought was funny.

David squinted at the television. The Elaki were tall, he could not see over their heads.

"David?"

String slid close, the Elaki doctor in tow.

"What's going on?" David said.

"Toilet paper," String said.

"At the Houston Stock Exchange," the doctor added. "Close it down one hour before time. A ton of toilet paper, dropping from the skies. Everything clogged."

"From ceiling," String said.

"Angel Eyes again?" David said. "The Guardians?"

"You need to ask?" Mel's voice was loud beside him.

"Is she not wonderful?" the Elaki doctor said.

"Childish," String said.

The Elaki doctor stiffened and twisted sideways, her eye stalks slanted at String. "I forget. You Izicho."

String said something in staccato syllables that David could not understand. It was rare for an Elaki to speak Home-tongue in front of a human, and it was only the second time David had heard it.

The Elaki doctor answered in kind, her voice a whistling hiss. David watched them grimly. So much for the heart-to-heart he wanted to have with the doctor.

He realized that the ER had gone suddenly quiet. He looked up and found them watching, looking from him to the television. He moved toward the screen.

He could not make out what the reporter was saying, but the image onscreen was clear. He saw himself emerging from the dark Elaki house, Dahmi in his arms.

He wondered if Rose was watching. He hoped she wouldn't notice the shirt.

FOUR

DAVID TURNED OFF THE TWO-LANE ROAD, BARELY MISSING THE deep pothole that festered outside his driveway. Gravel crackled beneath the tires.

Rose had been out doing yard work. There were pink begonias planted alongside the porch, and a hoe rested in the corner by the front door. She had set the lawn animals out. Mechanical squirrels and mule deer wandered sightlessly through the grass, chopping at the lawn with their sharply honed teeth.

The lawn animals made soft rustling noises. David didn't like them. No matter how often Rose told him the animals were safe, he insisted the children never be outside with them. He did not like to think of the sharp-bladed teeth anywhere near his daughters' plump, tiny toes.

God forbid little girls should wear shoes in the summertime.

For once, the children were waiting for him when he came through the door. They had given up waiting since the first cho invasion nineteen months ago, but tonight they were there.

They were ready for bed, all three wearing long, multicolored T-shirts, and all of them with plastic wires in their hair.

"What's this?" David said, bending down to hug them. In his mind's eye he saw the pouchlings, side by side, fins touching. "You get good reception with those things?"

"*Daddy,*" Lisa said. "Mommy says these curls will stay in two weeks, even when we get our hair wet. It'll just spring back."

"But they hurt." Mattie pulled at the wires that were already sagging in her fine, silky hair. "Come *mere,* Daddy. I got to kiss you." Her lips were soft and wet on his rough cheek. "And tell you I love you. Mommy says you have a bad day, and we gots to softy you up if we—"

"Shhhh." Kendra clapped a hand over her sister's mouth. "We saw you on TV, Daddy. How come you were holding that Elaki? Was it dead?"

"She," David said. "No. She's in the hospital."

15

"What's the matter with her?"

David looked at Kendra helplessly.

"She going to be all right?"

"Isn't it bedtime?" David said.

"I want a story," Mattie said.

"Kendra will read to you." David stood up.

"I want you, Daddy."

"Why can't she listen to a tape?"

"Do it," David said. He turned his back on his daughters and went to the kitchen. He ought to read to Mattie. He ought to read to all of them. He would do it tomorrow night, no matter how tired he was.

Rose had her back to him. "David?"

"Hi, sweet."

"Didn't figure on seeing you anytime soon. You home for the night?"

"Just a few hours."

She was crouched by the back door, bent over a new lawn animal. It was shaped like a calf, brown eyes and black nose painted wetly. The eyes blinked sleepily.

"What's wrong with it?" David asked. He opened the refrigerator.

"Its mother died."

"Ha. Did you cook tonight?" Dumb question, he thought.

"Just packages," Rose said absently. She glanced at him over her shoulder. "Saw you on the tube."

David put a hand over the bloody rip that had ruined the cotton designer shirt Rose had given him three weeks ago.

"I got hurt," he said.

"So I see. You ought to clean it up." Rose bent back over the lawn clipper. "Did that Elaki mother really kill her children?"

"Pouchlings," David said. "Yes."

"God, I wish they had the death penalty."

"She's in bad shape, Rose."

"Good. Don't try to make me feel sorry for her, David. Any mother who offs her kids. There's nothing that justifies it."

"I wonder," David said. He moved close to Rose, reached down to touch the curl that had come loose from the braid at the nape of her neck.

The lawn trimmer bawled and skittered its legs. David stumbled backward. The lawn animal looked at him, panic in the soft brown eyes.

"That's a *cow*," David said.

"Calf, David, just a baby."

"But it's real."

"Of course it's real. Another victim of Ridley's Petting Zoo. This was a bad one. Gag city. Operating down in Georgia this time."

"Jesus, I thought it was—"

"What?"

"A lawn animal. I saw you had them out."

Rose put an arm around the neck of the calf and scratched its ears. The calf's legs looked spindly and vulnerable. The calf bawled and butted Rose's shoulder.

"We had to destroy the mother," she said softly.

"Rose, we don't need any more animals."

She glanced at his shirt. Silence settled.

"Just awhile," Rose said.

"Awhile." David scratched the back of his neck, and winced. His shoulder was getting sore. "Where's the dog? And where's Alex?"

"Hilde is out in the yard. I don't know where the cat from hell is. I threw him out because he was upsetting this baby here."

"How many others are there?"

"Others?"

"Come on, Rose, I know you. How many?"

"Okay, one."

"What?"

"Just a llama. There *might* be an ostrich later, but it's bad-tempered and—"

David closed his eyes.

"The llama's in the barn," Rose said. "The children might could ride it, when its sores heal up, and it's filled out a little."

"Rose, there's got to be an upper limit. This is the third petting zoo you've shut down in the last year. What if—"

"It's all him, this Ridley. And he's out of action for a while."

"I don't want to know." David turned his back. "You heard from Haas?"

"No," Rose said shortly.

"Any idea where—"

"No."

The package in his hands was melting. David turned it over and looked at the label. Veal ravioli. He glanced over his shoulder at the calf. She blinked, lowing softly. He took the package back to the freezer.

David sat in front of the computer. He had taken off his shoes and put his reading glasses on. He scratched his heavy black beard.

"Code Shalom," he said.

The computer came to life. "Good evening, David Silver. Working late again?"

"Case name, Dahmi," David said.

"Searching . . . no case under that directory."

"Key word search, Dahmi, beginning with cases entered today."

"Searching . . . finding Elaki Shockee."

"Funny." David sighed. "Information dump to this system, code Silver XBC."

"One percent loaded, five percent . . ."

"Quietly, please."

David rubbed his eyes. Della and Pete's report on Dahmi came up on the screen.

The Elaki Mother-One had been a frugal shopper, according to her purchasing records. Tallied food purchases showed no indication of possible vitamin deficiencies or cravings that would indicate mental unwellness. All luxury items had come from Capo's, a store specializing in what Elaki called learning aids for children, and what David called toys. Dahmi's monthly budget was two times David's annual salary.

Dahmi came from a well-to-do Elaki family, was well educated, with strong social ties to Edmund University. She was not outgoing—par for the course from what David knew of Elaki mothers. They spent years concentrating their energies on their pouchlings.

If you wanted an Elaki pal, better choose a male.

No history of mental aberration.

Did Elaki go nuts? he wondered. Did they commit pouchling abuse? He would have to ask String in the morning.

David leaned back in the chair and closed his eyes. Something heavy landed in his lap. Alex. The cat purred loudly and settled on David's thighs, hind leg dangling. David shifted the cat's sixteen plus pounds so his leg wouldn't fall asleep. The cat twitched an ear and allowed David to stroke his enormous belly.

Cho invasion. Dahmi had said it at the hospital. And been afraid of Izicho.

David wasn't sure who had coined the title cho invasion. It had

never been proven that the Izicho, the Elaki police, had anything
to do with the brutal murders, where entire Elaki groupings—
Mother-Ones and pouchlings, sibs or roommates—were killed in
their homes in the dead of the night.

If Dahmi had been afraid for her children, why hadn't she come
to the police?

Maybe she didn't think she could.

There were rumors that the killings were politically motivated.
Rumors they were carried out by Izicho.

David put the cat out of his lap and brushed the hair from his
jeans. He powered the computer down and turned off the light on
his desk.

He was tired, but not sleepy. Just as well, he needed to get back
to the office—leaving, once again, before his daughters got up.

David walked down the shadowed hallway, guided by the bathroom light. It was a small house, a two-bedroom farmhouse on
seven trash acres, bought with the money Rose made hiring out
as muscle to animal rights activists. The girls were asleep in their
room, bedclothes askew, the floor barely visible under books, toys,
and wadded up clothes.

David tiptoed in, trying not to notice the brown apple core
and the half-eaten cookie with an ant on it. He shuddered at the
green-scummed glass of cloudy juice. He stood for a moment,
watching the girls sleep.

David sat cross-legged under their window, between the bunk
beds where Lisa and Kendra slept, and the single bed, for Mattie.
The girls breathed softly, evenly, except for Lisa, whose breathing
was heavy and deep.

Allergies, David thought.

He picked a book at random from the floor.

"Zeus," he said softly, holding the book under the night-light so
he could see. *"The Adventures of a Parrot in the Big Apple."*

Mattie stirred and sucked her fingers, but did not wake up.
David lowered his voice.

" 'Zeus,' " he said softly, " 'had never gotten over being abandoned, a lone egg, in the nest. Had his mother left him on purpose,
or had something happened to her? Whatever the reason, she had
never come back . . . ' "

FIVE

DAVID WAS PARTWAY DOWN THE SIDEWALK BEFORE HE REMEM-
bered to send the car on to the police garage. He opened the
driver's door.

"Follow the grid," he said. "PD garage."

"Acknowledge, David Silver," the car said politely. "I should
inform you that my gas tank is half-empty."

"Think of it as half-full." David slammed the door.

It had been dark when he left the house. The calf had been
tucked into the barn with the llama. The lawn animals had still
been stupidly chewing, though the lawn was thoroughly grazed.
Tufts of missed grass gave the yard an unkempt look.

The sun was coming up now, making the sky go pink, with overtones of reddish-brown that meant heavy air pollution. The city air
smelled sulfurous and damp. David looked up to the third-floor
homicide offices. Lights blazed, the blinds up. He felt a twinge
of guilt for going home.

In his mind he beard Dahmi's wistful voice. Little baby ones.

He frowned when he saw the Elaki standing like a sentinel near
the back entrance. She was early today—if she'd ever gone home.
Her usual place was at the front door, under the overhang and in
the shade.

Why had she moved?

She was immensely tall, even for an Elaki, and must have been
something to see before age had pulled her inward. Her scales were
dull, the normally pink inner coloring transparent, the black outer
layers faded and streaked with yellow.

String had warned him not to approach her. No, he did not know
why she chose to stand outside police headquarters day after day,
but her great age made it an impossible breach of etiquette to ask.
If she had something to say, she would say it.

David chewed his lip. The old Elaki looked ill. Her side pouches
hung open and loose—she had borne pouchlings.

20

"Are you all right?" David asked softly.

The Elaki did not seem to hear him. She swayed slightly. Her eye prongs drooped, and she did not look up from the sidewalk.

David shrugged and went into the building.

Upstairs, Mel was sitting on the edge of his desk. Two women and a man, all in uniform, slumped in chairs. Their shirts and pants were rumpled, jackets off, hats lying around. They had the up-all-night look. David knew it well.

Mel looked up. "Rose chew you up pretty bad about the shirt?"

David rubbed his cheek. He had forgotten to shave. He noticed that String stopped working when he heard Rose's name. Two years ago Rose had killed a serial murderer who had broken into their home, and she had a reputation among Elaki Izicho.

"She was very understanding," David said.

"Aw, right." Mel rolled his eyes. "My sister is known for being understanding."

David sat behind his desk. He nodded at the uniforms. "What you got?"

Mel cocked his head sideways. "These guys did the interviews, up and down Dahmi's street."

"Had to move our butts to get there ahead of the press punks," one of the women said.

David focused on her name tag. Officer Janet Kellog. She was a solid woman, dark-haired. She looked very tired.

"You related to Miriam?" David asked.

"Sister."

"You don't look—"

"Anything alike," she finished for him. "I know."

"And did you?" David asked. "Get there ahead of the press?"

She nodded, then grinned. "But only because Janvier—" She looked at the older, grey-haired man sitting backward in the chair next to her.

"What my partner here is referring to was simple misdirection . . . I mean to say, misunderstanding."

"You mean you lied and they believed you," David said. "This time, anyway."

"The captain said get there first," Kellog said. "We got there first."

"They talked to an Elaki Mother-One called Painter," Mel said.

"Her Elaki name?" David asked.

Kellog and Janvier shrugged.

"But she knew this Packer—what you call her, Dahmi? She

knew this Dahmi pretty well, before Dahmi got her eye stalks twisted. Said she was po-friggin'-litical. Went to all the lectures at the School of Diplomacy, over at Edmund. Started up last year when they let that Elaki take over."

"Angel Eyes?" David said.

Janvier nodded. "This Painter said that the Elaki mama knew her. Knew Angel Eyes. Like for a friend."

The silence was awkward. Tense.

"That's about it," Janvier said.

"Good." Mel waved a hand at the blond-haired officer who dozed, head on his desk. "Wake up your pal there and get some more sleep."

The uniforms got up, stretched, woke up their sleepy, disoriented partner. David picked a cap up off his desk and handed it to Mel.

"Yo. *Kellog.*"

The woman turned. Mel tossed her the hat.

"Next time you leave your hat on my desk, put your phone number in it."

She caught the hat, one hand on her hip. "Not a chance, Burnett. My sister already told me all about you."

"Good for you, David," Mel said, watching her go. "Lecture the troops on relations with the press. From the man who called a media blackout on the biggest story since Angel Eyes turned the city drinking water purple."

"There's no proof it was Angel Eyes," David said.

"Ain't going to be, rate they're moving on it. Word is, she's too old for that stuff these days anyhow."

"Anarchists do not retire." String had moved silently to the side of the desk. He held a thimble in one extruded finger fin. "Please to watch the thimble disappear."

"Where did you get a thimble?" Mel said.

"Antique flea market. Much human . . . human—"

"Junk," Mel said.

"Junk. Please observe."

Mel rolled his eyes. "String, you ain't even good at this kind of thing, let alone do we got the time."

String held up the thimble. "Now that you see it." He tossed it into the air. "Now that you do not."

The thimble disappeared. A moment later, something thudded on the floor.

Mel applauded. "Needs some work, Gumby."

String sagged.

The sound of knuckles on glass caught their attention. Halliday waved to them from his office and opened the door a crack. "Conference room. Five minutes. The whole team."

David checked his watch. He hoped it wouldn't take long. He wanted a talk with the Elaki Mother-One who knew Dahmi.

SIX

DAVID DID NOT KNOW THE THREE ELAKI AT THE BACK OF THE conference room. They were carefully poised on their bottom fringes, bellies rigid.

"I thought this was s'posed to be a team meeting," Mel said. "What's with the bellybrains?"

David looked at String. The fluidity of the Elaki's movements went stiff. String glided to the opposite side of the room, stopping behind the podium Mel had swiped from downstairs. Della and Pete, oddly quiet, looked to David. He shrugged.

Captain Halliday walked into a silent conference room.

"Good morning," he said. His tie was unknotted and slid sideways on his wrinkled shirt. He sat down, leaned forward, and laid his palms on the table. "My friends." He lifted his chin. "The department has been reorganized."

No one said a word. The closed set of Halliday's face, the uncompromising tone of his voice, deceptively mild, stilled their reactions.

"We will no longer report to Richer. Our chain of command now goes through Commander F. Angelo Ogden."

"Shit," Mel said.

Halliday gave him a look. "We're still Homicide Task Force. But we're adding three new members. I'd like to introduce—"

"I am Walker," one of the Elaki said, her voice youthful. She waved a fin at the other two Elaki. "Thinker."

One Elaki bowed slightly.

"And—"

"Stinker," Mel said under his breath.

"Ash."

Mel put a foot up on the table. "Now all we need's Grumpy, Dopey, and Doc." He looked at the captain. "You saying these belly—" He glanced at String. "Sorry, Gumby. These guys are part of *our* homicide team?"

24

"That's right."

"Says who?"

"Commander Ogden, Mayor Bianchi, and the Elaki proconsul."

"Oh, la," Mel said.

"It is, at present, a temporary assignment," Halliday said carefully. "It was felt—"

"By whom?" David said.

"It was *felt*," Halliday said, "that in light of the publicity we're getting over the cho invasions—"

"These *not* cho invasions," String said, voice high and hissy. A patch of scales slid from beneath his fins and landed on the table. "Is idea planted in media by anarchists, who make the advantage of a bad situation. Is nonsense perpetrated by Angel Eyes."

The Elaki named Walker made a noise. "Angel Eyes is old and harmless. Guest lecturer at School of Diplomacy. Must prove *not* cho invasions. Our job."

"*Our* job," David said.

"All our jobs," Halliday said. "We're one team. One Homicide Task Force, and—"

"Dream on," Mel said.

"The next person who interrupts me is out on his ass."

"Please to explain an ass," Walker asked.

"Give her a mirror."

"Let me show you something, folks." Halliday looked at Pete. "You got the tape?"

Pete nodded.

"Run it."

Pete slid a tape into a slot beneath the television. "Play."

Halliday waved a hand. "This was taped at three this morning. It will hit the air at noon, and six o'clock tonight."

The screen filled with static.

"Nice job," Mel said.

The static blipped away, showing the WKBC news set, and the avid face of Enid West. Beside her desk, curled forward, was an Elaki.

"Angel," one of the Elaki said softly.

David frowned. He had never seen an Elaki *sit* before. Was it crouched behind the desk? Having it on eye level with Enid West made the Elaki seem more personable. Friendly.

So this was Angel Eyes.

She had emigrated to Earth two years ago, amid a flurry of bureaucratic disapproval and mainstream support—Elaki, as well as human. Like all Elaki, the breathing slits on her belly formed a happy face pattern. But scars—torture scars from the bad old days of Izicho repression—made the almond shape of beautiful, long-lashed eyes. Angel Eyes.

A figure of mystery, legend, and wild speculation, she embraced Earth, human philosophy, and freedom, and had a history of trouble with the Izicho, and what she called community repression.

"Today we have with us a renowned Elaki lecturer and freedom fighter, founder of the political organization called the Guardians. Angel Eyes." Enid West's voice was raspy and grating. She turned from the camera and faced the Elaki. "Yesterday a prank shut down the Houston Stock Exchange. Rumors are the perpetrators were your followers. True?"

The Elaki waved a fin. "I am no longer the active political." Her voice was deep and strong. "I am very old Elaki, and such doings are beyond my capabilities. And, to be frank, my interests. But I will say I do admire the—"

"Pranksters?"

"Freedom fighters," Angel Eyes said. "Soldiers. For their methods are peaceful, but the intent, I think, is serious. And certainly the—"

"Terrorists," String muttered.

" . . . consequences for them may be most severe."

Enid West raised an eyebrow. "And what are the consequences?"

"I hesitate—" Angel Eyes fluttered a fin. "I am not what you would call a source of . . . objectivity? Yes. Objectivity. I have memories, so many memories, of bad times, and bad days."

"Are you talking around the subject of cho invasions?" Enid West said. "Do you think these invasions, these death hits, are a form of political retaliation?"

Angel Eyes faced the camera. "Is not proven such incidents are form of cho. The killing of Elaki students and host families, chemaki groupings, Mother-One and pouchlings. This is beyond any cho. This is the work of those who fear and hate."

"Do you think the Izicho have anything to do with these invasions?"

"Indeed, I do not know. That, of course, is the problem. And if Izicho investigate Izicho, if police investigate police, who will ever know?"

"Who indeed?" The camera closed on Enid West. "The Izicho, who are, in effect, Elaki secret police, would or could not send a representative to us today, on the grounds that information on their organization compromises agents in the field. We do, however, have Commander Angelo Ogden of the Saigo City PD here to give his opinion of the ongoing problem of these death invasions. Commander Ogden?"

"Yes, Enid."

David chewed his bottom lip. There was a bad taste in his mouth.

The man loved the camera, that much was clear. And, David had to admit, Angelo had a certain presence—accumulated, David thought sourly, from years of taking public credit for other people's work. Ogden was upper management at its best—one of those wily old survivors who worked the beginning of projects, when there was money and excitement, and rode out on a wave of promotion before reality hit, somehow managing to land on the tag end of another successful project, just in time to sop up the praise and kudos that rained on everyone except those who did the work.

David looked at Ogden's thick head of silver-white hair, the expensive suit.

"Have a heart attack," Mel muttered. "Massive."

Enid West was leaning forward. "First, Commander, do you think the invasions are politically motivated?"

Ogden shifted sideways. "There are indications that this is a possibility. At this point in time, I can't say for sure. We're following leads. It's a new crime in Saigo City—"

"The first was about two years ago, wasn't it?"

"Eighteen months."

"*Nineteen* months," David said.

West leaned forward. "And so far there have been three arrests."

"No arrests." Ogden leaned back in his chair. "We've had several people questioned, we're following leads, but—"

"Would you say any arrests are imminent?"

"No, I would not."

"Commander, are you looking into the possibility that these murders are committed by Izicho—Elaki secret police—to keep Elaki in line?"

"We're looking into every possibility. Every reasonable possibility. Please keep in mind that the victims are human, as well as Elaki."

"Don't most of the victims—human and Elaki—have some kind of tie to the Guardians? Don't you find it interesting that these invasions began eighteen months ago? About the same time Angel Eyes became a lecturer at the Edmund University School of Diplomacy?"

"It's an area we're looking into. One of many. I can't compromise the investigation by leaking sensitive information."

"But don't you have Elaki working on these cases? Elaki Izicho secret police? Elaki with a vested interest in—"

"In what, Ms. West? There's no proof, no hard evidence, that Elaki Izicho are responsible for the invasions. We're bending over backward to have a clean investigation. We've just now added Elaki officers whose politics are actually pro Guardian, or who *have* no politics, and who are unquestionably *not* a part of the Izicho, or *any* police or government hierarchy."

"So you *don't* trust your own people?"

Ogden smiled. "That's a cheap shot, Enid. Certainly I do. They wouldn't be there if I didn't. I'm new to this investigation, but it's going to be clean and it's going to be tough. The mayor has promised funds and support. So long as I get those funds, so long as I get that support, we'll get the job done."

"Commander, how can you run a clean shop, how can we, the people, be assured of a clean shop, when you call media blackout during a case? Just last night an Elaki Mother-One was found inside her home with four dead pouchlings. Why did you shut us out?"

"That was a piss poor decision made by a captain I will not name, but whom I assure you has been reprimanded."

David opened his mouth, then shut it. He looked at Halliday.

Ogden leaned forward. "And I will remind you the blackout was temporary, and that the captain himself reversed the order."

"Once the action was over."

"The officer on the scene makes the decision. That's standard operating procedure. If he makes a wrong one, we talk about it. We talked about it. He wasn't in my jurisdiction yesterday. He is today. It won't happen again."

"Word is this Mother-One killed her own pouchlings."

"Yes."

"And yet." West cocked her head sideways. "Here is one more incident involving an Elaki with ties to the Guardians." She turned to Angel Eyes. "Did you know this Mother-One? I believe her name is Dahmi?"

Angel Eyes was silent a long moment. "Yes," she said finally, softly.

"What kind of Mother-One was she?"

"I did not know her well. But she seemed quite devoted, quite loving."

"How do *you* explain what happened?"

Angel Eyes made an odd gesture with her fins. "Who is to judge? Who is to know the mind of a Mother-One most desperate? I can only ask that Elaki and human please to think carefully, and with compassion, toward a Mother-One in trouble. And, I can only say, it is my sincere hope that her association with me, her attendance and interest in my lectures, had nothing to do with what happen yesterday."

SEVEN

"ROGER." DAVID LOOKED STEADILY AT HALLIDAY. "HERE, OR IN private?"

"Meeting's over." Halliday stood up. "Pete, take care of Ash, Walker, and Thinker. Introduce them around. Find them some space."

Della picked up the scales String had shed near her coffee cup. "You want these back?"

String twisted toward her. "Odd request. Granted." He glided out of the room.

"David?" Halliday said. "My office."

"Give him hell," Mel said, under his breath.

David followed him out.

Halliday settled behind his desk, pulled the tie loose from his collar, and tossed it over the lamp shade.

"Sit down, David."

"I don't think so."

Halliday cocked his head sideways.

"You covered for me," David said. "Why?"

"It was a bad call, David. Under the circumstances. We're in deep right now. It changes things."

"The pouchlings might have been alive. There was no way we could know. It is *contraindicated*—look it up in the manual, Roger—*contraindicated,* in a hostage situation, for the perps to watch what's going on on *TV.*"

"This time—"

"This time *hell.* It's not done. You let them blackmail us into doing it, on the basis of political climate or a goddamn presidential decree, and you *jeopardize hostages.* I stand by that. When you cover for me, I *can't* stand by that."

"Exactly," Halliday said. "If you want to discuss it, sit."

David sat. He folded his arms, one shoulder higher than the other.

"I'm an administrator, David, and a cop. Most of the fieldwork falls to you and the rest of the team. My job is to field the bureaucratic crap, so you can do your job, you follow? I'm not here to see you punch your time clock. I'm here to see that people like Ogden don't tie you up in red tape and politics so you *can't* do what you do best.

"And you're not in his league, David. *I'm* not in his league. It would have made him look sweet in that interview to be able to say the cop that called the blackout has been fired. And he'd do it. And justify it with the politics, and never give a flying fuck about your years with the department, your depth and breadth of experience, your wife, your kids, or your state of indebtedness. You hear what I'm saying?"

"Why didn't he fire *you?*"

"Because I'm a captain. Some ways I'm easier to hit, some ways I'm harder. And I got friends. *This time* he didn't push. I figure he's biding his time. He may get me yet, before this is over. Depends on how the investigation goes."

David frowned. He thought of walking out the door. "I don't like the Elaki."

"Walker, Ash, and Thinker?"

"They're here to investigate *us* while we investigate."

"They're here to assist."

"That so? What are their qualifications? Past police work?"

"None."

"Law enforcement degrees?"

"Elaki don't have degrees."

"They don't have their *street* degrees, Roger. They're not like String, they don't have street eyes, they don't have instinct, they're not *cops.*"

"Then train them."

"*Train* . . . in the middle of an investigation like this?"

"I got no choice, David. If I got no choice, *you* got no choice."

David looked through the door, clenched and unclenched his fist.

The memory of Dahmi—netted, restrained, mourning her pouchlings—was strong in his mind. And the last cho invasion. He could see it at night when he closed his eyes. He could smell it.

He leaned back in his chair.

"If there's any way, David, any way at all. I'll jerk a knot in Ogden's tail."

"There won't be a way," David said. "I've been this road before."

EIGHT

THERE WERE THREE REASONS WHY THEY DIDN'T WIND UP AT THE usual bar or taco stand. They wanted privacy from other cops, the lunch crowds were thicker than usual, and Della had a craving for frozen yogurt.

David sat on a spindly metal chair that had a heart-shaped yellow back and a butter-soft cushion.

"This chair was made for smaller butts than mine," Mel said.

Della sat happily across from him, dipping a long-handled spoon into a waffle cone full of papaya yogurt. String stood beside the table, swaying back and forth. He crunched an empty cone, and pieces fell off and landed in his scales.

"I just love how you said that, David." Della scooped a large hunk of yogurt up in her spoon. She lowered her voice, sounding gruff. " 'You cover for me, and I *can't* stand behind it.' "

David finished off his coffee and set the cup down on the table. "How'd you know what I said?"

Mel looked at String, who looked at Della, who looked at Mel. David cocked his head sideways, remembering how they'd been huddled together at Mel's desk, pretending not to notice when he came out.

"Could everybody in the precinct hear us?"

"Ah, no," Mel said. "Della only told *us* what was going on."

"How did she know?" David looked at Della, who was rotating the waffle cone in her hands, steadily nibbling the edges.

"She can read the silent words," String said.

"What?"

Mel took a slurp of his yogurt shake and wiped his mouth with the back of his hand. "She reads lips."

David leaned back in his chair. He picked his coffee cup up, saw it was empty, set it down.

"Tell me." He looked at String. "Why does an Elaki Mother-One kill her pouchlings? What makes it happen?"

"It does not happen," String said.

32

"It happened." Mel looked at Della's cone. "That papaya any good?"

"String," David said. "People, *humans,* love their children. But strong as that is, people hurt their children. Sometimes they're evil. Sometimes they're reacting to pressures. And sometimes— sometimes they are so deeply disturbed, they do it for reasons no sane person can understand."

Mel waved a hand. "We get them like they go paranoid delusional. Like—you remember that one drowned her baby, David? And to hear her talk, she loved the kid. Loved it so much she killed it, so it wouldn't have to go to junior high school, I think she said. Isn't that what she said?"

"Elaki *not* like human." String puffed his belly slits and grew bigger. "Elaki not go out of the bonkers."

"Out of the bonkers?" Mel mouthed at David.

"We do not have the child abuse, as you have it. It is not to be a part of our society."

"You said before." David frowned. "Something about her chemaki. She was without her—"

"A chemaki is the sexual unit," String said.

The man sitting at the next table stopped eating.

"Five, six, maybe seven Elaki. Male and female. Usually four male to two female. This grouping is more than just the line copulation. We are not to be like the married the one on one. But the chemaki forms the base set of support. All to look out for the other. Pouchlings raised by the Mother-One, who becomes . . . um . . . there is no human word. Bepouched?"

"Impouchnated," Mel said.

"Impouchnated," String said thoughtfully. "The female can choose to become impouchnated at her own . . . um   timing? Timing. But all of chemaki responsible. Males to keep lookout. Available for whenever help necessary. Other females, too. All do not choose to bear young. But always one female in chemaki will. Choose to bear young. And that female is the . . . the spart? Spark. The beginning. Is hard to explain."

David folded his arms, one shoulder higher than the other. "If Dahmi was separated from her chemaki. Could she be under so much pressure she would snap?"

"No," String said.

"Just no? *Never* happens?" Mel asked.

String turned his back. Some of his scales slid to the floor. Della picked them up.

"What we going to do," Della said, "about these other guys? This Ash and Tinker and . . . what was the other one?"

"Dopey."

"C'mon, Burnett, be serious here."

He handed her a napkin. "Left corner of your mouth. No, sweetheart, higher. Lean close and I'll lick it off."

"Serve you right if I did."

"Chicken," Mel said. "Hey, Gumby, turn around here and tell us what you think of the new Elaki."

String twisted sideways. A slow steamy hiss came from his belly slits. "Not Izicho. Not police. Most stupid, sly, not to be trusted. You have the word. It is . . ."

"Snake?" Mel asked.

"No, not it."

"Pig?"

"What's with the animals, Burnett?" Della said.

"Runs in the family."

"How about spy? Traitor?"

"No no."

David rocked his coffee cup back and forth. "Bureaucrat."

"This is just the beginning," Della said. "Under Ogden? We're in for a lot of shit."

"One thing at a time," Mel said. "We got to decide about the Elaki-Three."

"Freeze them out," David said.

Della shook her head. "Ogden won't like it."

"Ogden don't have to." Mel drank the last of his milk shake, then tossed it in the trash.

"Clue Pete in, Della," David said. "Official reports that go to Ogden—make them long, dreary, no information."

"Just let Pete write them," Mel said.

"Burnett, you wouldn't know a good report. How about that one you wrote. Let's see. Went like 'guy died, stuck by some creep in an alley.'" She looked at David. "He actually *wrote* that."

"Dictated it."

"Whatever."

"That was an accident, Della. It got bumped out before my auto-editor turned it into proper police jargon."

David cocked his head. "Della. Is there any way you can tinker with the translator on the computers, so that when it compiles our input into a formal report, it doubles the jargon—gets murky and hard to make sense of?"

"Yeah, just let Mel do it."

"Seriously."

Della chewed her lip. "Maybe." She sat up. "We could use an earlier version—before they worked the bugs out. Let me talk to the software guy."

"Quiet on it," David said.

Della nodded.

NINE

THE ELAKI NEIGHBORHOOD WAS PEACEFUL, SLEEPY IN THE AFTER-
noon heat. String's van slowed as soon as it hit the narrow, resi-
dential streets. David took a breath. He would never get used to
standing up in a car. No matter how tightly he held the strap, he
swayed from side to side, slamming into Mel, or the side panel
of the van.

Mel grinned at him. "Imagine doing this drunk?"

"People used to *drive* that way," David said. "Before roads had
tracks, even."

"Ought to be illegal."

"It was."

"Blue fifty-two," the van said.

David looked out the window. He didn't see anything blue. He
would never understand Elaki addressing systems.

The shockee was tall and narrow, the yard hard-packed, reddish-
brown dirt.

String looked out the window. "*Nice* landscaping."

Mel looked at David, who shrugged.

The shockee was painted with an iridescent pastel glaze that
gave the raw wood gloss and glimmer. Mel stood back and cocked
his head to one side.

"I guess it's like if you glaze a cake, instead of ice it. Like
Rose does, you know? For the lemon ones."

David looked over his shoulder. Dahmi's shockee was still
sealed with crime scene stamps that winked and glimmered on the
doors and windows. He wondered if she was still under restraint.
He wondered if she knew what she had done.

She knew. Which meant she wasn't crazy. But in order to do
what she had done, and be who he thought she was, she'd *have*
to be crazy. Only String said Elaki didn't snap.

The door to the shockee opened and an Elaki Mother-One rolled
out. Two pouchlings followed a foot behind, jostling each other
for position. They craned around the wide, flowing fins of their

Mother-One. They were both small.

"You have brought the pouchlings?"

David looked at String, then back to the Mother-One. She had a beautiful voice: rich, deep, youthful. Her inner coloring was scarlet, her outer scales a soft dove-grey. Her fringe scales were like the ivory-pink inside of a polished seashell, and she was tall and straight. Her eye stalks were short, close to her head, symmetrical.

"I'm David Silver." David flipped his ID card. "Homicide Task Force, Saigo City PD."

The Elaki Mother-One puffed her belly slits and swelled.

David took a step backward. "Uh, my partner, Mel Burnett."

Mel nodded.

"And my associate. String."

"*Izicho,*" the Elaki Mother-One said.

"You're Painter?"

"Yesss. You are here about Dah . . . about Packer?"

"About Dahmi, yes," David said. "May we come in?"

"No. Am expecting pouchlings. Packer's little baby ones have not had the death watch. I have much to prepare. Must ask you to leave."

String bowed slightly, and turned back to the van.

Mel shifted his weight. "Sec, Ms., um, Painter. We got to talk to you now. We can talk here, at your convenience. Or we can ask you to come down to our office and make a statement."

"I have made statement already to flatfoots."

String turned to her. "Is term of insult, this flatfoots. Please to say uniformed officer."

The Elaki hissed. "I have already made statements to flatfoots."

"Okay," Mel said. "You want to pack up your pouchlings there, and come on down to Izicho headquarters—"

David winced.

The Elaki skittered back and forth on her fringe, then became still. She expanded her fins, hiding the pouchlings from view.

"I talk to the David Silver," Painter said. "Him, only."

Mel snorted.

"Is not for you choice," String said. "For not to be necessary a difficult."

Painter's scales took on a yellowish cast. David, standing to one side, could see one of the pouchlings, rigid and still behind the Mother-One. David thought of his daughters, afraid of strange men at the door. Impossible to imagine Rose afraid. But the Elaki Mother-One certainly was.

David inclined his head. "Wait for me."

Mel looked at String, then shrugged. "We're going to wander down the street. Honk the horn when you're ready."

The Elaki Mother-One watched String and Mel leave the yard.

"We don't have to go in," David said. "We can stay right here, if you want."

"I see you on the television box," Painter said. "You carry Dahmi out. No one will tell for me. She is hurt? They have . . . they have plugged her?"

"Shot her?" David said. He wiped sweat from the back of his neck. "No. She wasn't hit."

"There was *much* gunplay."

"Gunshots? You heard a lot of shots? That scared you, didn't it?"

Most Elaki were afraid of guns. David took off his jacket and loosened his tie. He moved past the Elaki Mother-One, taking care to stay clear of the pouchlings, and sat on a landscape timber that separated a clump of dwarf trees from the sidewalk. It was cooler under the little trees. Cedar chips beneath their base gave off a pungent, woody scent.

"Dahmi wasn't shot," David said. "But she had a gun. Her pouchlings were in the room and so was I. Some of the officers were afraid. They fired."

"They must have been *very* afraid."

"Yes." David stretched his feet out. "They were trying to protect the pouchlings."

"Protect the pouchlings—or you, their brother flatfoot?"

David folded his arms and considered her. "Likely? Protect me."

The Mother-One rocked from side to side. "A truth teller," she said. "Many hot dogs tell lies."

"Where'd she get the gun?" David asked.

The Elaki Mother-One glided past him into the house. "Please to come in."

"Thank you," David said. It would be good to get out of the heat.

"Most welcome. Must clean shockee anyway, to prepare for death watch."

It hurt his feelings.

The inside hall was narrow, the ceiling high, and David got a panicky feeling in his chest. Small, tight places bothered him now. He wished they'd stayed outside.

Inside was cool, at least.

The lime scent of Elaki was strong, but not unpleasant. The pouchlings followed their mother like baby ducks. The hallway snaked to the right, then curled left. There was one door on the left, but it was closed. Going through Elaki houses—shockees—was like falling down the rabbit hole.

The hall widened into a large room with a tile floor and a glass ceiling. David's heart quit pounding. He could breathe here. There were squared-off areas filled with small pebbles. David wondered if they were the start of a new project, or a completed scenario that only an Elaki might appreciate. String would know. It would have been good if he'd been able to come along. This hostility to Izicho was new, judging from String's bewilderment. Kind of like what cops put up with in the 1960s.

Poor String.

There were reasons in the sixties. Were there reasons now?

The Elaki Mother-One stopped abruptly and David expected the pouchlings, following so closely, to run into her. They didn't. He veered to the right to avoid tripping over the one ahead of him. His reflexes were good—honed by years of going places with his own kids just ahead.

Painter scooted to the center of the room. She swept sideways gracefully and turned to face him. Her left wing went out. The pouchlings seemed to find the motion meaningful.

"But, the Mother-One," a pouchling said—the one with the reddest inner coloring.

"Please, please, please," said the other, smaller pouchling.

Interesting, David thought. Even alien children chanted at their parents.

"Conversation not of interest to young ones," Painter said calmly.

"Oh, but, Mother-One, it is, it is. Very much interest."

Painter's voice took a hard note. "Conversation not proper for pouchlings. Please to use new construction materials in vid room."

"Yes, Mother-One." The small pouchlings swayed. "What shall we build?"

"You must decide."

"Yesss, Mother-One." The pouchlings moved their fringe scales slowly.

David laid his jacket over his arm. It was an Elaki home—no chairs.

"Dahmi's pouchlings were younger," David said.

"Yesss. Baby ones. Tonight I do the death watch. No one from the chemaki will come. Cannot be reached. Out of town."

"Where are they?"

"Home planet," the Elaki said. "Dahmi's pouchlings. Please to tell—she did this? She kills them?"

"I'm afraid so," David said.

"Hard for to believe. And yet—"

"Yet?"

"They did not suffer?"

"No," David said. He thought of the pouchling who had opened his eyes. "No. Tell me. Where did Dahmi get the gun?"

The Elaki twitched an eye stalk. "Very good question, yes. I have no knowledge here. I know Dahmi very little. Live near, but both involve with pouchlings too much for the close association."

"Where would you get a gun? If for some reason you were desperate to have one."

"I do not think it would be possible for me to secure such a thing. Not common to Elaki. Complicated and dangerous."

"Suppose it was a matter of life and death. What would you do?"

"What could be such a matter?"

"Suppose you needed it to protect your pouchlings?"

"Ah. That then. I still do not know. Perhaps to ask a friend. To ask Dahmi."

"Why Dahmi?"

"Because now she had one."

David gritted his teeth. If it suited her to play stupid there was nothing he could do.

"Dahmi, then," David said carefully, "was the kind of Elaki who knew about guns."

"But no."

"You said—"

"I meant just. I mean if I had to find gun, I would ask a friend who knew such things."

"Did Dahmi have any friends who knew about guns?"

"I do not knowledge."

"Why'd she do it, Painter? Was she crazy?"

"Dahmi not crazy. Elaki not crazy."

"Was she a good Mother-One?"

"You can ask?"

"Yes. Tell me." David folded his arms.

The Elaki swelled. "Very good Mother-One. *The best.*"

"Why did she do it?"

"You do not know?"

"Tell me."

"To protect, David Silver. To protect."

"To protect from what?"

The Elaki scuttled to the other side of the room. "There are worse things than dying in the sleep, David Silver. Much worse things."

"What was she afraid of? Did she tell you?"

"No. She would not."

"Why not?"

"Would not involve other Mother-One, other pouchlings."

"Why didn't she go to the police?"

"I do not knowledge. I can only think of things. I *know* nothing. Talk to the Angel Eyes."

"Angel Eyes? Was Dahmi involved with the Guardians?"

"She was . . . interested. A lecture attendance. Wednesday-day. That is as far as it would go; she have pouchlings."

There were loud, scraping sounds from the hallway, and a high-pitched series of squawks. The smallest Elaki backed through the door, pulling a bench made of a malleable plastic, bright red and shiny.

"Please to interrupt, Mother-One. But the human needs a sit. And I have made one with new materials." The small Elaki straightened, belly rippling.

"You were told—"

"Humans get tired, Mother-One. I have studied them. It would be bad hospitality not to bring sit."

The Elaki stiffened, but she waved a fin tip. "Permission."

The small Elaki turned to David. "Please? Have a sit?"

The bench did not look like it had a prayer of holding him.

"Thank you." David pressed his palm on the plastic. It was soft. The pouchling skittered back and forth, watching.

David sat down carefully. The bench held, damp on the seat of his pants. It was low to the ground, and David's knees rode high. He felt ridiculous, but touched.

"Good sitting, David Silver," the pouchling said, voice high and fluting.

"Good sitting," David agreed.

The pouchling rippled and slid from the room. The Elaki Mother-One was silent.

"What was Dahmi afraid of?" David asked. "Cho invasion?"

"I will not speak of such things. It is not safe."

"When's the last time you saw her?"

"On TV."

"Before that?"

"Outside with pouchlings. Throwing them into trees."

"Doing . . . into trees?"

"It is game. She did not *throw* them into a tree. She . . . it is a game."

"When was this?"

"Nine days before last night."

"Nine days." David rippled his fingers, counting. "Sunday? Sunday, you saw her?"

"Sunday-day. Yes."

"Did she play with the pouchlings outside a lot?"

"Infrequent. Only when she was . . . the word? Happy. Only when she was happy, David Silver."

TEN

DAVID GLANCED UP AND DOWN THE STREET. NO SIGN OF STRING or Mel. He stepped up on the running board of the van and leaned in the open window.

The horn seemed overly loud in the quiet neighborhood.

"What's up?" the van asked. "Problem?"

"Mind your business." David draped his jacket over the headrest and looked down the street to Dahmi's house.

The sun was high and hot. David rolled the sleeves back on his shirt, wondering if it was worth the trouble to wear a suit to interview Elaki. They didn't care what people wore. No scales no sales. As far as Elaki were concerned, people had strong cheesy odors, and it stank in a suit or a pair of jeans. Painter was going to clean her house this afternoon just because he'd been in it.

He stood outside the shockee where Dahmi/Packer had killed her pouchlings because she loved them. Was the danger real, or in her mind? What kind of danger could an Elaki Mother-One be in?

She had not gone to the police. Elaki were orderly, rule followers. Dahmi was afraid of the police.

Cho invasion. Enough to frighten any parent, Elaki or human. They were very like the home invasions of the past. The bastards broke in while the families were home and took what they wanted, trashed the house, and, worse, tortured the families. Men, women, children—rape, pain, twisted pleasures. Usually they left them alive.

Cho invasions went a step further. They didn't leave them alive. But they took their time with the killing.

Motiveless sprees was the official line of thought. Very sick clusters of criminals, creating a twisted synergy. There had been two in Saigo City in the last nineteen months.

Could the Izicho be responsible? Both Saigo City victims had been predominantly Elaki groupings, with tenuous ties to the university, and stronger ties to the Guardians. But neither was deeply involved with the organization. Their connections were almost peripheral, very much on the fringes, nothing more serious than being, say, registered Democrats.

As far as he knew.

The killers were Elaki. Were they Izicho?

String, in the midst of the investigation.

David bit his thumbnail and looked at the house.

The ivy ground cover was trampled and torn, and bits of waxy green leaves spotted the gravel walk that led to the door. The front yard was crisscrossed with deep tire ruts, and there was broken glass near the front door. David walked around back.

The back window was sealed with thin plastic that had bowed in the hot sunlight. Shards of broken glass were scattered in the dirt beneath the window. David looked inside. The room was bare. In his mind's eye, he saw the four pouchlings side by side on the floor.

David heard voices.

"But yes, the human mind is easy to read."

"Sure, String, sure."

"Pick any number between one and ten."

"Four."

"Do *not tell* the number. Pick another one."

"I know I heard that horn honk. David?"

"Pick any other number."

"David?"

"Back here." David moved around the side of the house to the front yard.

Mel grinned at him. "So what? She put the moves on you, partner?"

"The moves?" String said.

"Slang for a pass." Mel sighed. "A sexual advance."

"Between human and Elaki? You must joke."

"Yes, he must," David said.

"What did you learn?" String asked.

"That she was a wonderful mother, very happy, no access to a gun." David looked at String. "She was playing with her children Sunday week. She was happy. Throwing them into trees."

Mel grimaced. "Already snapped, huh?"

"It is game, Detective Mel. Play it with the little baby ones."

"Much belly rippling," Mel said sourly. "I didn't know Elaki played."

"The point is," David said, "she was happy. Do you think it's likely . . . String, say Dahmi was convinced that she and her pouchlings were going to be the target of a cho invasion. How likely would it be for her to be outside, throwing her pouchlings into the trees?"

"There aren't even any trees around here," Mel said.

"Not all likely," said String.

"Humans . . . a human mother, or father, still might play with their kids, even if they were upset."

String teetered back and forth on his fringe. "Human would ignore pressing matters and play?"

"People, *parents*," Mel said, "might still play with the kid if nothing could be done about it then. Why drag the kid down with you? Let them be normal."

"And the pouch . . . the child has no idea the problem or upset?"

Mel shrugged. "A lot of the time they know something's up. Depends how bad it is."

"Ah. This is when the pretending is taught."

"Just answer the question, String," David said. He wiped sweat from the back of his neck. "Likely or not?"

String considered. "Hard to say. But this outdoor game. Is it part of the usual regimen? Mother-Ones often most organized the day."

"No," David said. "Painter said she only saw them out playing like that now and then."

"Ah," String said. "More sense. It is a spur moment thing. Would be like human female, walking down street, swinging her purse."

David was quiet.

"Something happened, then," Mel said. "Something major happened between the time she was doing whatever weird thing she was doing out here with the kiddos. Yeah, I heard you, throwing them into the trees. And between the time she killed them. Miriam tell you how long they'd been dead before you found them?"

"Ninety hours."

"This is Wednesday, then. She kill them Friday night?"

"Afternoon or morning," David said.

"And when was she throwing them around?"

"Sunday."

"So whatever it was happened between last Sunday afternoon and Friday morning."

"She had to get the gun," David said. "It happened before Friday."

"I wonder what it was."

ELEVEN

THE WAITING ROOM OF BELLMINI GENERAL WAS FULL, AND THE cacophony of distressed Elaki gave the air a frantic flavor. One Elaki moaned. The others politely turned away.

David wondered if there was coffee this afternoon. He must be an addict to want coffee in this heat.

Two pouchlings skittered in front of him and he stopped just in time. Another Elaki cried out and teetered sideways. The other Elaki turned away as one, only to find themselves facing a sick pouchling. Elaki hisses filled the air, as Elaki twisted and turned in doomed efforts of courtesy.

The same blonde sat behind the reception desk. Her hair stuck up in clumps around her head, and her lipstick was worn and chewed. She spoke in soft, careful tones to an Elaki Mother-One who held a tiny pouchling.

"Yes, yes, ma'am." Her voice was shaky. "We are giving proper priority. We're shorthanded, excuse me, short on staff." Her voice became tearful. "We're usually not this busy Wednesday *mornings*. Yes, ma'am, yes . . . it *would* be good to plan for such things." The blonde looked up and saw Mel over David's shoulder. She flinched.

"Doctor . . ." David frowned and looked at String. "What was that doctor's name?"

"Aslanti," String said. "Please to see the Aslanti, medical."

The blonde frowned. "You'll have to wait."

Mel smiled with his teeth. "Sweetheart, just tell us if she's on duty."

"Yes. But she's—"

"Get me some coffee, will you, hon?"

"I most certainly will not." The blonde straightened her back and raised her chin.

Mel grinned and led David and String through the swing doors to emergency.

46

There was no television in the ER this afternoon. David leaned close to String.

"Wednesday a big day for Elaki accidents?"

String drifted slightly sideways, the equivalent of an Elaki shrug. "Not for me to know the experience of."

"Gumby, if you mean no," Mel said, "just say no."

String hissed. "There." He slid across the tile floor, belly plates rippling. "Aslanti, medical."

Her answering hiss was audible.

Mel looked at David. "Looks like love to me."

"Dr. Aslanti?" David said.

"Yes, police detective. Please to hurry, much to do."

"We need to talk to Dahmi. And I'd like an update on her condition."

"Yes?" Aslanti teetered back and forth on her fringe.

There was a short silence.

David tried again. "Can you tell us—"

"Why you ask?"

"Cops are irritating, aren't we?" Mel said.

"No. No, why you ask to me?"

David had a sudden bad feeling. "Where is she?"

"Not here."

He gritted his teeth. He'd had one too many literal Elaki today. "What room did they give her?"

"Fifth floor, mental. I tell all this to other of the police. Why not to speak for them?"

David glanced at Mel. He felt a chill at the base of his spine.

"What other police?" Mel's voice was rough.

"Other ones. I not remember names. One say . . . oh, I not know. Am busy, please to—"

"What other cops?" David put a hand on her soft scaly side and she skittered backward, out of reach. "Human? People cops?"

"No, not hot dog flatfoot." She turned to String and hissed. "More Izicho."

"I'll take the stairs," Mel said. He ran to the door, then turned. "Where *are* the stairs?"

A woman holding a basket of plastic specimen bags, one Elaki scale to a bag, looked at him curiously. She popped her gum.

"Best way is, you go like through there—"

"Show me." Mel grabbed her arm and pulled her along.

"Parking lot, String," David snapped. He looked at Aslanti. "Show me the staff elevator."

"Elevator?"

David gave her a push. It was like rolling a heavy vacuum cleaner. *"Go."*

Aslanti swept ahead of him, shedding scales. She glided out of the ER into a main hospital corridor, then made a sharp left.

An Elaki mounted upright on what looked like a scaled-down fork lift was being propelled into a open elevator.

"Priority," Dr. Aslanti called. *"Please* to scram out of the way."

A startled boy in green cotton scrubs pulled the fork lift back out of the elevator and watched David and Aslanti scuttle in.

"Five to mental, code secure Aslanti," she said. "Priority speed."

David grimaced. Priority speed on a hospital elevator? They might make it by dinnertime.

"Brace yourself, Detective."

The door slid shut and the elevator shot upward like a rocket. David grabbed for the side handle that wasn't there, and fell backward. Aslanti, lightweight, no ballast, her frame no more than three inches thick, spun sideways past him.

"Gabilla," she muttered. "Most stupid system."

David caught her in one arm and held her close. She smelled citric and was soft to the touch. He wondered if she was offended by his human odor. The elevator jerked to a stop and he let her go.

The door slid open and Aslanti glided through. She was moving fast now, he could just keep up. The floor was polished and slippery and he skidded once, Elaki staff looking up at the squeak of his shoes.

Aslanti paused outside a narrow black door. "Secure, Aslanti," she said. The door opened a few inches, and she pushed her way in. David turned sideways to fit through.

The room was tiny and close, the walls dark brown. The S-shaped bed was shoved crookedly against the wall. A leather buckle dangled over the headboard. A smattering of scales trailed across the floor.

No Dahmi.

David wondered how she'd stood it, restrained and netted in this narrow nightmare, alone with her thoughts.

Perhaps it was different for Elaki.

He looked up at the sound of pounding feet. Mel's face was red and he was breathing hard.

He stopped when he saw David's face. "They got her?"

TWELVE

DAVID SAT AT THE OVAL TABLE IN ROGER HALLIDAY'S OFFICE AND watched Enid West on the news. Was it his imagination, or were her teeth unusually sharp?

"And in a startling development, Dahmi/Packer, the Elaki Mother-One *alleged* to have committed infanticide by smothering her four pouchlings—"

"How'd she know they were smothered?" Mel said. "We didn't release that."

"—was kidnapped from Bellmini General Hospital today, where she was undergoing mental evaluation. The Saigo City Police Department will not—"

"Turn it off," David said softly. He leaned back in his chair and stared at the ceiling.

Della peeled a tangerine, carefully placing strips of deep orange skin on a white napkin. She looked thoughtful.

"Off," Halliday said. The television blipped off and the overhead light went out. String looked up. Halliday sighed. "Lights on." He glanced warily at the television. The screen stayed blank. He looked around the room. Mel was slumped in his chair. Pete had his arms folded and his eyes shut.

"Where are the Elaki?" Halliday said.

Della delicately spit a seed into her palm. "String's right there, Captain."

Halliday eased into the chair behind his desk. "The *other* Elaki."

"The Elaki-Three," Mel said.

"Where *are* they, Mel."

"In the waiting room at Bellmini," David said.

"Doing what?"

"Interviews. The waiting room was full. We thought some of the Elaki there might have noticed something."

"Yeah, when they didn't have their backs turned." Mel grinned and David gave him a warning look.

49

Halliday put his fingers together. When he spoke, his voice was flat, words carefully enunciated. "This was a professional job, wasn't it? That was your take, David, as I understand it."

David nodded, unsmiling.

"Based on?" Halliday said.

"No witnesses, except the doctor, um, I can never remember—"

"Aslanti, medical." String hissed. Halliday looked at him.

"And there was one nurse who talked to them," David said. "I interviewed the hospital bed, the clock, the elevator. Nothing in the room knew anything—memory erased on each one. The elevator didn't know anything either, but it doesn't look like anybody did anything to the memory. So they likely took the stairs. In and out—took a patient out of a secure, psychiatric floor. And nobody knows anything. That doesn't happen by accident, Roger."

"It's not likely then, is it? That the Elaki in the waiting room saw anything?" Halliday said.

"A thorough, methodical investigation," David said. "You have to ask."

The silence was heavy.

"Seems a poor use of manpower, Detective Silver."

"Remember, *Captain,* that the Elaki-Three—"

"Will you quit calling them that?"

"Were appointed to see that there were no cover-ups. The Elaki doctor—"

"Assslanti."

"Aslanti said whoever it was, was cops. Elaki cops. Izicho."

"Isss *not* Izicho." String spread a wing tip and a scale fell, landing at Della's feet. She bent down and picked it up.

"What for you do this?" String said.

"We don't want anybody to think we're hiding anything," David said.

"And we don't want to fuck up the investigation," Mel said. "And these guys *aren't* cops, and they don't know squatola. Even Gumby don't like them. Do you, String?"

String hissed.

"Well he wouldn't, would he?" Pete said.

Mel frowned.

"So they get access to witnesses," Della said. She daintily wiped her hands on Mel's jacket, which hung from the back of his chair. "But nothing critical."

"Nothing they can screw up," Mel said. He looked from his jacket to Della.

"And what have the *professional* cops come up with?" Halliday said. "A secured prisoner who vanishes from her hospital bed. What kind of security was there, anyway? She—"

"She was in restraints, Roger," David said. "Nets and leather buckles. Somebody let her out. When, I don't know. Aslanti thinks it was just before lunch. Around ten-thirty, or so."

"That's just before lunch?"

"Hospital schedule," Mel said.

"But they got great elevators," David added.

Halliday leaned back in his chair. "Theories, please. Who and why?"

"Izicho?" Pete said. "Sorry, String, but that's what the doctor said."

String moved from side to side.

"Get a grip, Gumby," Mel said. "We got to be objective."

"Why objective? I know things. Is good to know, then not the time wasted."

"We got to prove it," Mel said. "Best favor you can do the whole Izicho secret police bunch is prove they had nothing to do with Dahmi, or the cho invasions."

String turned sideways, both eye prongs stiff. "That may a point be made."

"Sure it is, Gumby. And you got to at least admit the possibility of some kind of extremist group of Izicho involved. I mean, what do the Izicho think, String, of the Guardians?"

"Anarchists," String said.

"Yeah, well, see, most people think the Guardians have the right idea. Personal freedom—it's a hangup with hot dogs, String."

"Much trouble."

"Okay, say you're right. What kind of trouble?"

"Not obey community rules. Laws. People hurt when this to be case. Follow Guardians, no rules, then what? Killing allowed? Theft?"

"Okay, String. Suppose you got a group of Izicho who are real worried about the Guardians. Maybe they think the combination of Guardian politics and Earth freedom are too dangerous. Maybe they decide to do something about it."

"What does this have to do with Dahmi?" Della said.

"The neighbor—Painter—she said Dahmi was a big fan of Angel Eyes."

Pete snorted. "Angel Eyes. She's too old for this stuff, she's retired."

An old Elaki. David wondered if the ancient Elaki Mother-One was still on the sidewalk outside the office.

"She used to run the Guardians," Della said. "She's still got lots of popular support."

"Yeah, well, so does Reagan," Mel said.

"He's dead."

"Finally."

"That could be attractive," Pete said. "Blaming it on Reagan."

String looked from one to the other. "What is Reagan?"

"Trust me, Gumby, there's some things about humans too horrible to know."

David rubbed his eyes. "Suppose it was Izicho. Suppose it was just like Dahmi said. She finds out, somehow, she's a target for a cho invasion. Why would the Izicho take her now? They've accomplished what they want."

"She would be most dangerous," String said.

"Aw, come on."

"No, Detective Mel. Please to hear this. She not irrational if follow the theory. Soon to recover from shock. Soon to have nothing to lost. Soon to be most dangerous. Mother-One with pouchlings to avenge. Could be much trouble."

"I believe it." Della pointed at David. "We all know *his* wife."

String bowed deeply. "Rose Silver much admire."

David bit his thumbnail. "What about the Guardians?"

"Them?" Pete frowned. "Why? They should be on her side."

"Ohhhh," Della said. "I see it. Sure. They are on her side. They took her to protect her."

"What do we know about this group?" Roger said.

David shrugged.

"Maybe we better find out."

"I think it's time I met Angel Eyes," David said. "Maybe I'll stop in for a lecture."

Pete pushed his chair back. "Are we wrapped here? 'Cause if we are, I haven't had my lunch."

"You bring that garlic salami again?" Mel asked. "You did, we're moving your desk downstairs."

"Pastrami, today. Pastrami and cheese. And . . ." He faltered and looked at Della. "A tangerine."

THIRTEEN

THE RECEPTIONIST AT THE SCHOOL OF DIPLOMACY WAS HUMAN, and the waiting room had comfortable chairs, people, and no elusive scent of lime. Edmund University had Elaki faculty members, but not very many.

The boy behind the desk was young. Most likely, David decided, a student on a work/study scholarship. He wore blue jeans, and squinted over a book on physical anthropology when he wasn't answering the phone or admitting ignorance to people's questions. He had a trace of acne, innocent blue eyes, and a tendency to push the wrong button and disconnect people when the phone rang.

Every time the kid screwed up, David felt a twinge of satisfaction. He was beginning to cherish human incompetence.

Mel was humming. David could not quite recognize the tune. String was quiet in the corner, and no one stared at him. Elaki were part of the fabric of the university. As were humans. String had that stillness about him, that look of waiting, of patience, the Elaki ability to go inside himself. Becoming one, they called it.

Mel always said one what.

David cleared his throat. He glanced back at the coffee table. His choices were *Package Gourmet,* the December issue, and the latest *Saigo City!,* the smarmy local glossy.

He leaned forward and took the *Saigo City!.* Nothing about the cho crimes, this was strictly a chamber of commerce effort. Their ideas of *Saigo After Dark* bore no relation to his own experiences. He flipped the pages, yawning, wondering how a local horoscope was different from a regular one, but not interested enough to find out. One of the pictures caught his eye, and he turned back.

He did not expect to find a shot of Little Saigo, no matter how cleaned up and airbrushed. The usual garbage was gone, and except for an overly relaxed man sprawled next to a bush, there were no obvious derelicts. A grey-haired woman in a baggy, forest-green sweater grinned at the camera. Her face was slightly out of focus, but it was obvious that she was missing teeth. She held up a necklace that caught the sun, sending a sword of reflected light across the page. The headline said "JEWELRY FOR SCALE."

David skimmed the article, then glanced up at String. Was that why Della was saving his scales? To make jewelry from?

David stood up, tossed the magazine in the chair behind him. He glanced at his watch, then frowned at the boy behind the desk.

"It's been twenty minutes. You sure she didn't have an appointment or something after lunch?"

The boy opened his mouth and closed it. "I don't think so." He turned to a computer terminal and typed in a command. He shook his head. "Nope. No appointments."

"She prone to taking long lunches?"

"Ummm. I don't know. I've only been here a couple weeks." The boy swallowed and smiled. "I'm sorry. She should be back real soon." His voice was hopeful.

David nodded curtly. He moved from the desk and bent down to Mel. "I'm going to head out a minute. I'll check and see if there's a back door she can come in and out of. I'm not in the mood to sit pat while she plays games with us."

"Um," Mel said. He didn't look up from his magazine. David bent down and looked at the cover. *Aquarium Fish*?

David let the door ease shut behind him. If the office complex had a back door, it would likely be to the left and down the hall. Instead, David crossed to the side doors that led to the quadrangle gardens.

It was getting late for lunch, and the benches and walls that had been clotted with students, faculty, and staff were free now. A pink paper napkin was picked up by the breeze and swept past David's foot. The sun was high, but it might be semipleasant in the shade. David shed his jacket, unknotted his tie, and unbuttoned the top, tight button of his dress shirt. He took a breath. If he remembered right, there was a fountain and a statue down the worn brick walkway, and a thick knot of tulip trees.

The fountain was still there, and water rose and circled in a fine spray. The tulip trees, ancient and lush, arched over a concrete bench. David sat down. It wasn't till he was settled that he saw the Elaki.

She was extraordinary—coal-black from the back, side pouches loose enough to indicate a female who had borne children. She stood under the trees, swaying slightly. She turned suddenly and saw him.

Angel Eyes.

Her inner coloring was rose-petal pink, the scars that laced her belly stark white. Her eye stalks were close to her head. She was holding a brown bag with the sides turned down. David smelled popcorn.

"Excuse me," David said.

"Good of the afternoon."

He knew the voice, of course. Too young and strong, for her supposed great age. Actually, no one ever said she was old, exactly. Just that she was retired. But if she'd been active in the bad old days the Elaki never liked to talk about, she'd have to be at least . . . He had no idea. He'd have to ask String.

She moved steadily toward him, moving off the grass to the brick walkway, and David wondered what age meant in an Elaki.

She swept by him. She was graceful, he thought. He stood up.

"I'm sorry," he said. "But—you are Angel Eyes, aren't you?"

He wondered if he should use a title of some kind, the Elaki were sticklers. Did she have a PhD? Dr. Angel Eyes sounded ridiculous.

She gave him a second look. "Do I . . . I do know you, don't I?" She turned and faced him.

He had never seen eyes like hers on an Elaki. Not the Angel scars on her belly, but the purple-brown eyes on the stalks.

David frowned and shook his head.

"I do *not* know you? But—" She moved slightly to one side. "Ah. You are the police captain who rescued the Elaki Mother-One. You brought her from the house of bullets."

"David Silver," he said. "*Detective*. Saigo City PD." He took out his ID.

Her belly rippled and she made little noises, like laughter. Except Elaki didn't laugh.

"Not necessary, David." She held up the grease-specked bag. "If you like it salty with butter, please have some. You have caught me. I was supposed to lunch on red snapper at the faculty club. But I had this urge to eat popcorn and be out of doors. Please." She pushed the bag toward him.

David took a handful of popcorn. It was crunchy and sun warm, and a piece fell through his fingers to the ground.

"It is easier with fins," Angel Eyes said.

David smiled.

"Are you here to see me?" she asked. "How did you know where to look? This intrigues me. I did not even know where I was going, until I got here."

David gave her what he hoped was a mysterious smile. He wondered if an Elaki would recognize a mysterious smile.

"I have some questions to ask you."

"I imagine so," she said. "Please, let us sit." She folded in the middle and perched on the edge of the bench.

David cocked his head to one side. "I've never seen an Elaki sit before."

"And it is most uncomfortable. But so rude to tower above people when talking, and so uncomfortable for the hu . . . person to be always standing on the feet. I have heard folk songs about the aching feet, and I do not wish to cause them."

David wondered what songs she meant.

"How about this?" He climbed onto the bench and stood up. Angel Eyes unfolded. For once, he was able to look down on an Elaki, if only a few inches.

"Unique," she said. "If you are comfortable?"

"Tell me about Dahmi," David said. "How well did you know her?"

Angel Eyes set her bag of popcorn on the bench. "Not well. She came to the Wednesday night lectures. Then, sometime, she would hang about after the lecture—there is always a group like that— and continue with questions for me. There is little restaurant across the street from lecture hall. Students might go there, afterward. There were nights she seemed to hurry away. I assume she was needed at home by the little baby ones. How many pouchlings, David?"

"Four," he said.

"Ah. Is there anyone to do the death watch? I understand she alone of the chemaki is here?"

"It's taken care of."

"Oh?"

"A friend." It seemed churlish, but David did not say who. "Was she there? At the last lecture?"

"Yes."

"You remember?"

"Yes. I checked roll sheet, also. I wanted to know for sure."

"Did she seem upset?"

"No. But how to tell?"

"Did she stay after the lecture that night? Ask questions?"

"I try to remember. And I ask other Elaki. She did stay, and she did go to restaurant. I did not go."

"Did she ask anyone about a gun?"

"A gun? Ah. I do not know. I did not go to the restaurant. Where would Elaki get gun? Back of magazine?"

"Good question. Who did go to the restaurant that night?"

"Try Tate Donovan. Human, in the senior dorm. And Dreamer. His Elaki name is Tati. He would have been there. He is also in senior dorm."

"Why do you think she killed them," David said softly.

"I do not know."

"You seemed to know the other day. On television."

"I have my theory. If you saw the television broadcast, then you know the theory."

"What would make Dahmi think she was the target of a cho invasion?"

The Elaki moved slightly to one side. "I do not know. But if she did think so, would that not explain?"

"Not really," David said. "She could have asked for help."

"From Izicho?"

"From you. From the Guardians. Did she ask you for help, Angel?"

"She did not," Angel Eyes said, voice nearly inaudible.

David bit his lip. If he didn't know better, he would have sworn that her eyes were glistening with tears.

FOURTEEN

DAVID COCKED HIS HEAD TO ONE SIDE, WHISTLING. HE ABSENTLY crammed a handful of popcorn into his mouth. Rose didn't much like popcorn, but that was because she didn't eat it properly. You had to eat it in fistfuls for it to taste right. One piece at a time wouldn't give the proper effect. Popcorn was as much texture as taste.

David tipped the final contents of the brown paper bag into his mouth. It was salty down at the bottom. He licked butter off his lips.

A girl walked by, carrying a small pack of diskettes and books. Something glistened at her neck and David did a double take. The girl wore a gold chain strung with Elaki scales.

"David?" Mel stood outside the doorway to the Farnum Building. "Where you been?"

David wadded the empty bag, and looked around for a trash can. "In the gardens."

Mel narrowed his eyes. His voice was flat. "We got to go."

David felt his heartbeat pick up. "What's up? Where's String?"

"Already on his way in the van. We got a car, should be out by the curb."

"Dahmi?" David said.

"Cho invasion," Mel told him. "Not too far from here, as a matter of fact."

The neighborhood was as old as the university, older. The houses were meticulously tended, many of them landmarks on the historical tours. It was a neighborhood popular with the tenured faculty. Close by were houses that had been converted into apartments, various sororities and fraternities, all bordering the university proper.

The driveway had been roped off, and there were cars up and down both sides of the street. Neighbors stood quietly in groups in adjoining yards. The car let David and Mel off in the road, then went on without them.

"Aw hell, Daley's standing outside." Mel groaned. "Must be a ripe one."

David wished he'd left the sport coat and tie in the car. He headed up to the porch. Daley was a big man, blond and hefty, and he looked forlorn. Sweet disposition, for a cop.

David frowned suddenly. "These aren't Elaki."

Mel met his eyes. "We got people this time."

David looked for bicycles and roller skates and was happy not to see any. There was a stack of rolled-up newspapers in a neat mound on the porch, and the small black mailbox was ajar, stuffed with mail that hadn't been picked up. Flies clustered in the corners of the window. The porch light was on.

Happened at night, David thought. Behind him, Mel muttered into his recorder. David turned and pointed to the porch light. Mel nodded.

Daley smoothed the thin blond hair that was combed over his pink scalp. He nodded at David.

"How you doing, Daley?" David said. "You take the call?"

Daley nodded. "That old-time favorite, check out the suspicious odor."

"How long?"

"A week at most. Hard to tell. Been a lot of decomposition."

Mel grimaced. "Air-conditioning on, please God?"

"Turned off. Just like the other two."

"Shit," Mel said. He unwrapped a pack of small white filters, handed two to David, and put one in each nostril. "Let's do it."

"Watch out for—"

They went in fast, tramping through a dried oblong of black blood.

"The blood," Daley said.

David looked at Mel, who shrugged. "That's what cops are for. Fucking up the crime scene."

"A time-honored tradition," Daley muttered.

David smelled hot death, and coffee. He turned to Daley. "You put the grounds on?"

"Helps, a little bit," Daley said. "Wait till you get upstairs."

In the kitchen, the floor and the back wall were liberally splashed with blood. A woman in a thin blue negligee was limp and battered on the floor. Her face was gone, blown into bits. Blood had fanned and dried in Rorschach patterns beneath and behind her. A wall calendar was specked with blood. The woman had been hog-tied with fishing wire that had been looped several times around her ankles, run between her legs to her hands, crossed behind her back, and tied around her neck. Her fingers were cut and bloody. The hole in her face was about two inches in diameter, the edges scalloped.

Her skin was blue and swollen, and flies buzzed in the carnage of her face. Her breasts were visible under the thin nightgown. Her hips were generous, belly overlarge and flaccid. The night-gown was twisted around her thighs—she had spent some time struggling with the fishing line. David squatted down. The filters in his nose were not effective. He knew he would carry the smell home with him.

The skin of the neck flapped open from the gouge of the knife that had severed her vocal cords. Whoever did these killings didn't like to hear them scream.

He stood up, looking around the kitchen. The garbage can was overflowing, and on top were the remains of brightly colored wrappers with cartoon characters.

Kids in the house, he thought. David left the kitchen and headed through the living room.

The first thing he noticed were the books. Stacked everywhere there was a surface, two to three feet high, laced with magazines, computer printouts, disks. The furniture was old, the kind that stayed in the family, a few nice pieces, dusty. The clock on the wall watched.

David went up the stairs.

There were stacks of magazines on the steps, like someone had tossed them there to get them out of the way. Streaks of dried brown blood stained the carpet, the handrail, the baseboard of the wall. David recognized the bright yellow cover of a *National Geographic* and a *Children's Hour,* both splotched with blood splats. Several bloodstained magazines were strewn across the second and third step, and David and Mel stepped over them.

It was hot upstairs, the air putrid. The first door, on the left, was closed. David snugged rubber gloves over his hands, and opened the door.

Bunk beds. The smell was strong here. David clenched his jaw and walked in.

The Elaki on the floor was quite dead, and it would take some time to reconstruct the pieces. There was enough upper torso intact for David to see that the vocal chamber had been slashed.

"What's the Elaki doing here?" Mel asked.

David shrugged. He walked to the bunk beds. Empty. He opened the closet door. Stuffed animals cascaded out, and something fell and scattered, sounding like marbles. No children.

"Detective David?"

"String?" David moved into the hallway. "When'd you get here?"

"Just now." String extruded his fin. "Here. In the bathtub. I believe this to be the man of the house."

"*Was* the man of the house," Mel said.

The green tile of the bathroom floor was streaked with blood. The walls were tastefully covered in floral wallpaper, no stains. The sink had clawed feet and no cabinet underneath. The shower curtain had been pulled off the rings, and was crumpled in the corner. The toilet lid was up.

It was odd, David thought, that bodies looked bigger underwater.

The man in the tub was naked, swollen, skin white and bluish. The only visible wound was on the man's throat, where the vocal cords had been cut, signature of the cho invaders. The eyes bulged, the hair floated in the pink-stained water. The skin looked loose, like ham that has baked so long it falls tenderly off the bone. White foam caked the nostrils and open mouth. Lividity in the head and neck was marked.

David knelt and peered into the water. There were fingernail marks on the right hand, and the left was bunched into a fist.

He looked at String. "Miriam here?"

"Downstairs in kitchen."

David moved into the hallway and down the stairs. He looked again at the trail of scattered magazines and blood and imagined the man in the bathroom, vocal cords cut, being dragged up the stairs by the killers. He nodded at Daley, who stood in the doorway.

"Nano machines?" Daley had the proprietary nervousness of the crime scene man.

"Not yet," David said. "Soon."

Miriam was kneeling next to the woman's body. She glanced at David over her shoulder.

"Shotgun?" he said.

"Twenty gauge," Miriam said. "Killer stood three to six feet away. More like three would be my guess. No separation of pellets, wad propelled into the body. Edges of the wound are scalloped.

Some powder tattooing." She lifted the woman's hand. "Defense wounds on forearm, and—" She clicked off her recorder. "You see this, David?"

He stepped closer. "Middle finger missing." He peered at the bloody stump. "Defense wound?"

"I think so. It hasn't been cleanly severed, like it would be for a torture thing. Gouged and pulled. Possibly when her vocal cords were cut. She put up a fight." Miriam frowned. She peeled down the shoulder straps on the nightgown. "Maybe someone held her shoulders. The lividity here may be bruising. I wouldn't expect much pooling here along the top."

"Bruised by fingers? Or fins?"

"No finger imprints. Not sure, could be fins. My guess is someone held her, while the other one slashed the vocal cords, but she broke away and fought back. She was tied after, there's blood pumped everywhere here, but she was still alive, I think, till the shotgun blast." Miriam pointed to the stove. "My guess is he, she, or it stood right there. Fired while she lay on the floor."

"Any idea how tall the killer was?"

"Not yet. Wait for the autopsy. You see that finger anywhere?"

"Nope."

"Bet the killers kept it."

David nodded. "Can you come upstairs with me? Guy in the bathtub has something in his fist. I want to take a look at it. You want to do the honors?"

"A man after my heart. Let me at it."

Mel and String moved out into the hallway. Miriam peered into the tub.

She chewed her lip. "I can't risk it. There's a surprising amount of skin slippage here. And I don't want the water contaminated until we run it through the nano filter. Sorry, David. You'll have to wait."

The sudden ring of the telephone was jarring.

"I'll go," David said.

"Probably my office," Miriam said. "There's an extension in the kitchen."

"Also bedroom at end of hall," String said.

David left the bathroom. The phone was shrill. The hallway had wood floors that creaked when he walked. David opened the door to the bedroom.

Here, evidently, was the master bedroom. The bed was enormous and old, the mahogany dull and dark. A simple, white cotton bedspread was bunched at the bottom and pulled to one side, and the grey top sheet had been pulled back, as if someone had just gotten out of bed. Got up to answer the door, David thought. He wondered why anyone went to the door after dark.

Unlike the living room, the bedroom was Spartan, all surfaces clear. A woman's dressing table was the only exception. Cosmetics and wadded tissues were grouped around two or three books and a notepad. A narrow oak dresser, scarred and not matching anything else in the room, had a wallet, a set of keys, and an identity badge arranged carefully on the top. A skirt and a sleeveless top had been tossed into a mahogany rocking chair, and a bra was splayed on the floor. The man was neat, David thought. The woman was not. Undoubtedly there had been words.

The phone was beside the bed, next to a glass of water that had dust scummed in the top. A bottle of capsules was open next to the water, as if one of them had been interrupted in the act of taking a pill before bed. Just before David took hold of the receiver, the answering machine clicked on.

"You've reached the McCallum residence," a male voice said. "Leave a message, and we'll get back to you."

David heard static, then a female voice. "Mark, this is your mom. The kids just wanted to say hi. We'll be back home tomorrow, after lunch. George caught a . . . *okay,* sweetheart. He wants to tell you himself."

There were scuffling noises, then a child's voice, sweet and pure. "Hi, Daddy! I caught a big one. Grampa says it's probably eight inches. Mickey caught one too, but it was a—what you call it?—fingerling. That's a baby one. You got to throw them back, but Mickey cried. We had onions for lunch, want to hear me burp? Wait, here's Grammie."

David sighed and picked up the phone.

FIFTEEN

WENDY AND LAWRENCE MCCALLUM LIVED IN AN L-SHAPED RANCH house, red brick. The front lawn was high and ragged. The garage door was open, showing an antique gas eater—some kind of Oldsmobile, on blocks and under wraps. Recycle bins were lined neatly on one side, next to an assortment of lawn animals. Small tools were scattered amid oil stains, and a pile of stained blue rags had spilled out onto the driveway.

David's thoughts were back at the scene, with Mel, String, and Miriam. He tripped over a crack in the sidewalk. The front door opened.

"Are you okay?" A small, grey-haired woman ran out onto the porch. Her voice was thick, congested. Her eyes were swollen and red-rimmed. The screen door shut behind her. "Did you hurt yourself?"

David's face felt warm. "Fine, yes, I'm okay. Mrs. McCallum?"

She came forward and held out her hand. The pupils of her eyes were dilated. Her chin trembled.

David took her hand. It was cold. "I'm Detective Silver. We talked on the phone? I am so very sorry."

Tears ran down Wendy McCallum's cheeks. "Thank you."

"I need to ask you some questions."

"Come in." She turned to the house.

David hesitated. He'd come straight from the scene, and he smelled of death. She turned and looked at him over her shoulder, and he could see the whites of her eyes. He followed her into the house.

The living room was crammed with furniture. He wound his way carefully between the love seats, the wingback chair, and two ottomans, then jammed his knee on a recliner. The walls were covered with framed family portraits. David took a good look at the McCallum children.

Boys, both of them, no more than a year apart. Smallish, slight, one with black hair, one light brown. Blue eyes and freckled noses now, round-faced and hairless at birth.

The portraits told him what the bodies had not. That Charlotte Arnold was plump and pretty, her brown hair short and flipped under. That there was a trace of something knowing and naughty in her eyes, even in the family groupings, where she hugged her children. And that Mark McCallum was a plain-looking man, serious and remote, oddly stilled, with a large square hand heavy on his wife's shoulder. The baby pictures of the boys were remarkably like Mark McCallum's own old-fashioned infant portraits, with their multicolored background of fake fall foliage. The older boy still resembled his father, though his eyes were impish, a legacy of his mother. The littlest boy had the father's look of serious heaviness and discomfort under the camera's eye.

David realized he'd been staring too long. He glanced at Wendy McCallum, feeling a rush of gratitude for her. She had taken her grandsons fishing, and spared them.

"The boys?" David said.

"Back in the bedroom with Law. Lawrence. Their grandfather." She wiped her eyes. "Doped to the gills all three of them, and curled up on the bed together, watching cartoons. Anything, to take their minds off—" Her voice cracked. "Detective Silver, please. What exactly happened?"

"Someone—more than one, we think. Came in at night, probably just after your son and daughter-in-law had gone to bed." David pictured Charlotte McCallum tangled on the floor in fishing line and blood. "And killed them," he said lamely.

"What about Stephen? No, my gosh." She put a hand to her mouth. "He wasn't there. He's out of town. I need to call him." She bit down on the back of her hand. "Oh, God."

"Who is Stephen?"

"Stephen Arnold. Charlotte's father, he lived with them. He teaches at Edmund. They both do—he and Charlotte. Oh, my God."

"Mrs. McCallum, we found the body of an Elaki juvenile. We think maybe this Elaki may have—"

"Probably Barran. Sitter, they called him. He lived with them. Kind of greyish on the outside, and red in the middle?"

David raised a hand, noncommittal. There had been little left to ID.

"He gets room and board in exchange for helping with the boys. Kind of like an Elaki au pair, though I understand he was studying the boys for some kind of project. I . . . so he's dead, too?"

"If it's him. We don't have a positive ID yet." He looked at her. Her face was blank. She hadn't taken the hint. No matter, David decided. He wouldn't ask her to look. There wasn't enough left for her to tell for sure anyway.

"How . . . how did they do it?"

David put a hand on her knee. "Charlotte was shot. Mark was drowned in the bathtub."

She whimpered, swallowed hard, making a kind of gurgling noise.

"Let me get you a glass of water," David said.

She shook her head. Her bottom lip quivered and she caught it between her teeth. She breathed hard, through her nose. "How long did they suffer?" She looked puzzled. "How long does it take to drown?"

"He would have lost consciousness fairly quickly." David did not elaborate. She'd find out soon enough. He'd make sure Miriam talked to her before she got details from news reports. For the moment, he needed her mind as clear as possible.

"I have videos of them. Charlotte and Mark, and the boys. Do you need them?"

"Not just now," David said. He shifted sideways in the chair. "Tell me. How were things going? Between Charlotte and your son?"

"What do you mean? Do you mean their marriage?"

"Any problems? Did either of them seem worried maybe, or preoccupied?"

"Um, no. Well. Charlotte was . . . had something on her mind. But it didn't have anything to do with this."

A door opened and a toilet flushed. David heard the faint rumble of a television before the door shut.

He smiled at Wendy McCallum. "What was Charlotte upset about?"

"She . . . her period was late. She thought she might be pregnant. I think she was pregnant. And she hadn't made up her mind what to do about it."

"Did Mark discuss this with you?"

Mrs. McCallum shook her head. "Mark didn't talk to me about things. He was very reserved. But Charlotte . . . she was close to me. Truly a . . . a daughter. She lost her own mother when she was so very young, and she seemed—" Wendy McCallum's voice broke. "She seemed genuinely pleased to . . . to kind of let me be her mother."

"Did either of them ever mention upsetting phone calls? Crank calls or—"

"Someone had been calling and hanging up. It was traced, of course, to some kind of phone booth. They didn't think much of it. You think it had something to do with . . . with this?"

David shrugged. "Probably not. Mrs. McCallum, how were the two of them getting along? You said Charlotte was pregnant? Would that have been a problem, between the two of them?"

Wendy McCallum drew back. "It was Charlotte that didn't want any more children. Actually, neither of them did. But I honestly don't think Mark knew. She was only a few days gone."

"Any other problems?"

Wendy McCallum bit her bottom lip. "They had a *good* marriage."

David looked at her.

"There were the usual tensions, of course. Nothing major."

"Such as?"

She curled her feet up under her on the couch and squinted. Fine lines crinkled the parchment-thin skin around her eyes. She was aging, right in front of him.

"The toilet seat thing." She sounded exasperated. "He always left it up. Charlotte thought it was on purpose and she teased him about it, because he was usually so meticulous. And she and her father had books and papers and disks *everywhere*. Stephen was a pack rat, and Mark grew up to be a neat freak, though heaven knows I didn't raise him that way."

David glanced at the dark and crowded living room. His sympathies were with Mark, an orderly man surrounded by a chaotic family.

"Charlotte was the same way. Messy, and kind of stacked things up. But that was just Charlotte, don't think badly of her. She was a very exuberant person, very good for Mark, who could be a stick sometimes. They drove each other crazy once in a while, but . . . but . . ."

David raised a hand. "I understand. I'm married myself."

She sighed. "Then you know."

"Had they been robbed recently? Cars stolen or broken into? Interference with credit, or ID?"

She shook her head. "No. Nothing like that."

"You mentioned Charlotte's father. He lived with them?"

"Yes. He and Charlotte both worked at Edmund, both taught there. And it was a nice arrangement. He'd be there for the boys if they wanted to go out. And he liked the hustle and bustle of the household, and not having to eat alone. He's an interesting man, quite brilliant. Dotes on George and Mickey . . . the . . . the boys. He always says they keep him tied to reality. He's a very scholarly man. Quite well thought of, in his field."

"What is his field?"

"Political science. He's a full professor at the Edmund School of Diplomacy. Chairman of the department, at one time, though he moved away from the administrative side, to have more time to write."

"Ah. How well do you know him? How would you describe him?"

"Well, he, he's very . . . intense. Youngish and interested in everything. Very capable, you know. Not the professor stereotype." Her cheeks turned pink. "But still absentminded, the way brilliant people can be. You know?"

David nodded.

"He smokes. I know that's been a problem between him and Mark."

"Can you tell me where he is?"

"It was some kind of last-minute thing. And Charlotte and Mark had plans to go out—I think she was going to talk to Mark about the baby. So I told Charlotte we'd take George and Mickey for a few nights. We took them fishing. Out at the pay lake on Tonner Mill Pike."

"I see. So it was a last-minute trip? Of Stephen Arnold's?"
She nodded.

"When did it come up?"

"Four, maybe five days ago."

"Otherwise he would have been there?"

"Yes, but . . ."

"But what?"

"It's just good. That he wasn't there."

"Yes," David said. "Tell me, was Dr. Arnold political?"

"Well, of . . . oh, you mean *political*." She tilted her head to one side, narrowing her eyes. "He had strong viewpoints. But he was always *very* good at seeing both sides."

"Did he have many Elaki friends?"

"Oh, yes. Professionally, and personally. Students. He was very popular with the young ones. And colleagues, of course."

"Did he have any affiliation with the Guardians?"

"The Guardians? Funny, now, that you should bring that up."

David sat forward.

"He did a piece on them—some kind of paper he presented at a conference a few months ago. It was in Austria, I think. Yes. Because he said he ate a lot of pastry there and it wasn't sweet. There wasn't much sugar in it. Like here."

David nodded.

"It got a lot of attention," she said. "They had his picture in the papers. Charlotte said it was major work, but she did tend to . . . well, to exaggerate her father's importance. Which I think is sweet in a daughter."

"Yes," David said. "Yes, it is."

She was quiet for a long moment. David watched her patiently. She was thinking about something. She closed her eyes, then opened them wide.

"Detective. Can I go there? To the house?"

David chewed his lip. "Just now it might be best—"

"But, you see, he'd leave his itinerary. Stephen, I mean. One of the note minder chips—these ones with the magnets on the back? Press it and it would reel off where he was going to be. Name and numbers. He always did that. He'd leave it on the door of the refrigerator. So Charlotte could find him if she needed him. I could get that for you and then we'd know where he is."

"Why don't I take care of it?" David said gently.

"You don't want me in the house."

David frowned. "I won't stop you."

"Oh, but . . . my son. I almost think I should. Don't you?"

"No, ma'am. I don't."

The skin of her face sagged. The veins in her neck seemed to stand out, blue under crepe-thin, white skin.

"Why do these things happen?" Her voice dropped to a whisper. "Why would anyone hurt them? Do you know who did it?"

The thought hit her suddenly. He'd expected it sooner.

"Home invaders?" she asked. The implications sank in, and her voice moved up a register. "The cho invaders?"

"Too early to know for sure," David lied.

"Oh, no, oh, God." She waved a hand in the air. "You *get* them. The bastards." She sobbed. *"Get them."*

David nodded. It was always the women who wanted revenge.

"I'll get them," he told her solidly. He inclined his head toward the hallway, and the bedroom where two little boys huddled with their grandfather, filling their minds with cartoons. "And you look after *them*."

Wendy McCallum stood up, gritted her teeth, and shook his hand, her own trembling hard. David knew she would take the bargain seriously.

SIXTEEN

FROM A DISTANCE THE HOUSE LOOKED INNOCENT.

The word stuck in David's mind. It was an odd aspect of this case—the innocence of the victims. This was not a crime where John Q. Public was out where he had no business being. These were Elaki and humans, locked away in their homes, unsafe in the night.

He thought of Rose and his daughters, alone on the farm in the dark.

David told the car to wait in the driveway. The yellow crime scene stamps glowed in the windows of the house, like lighted jack-o'-lanterns on Halloween. The flies were gone—sucked in by the nano machines for analysis of stomach contents. The mailbox had been emptied. David passed his badge across the stamp on the front door. The lock released and let him through.

The bloodstain was gone, recorded, absorbed, and tagged by the nano machines that had swept through the house. The smell of death was officially erased, though David could detect it in the air. Perhaps the odor came from his own clothes.

He went to the kitchen. The garbage can was empty. Daley did a good crime scene, no slop. Cops like Daley were unusual.

The body was gone, but David felt the presence. Memory, he thought. Imagination. Fatigue. All a beautiful dream.

He never had beautiful dreams.

But he was glad the body was gone. For a moment his mind superimposed Charlotte's framed portrait over the ravage of her face. The gaping bloody image won out. It was always that way, and David didn't fight it. The forensic psychiatrist on staff would never give more than a glance to the faces of the victims. David was convinced she immediately forgot them. Certainly she never remembered their names—it interfered with her empathy with the perp.

He would let Charlotte be pretty again after he caught her killer.

Killers. He could see them, vague images, Elaki images. He picked up the phone and dialed Miriam's extension.

"Forensics, Miriam Kellog."

"Miriam? It's Silver."

"C'mon, David, I just gave it all to String. Can't you guys coordinate? I got work here."

"The killers were Elaki—weren't they?"

"David. Yes."

"The same three?"

"Too early, David. I'm just getting started."

"You sound tired."

"So do you."

"When you do get some information—will you hold the release?"

"David, I've got Ogden to deal with."

"Della will be giving you a call, by the way. She's got some new software to pass along."

"How nice."

"Pay *attention,* Miriam. Give the software a chance. No, hush, listen. Let Della show you what she's got. Will you do that? As a favor to me?"

"Yeah, okay."

"And no details to the press until—"

"David—"

"Until you talk to Mark McCallum's parents. And until Charlotte's father's been notified."

"Right. Of course."

"And until you hear what Della has to show you."

"Ummm."

"Thank you, Miriam."

David went to the kitchen. The door of the refrigerator was scoured clean. He went back to the phone. Daley was home.

"Hope I didn't get you up."

"Nah. Just doing a book tape," Daley said. "What's up?"

"I need to know if there was any kind of memo chip—you know those ones with magnets on the back? Were there any of those on the refrigerator door?"

"I don't think so. Have to access the list. Can you hold a few minutes?"

"Sure."

David wondered if Daley was married, if he had kids. Home late at night doing a book tape? No kids, likely. Probably no wife.

David tapped his foot. He always seemed to be waiting. He hated waiting.

"Sorry, David." Daley sounded out of breath. "Baby woke up and I had to stop and pick him up."

David heard the soft voice of a young baby who has the four A.M. sociables. Daley muttered sweet witticisms that would go unappreciated by anyone over the age of six months, then his voice shifted into a lower register.

"Nope. No memo chips on the fridge or anywhere else. What brought this on?"

"Just a thought. Thanks for checking."

"No problem." The baby squawked. "Somebody's out of patience here. Better wake Miss Mama up."

"Good luck," David said, and meant it. He remembered, with comfortable nostalgia, long wakeful nights with his own daughters.

The phone rang as soon as he hung up.

"Silver," he said, picking it up.

"Oh. Detective. This is Wendy McCallum."

"Are you all right, Mrs. McCallum?"

"I just . . ."

"Is something—" He was about to ask her if something was wrong, but the question seemed monstrous in its stupidity.

"I was calling the answering machine." Her voice was thick. "I wanted to hear my son's voice."

David was quiet a long moment. "Of course. I won't be here too much longer if you . . . if you need to call again."

"Good night," she said, barely mouthing the word.

David hung up. He frowned, then punched in one more number.

"Homicide Task Force, Detective Martinas."

"Della? David. Listen, I need you to get a hold of the department chairman of the Edmund School of Diplomacy. Charlotte McCallum's father, Stephen Arnold, is a full professor there. He's on some kind of business trip right now, and I need to find him."

"Sure, David."

"And, Della, there's more to this than notification and questioning. Wherever he is, you get the local cops in and explain that we have a situation."

"You think he did it?"

"I think he was the target. I want him protected and brought here."

"What makes you—"

"Not now, not on the phone. Mel around?"

"Captain's office. You want to talk to him?"

"Ask him to meet me at . . . say, Cooper's, in half an hour."

"Sure."

"One more thing. Call Miriam in forensics—but not until Arnold is squared away. Then get to Miriam and explain our new software to her."

"Our . . . you mean what we talked about in that yogurt place?"

"You had time to look into that?"

"Hell no."

"*Look* into it. Get Pete to help you."

"In our copious spare time."

"Do it, Della. We're going to be taking it from all directions starting now."

"We already take it from all directions."

"It's going to get worse. Trust me on that."

"And you're saying the best defense is a good *bureaucracy*?"

"Trust me on that, too."

SEVENTEEN

COOPER'S WASN'T CROWDED AFTER THE DINNER RUSH ON A WEEK night. Most people in now were there for beer and appetizers, or dessert and coffee.

David was eating onion rings, ignoring the cup of pinkish-white sauce they came with and dipping them in catsup. Mel slid into the seat across from him.

"Suppose to use the sauce, David." Mel looked at the waiter. "Beer. A Gornsby." He took an onion ring and dipped it in catsup.

The waiter brought a brown bottle and a fluted glass. "Something to eat?" he said. He wore glasses and his hair was cut short, with a trendy divot in back.

"Chili dog," Mel said. "Onions, cheese, and kraut."

"More onion rings," David said.

"Another beer?"

David nodded. He took a bite from his cheese steak sandwich.

Mel closed his eyes and leaned back in the booth. He looked older, David decided. His hair was curly and getting too long.

"When'd you eat today?" David asked.

"Today?" Mel opened his eyes. "Had a sandwich brought in this afternoon. Looked good, too. Ham and . . . mozzarella."

"Didn't you eat it?"

"Della. She got the pickle, too."

David shoved the onion rings in Mel's direction.

"Della says to tell you that Stephen Arnold is in Minneapolis. The cops there got him under lock and key. So what's up?"

A piece of grilled onion fell off David's sandwich. He picked it up and put it in his mouth. A burst of laughter sounded from the booth at the end of the room. Mel glanced over his shoulder, then back to David.

"Stephen Arnold lived with the McCallums. He's Charlotte's father. He's a full professor at Edmund University and he

75

presented a paper a few months ago, some conference in Austria. Care to guess what about?"

Mel chewed an onion ring. "Angel Eyes?"

"The Guardians."

"Same thing. He pro or con?"

"Not sure. Pro's my guess. But his daughter's mother-in-law says he always left a memo chip with his itinerary on the refrigerator door."

"You find one?"

David shook his head.

"You thinking the killers took it?"

"Could be."

"So in one pocket they got Charlotte's finger, and in the other her Dad's itinerary."

David set his sandwich back on the plate. "Something like that."

An alarm bell went off and the conversational roar quelled. The man behind the bar made a hand motion to the waiter, who nodded and disappeared down the hall toward the men's room.

David and Mel turned around to watch the hallway. A man, potbelly swelling over cheap blue cotton pants that were belted below the waist, came loping from the hallway, wiping grey foam off his neck, forehead, and arms with a wad of paper towels. The waiter followed, towel roll in hand.

Mel frowned. "That's new. When did they get the smoker's friend installed?"

"Had it since last summer," David said.

"I didn't know that."

"City ordinance. Everybody had to have them by spring."

There were hoots of laughter, but the man with the paper towels ignored them. He tossed towel wads in the center of the floor and left, disgust etched into his ruddy face.

Mel's hot dog arrived. He opened the bun.

"There's no mustard on this. No catsup, either."

The waiter consulted his order form. He ran a fingernail across the bottom of the pad, and Mel's voice could be heard, sounding grainy.

"Chili dog. Onions, cheese, and kraut."

Mel grimaced. "Anybody orders kraut, onions, and cheese, kid, it's a given they're going to want mustard and catsup."

"I thought so." The waiter pulled a jar of mustard and a bottle of catsup from his apron pocket.

David grinned.

Mel picked up the jar and gave it a sour look. "What's this Dijon shit?"

The waiter, expressionless, took a jar of yellow mustard from another pocket.

Mel shook his head, a reluctant half smile on his face. "You new here, kid? 'Cause you're born to the business."

The waiter permitted a small smile and left.

Mel doctored the hot dog and took a bite. "No question, is there, David?"

David shook his head. "Political hits. Teams of two or three. We let it out—FBI will take the case."

"Then they'll bury it, like cats in a litter box."

"We keep it quiet and the press finds out." David shook his head. "If *Ogden* finds out—"

"Same difference."

"*We* get buried. Same analogy."

Mel took another bite of his hot dog. It was two-thirds gone. Clumps of kraut and chili dotted with cheese and onion fell to the plate in mounds. Mel picked them up with his fingers and shoveled them into his mouth.

David frowned. "Where did String go this afternoon?"

Mel cocked his head sideways. He chewed heavily.

"You said he went ahead of us—to the murder scene in his van. But we were there a long time before he was."

Mel frowned. "So where did he go? Not right, is it? Go somewhere else first."

David nodded slowly.

"Van's in the lot," Mel said. "You want we should take a look?"

"Soon as you're done." David handed him a napkin.

EIGHTEEN

DAVID SLID HIS ID INTO THE ELEVATOR SLOT AND THE DOOR jerked, hesitated, then opened partway. Mel started to squeeze through.

David shook his head. "Take the stairs."

"Claustrophobia getting worse?"

"I'm not getting in any cranky elevator."

"Claustrophobia," Mel said.

They headed left, to the stairwell. The overhead light was harsh bright fluorescence. The concrete steps were slick, worn, and grey—treacherous when wet. Small cracks ran like veins of old age. The walls were cinder block, musty-smelling.

The underground lot was cavernous, well lit in the center, with dark corners. Here their footsteps echoed. Oil stains had dried like black velvet mold. The air was soiled with the smell of exhaust.

"When you love the love you've loved so long—" Mel sang loudly.

"Give it all you've got," David said. "There might be somebody out there doesn't know we're here."

"And wake to find that love is GONE . . ."

David looked for the blue Chevy van with the rusty bumper— String's favorite. It was easy to find—parked at an odd angle. The rest of the PD vehicles were lined up with mechanical uniformity, though there were no guiding parking stripes. The vehicles knew where they should be berthed. The van had skewed the lineup.

Likely, David thought, String had parked it himself. He was a tearaway driver, tending to leave the van in odd places, leaping out the instant the urge hit him. He had none of the driving habits instilled by the rules of the game during pre-grid days.

David absently felt the hood of the engine. Cool.

Mel ran his ID past the door handle, releasing the lock. The door hinges, large, unwieldy, and shedding rust, creaked loudly.

78

David looked back over his shoulder, but the garage was empty.

Mel sat on the floor of the car, and leaned sideways to fiddle with the navigator. David rested his arm on the open windowsill of the van door.

"Hello, Detective Burnett," the navigator said suddenly. "Navigator operational. Need something?"

"I got a query," Mel said. "Give me a list of locations. Anywhere you went today after twelve noon." Mel took a notebook from his jacket pocket.

The navigator's light glowed green. "First location after twelve noon—left parking garage, Saigo City Police Department. One-fifteen P.M. stopped at Clarissa Sarkey Building that serves as the political science hub of Edmund University. I then went to the overflow visitors' parking, twelve miles away on Hudson Avenue. At two-thirty I was again summoned to Akers Drive, which circles the Sarkey Building, and went from there to the Taco Stand on Mill."

Mel glanced at David. "Maybe he was hungry."

"I idled my engine at the corner of Mill and North Upper until three-fifteen."

David raised an eyebrow. "Picked somebody up," he said softly.

"Proceeded to the Museum of Human Behavior. Idled ten minutes on Sidley Alley. Proceeded from Sidley Alley to Napier Street, on priority one, arriving at four-eighteen P.M."

"The McCallum house," Mel said.

"I was sent to wait on Ridge Road, a nearby side street, by uniformed officer Berkson, until—"

David caught movement from the corner of his eye. The elevator door was opening.

"Elaki coming," he said. People would take the stairs, quirky as the elevator was. But stairs were hard on Elaki.

"String?" Mel asked.

The door slid open.

David shook his head. "Not String. One of the Elaki-Three."

Mel bent toward the navigator. "Emergency computation—figure the best route between Deerfield, Ohio, and Madison, Wisconsin, including as many Polish vegetarian restaurants in the route as possible."

The navigator made an odd hiccup. "This will require all memory, possibly resulting in the loss of—"

"Shut up and do it," Mel said. "Priority speed."

David watched the Elaki. Walker, he decided. The female.

"What you do here?" Walker's voice was rough and overly loud.

David's first inclination was to bring her to heel. He heard Mel take a deep breath, and decided to sit back and watch.

Mel poked his head out of the van. "Hey, there, sweetheart. You been looking for me?" He untangled his legs from the van and shut the door. The slam echoed.

She was very dark, this Elaki. Dark and thin.

"If I look for types of you, Detective, I go look in alcoholic serving houses."

Mel glanced at David. "I think I'm in love." He studied his fingernails, and stopped to scrape dirt from under the rims. "So what you doing down here, then?"

She was still for a long moment, stiff beneath the scales, in the way of distressed Elaki.

"Took wrong floor on elevator. And you here why?"

"We're here to meet String," David said.

Mel winked. "This is String's van."

The Elaki's eye prongs swiveled to the van.

"How did the interviews turn out?" David said. The Elaki faced him, but stayed quiet. "In the hospital waiting room? Any leads?"

"Leads? You mean the clue?"

"Yes. I mean the clue."

"No one is to see Izicho who take Dahmi."

"If it was Izicho," David said.

"It is you that needs convincing."

"And you that needs evidence."

"Interesting thing come up."

David leaned against the van. "Tell me."

Walker canted to one side. "This overflow of the waiting room. It is most unusual. This I got from the . . . the *acid* mouth."

"The blonde." Mel nodded. "Would have liked to been a fly on the wall for that encounter."

"So I talk with Elaki patients. And learn they have been misinformed to be there."

David folded his arms. "How so?"

"Call in to one health care farm for the problem—told to come here instead."

"You're losing me," Mel said. "Health care farm?"

"For animals."

"Hospital?" David said.

"Procedures for *animals*. Human influence." The Elaki skittered sideways. "Is *farm*."

Mel looked at David. "She been talking to Rose? How'd we get farm animals in here?"

David leaned forward. "What you're saying is they called their problems in to one hospital, but got told to go to Bellmini General?"

"Yesss."

"It's like playing charades," Mel said. "Figuring out what she says. Next thing you know she'll be wanting to throw us all into trees."

"And *you* will want to say that the London Bridge is falling. And it is not here London. And bridges falling on children is funny?"

"About as funny as throwing pouchlings into trees."

"What hospital?" David said. "What hospitals did they call when they got directed to Bellmini General?"

"Is just one. Edmund University Health Center."

"Hot damn," Mel said. "She *does* got a lead."

"This is clue?"

"This is clue," David said.

"Then we find Izicho at Edmund?"

"Izicho didn't take her," David said.

"Gabilla." Walker turned her back on them, but her voice was loud. "I think that you only wish to hide their rectums."

Mel looked at David and grinned. "Translate *that* one, I dare you."

The elevator groaned and the door slid partway open. Walker hissed and David looked up.

String sidled through and stopped. "Is department meeting?"

NINETEEN

STRING FACED DAVID AND MEL WITH THE ACUTE STILLNESS ONLY an Elaki could achieve. Unconsciously, David and Mel moved closer together.

"Ah," said String.

An engine started, and one of the parked cars inched forward. It emitted a warning beep. The car tires crackled against the concrete, and the car made a sharp right, then trundled toward the exit. String skittered sideways out of the way. David grimaced at the sulfurous exhaust.

"Miriam has sent me to find you, Detectives. There is news from the morgue."

"What's up?" David was aware of the blinking nav light, inside the van.

"The object in Mark McCallum's fist hand."

Mel leaned forward. "What?"

"Is a memo chip," String told them. "Itinerary for the business voyage of Stephen Arnold. The in-law father of Mark McCallum."

Mel headed for the elevator.

"Meet you upstairs," David said.

String swiveled an eye prong toward David. "You do not accompany?"

"He's got claustrophobia," Mel said.

"I do *not*."

TWENTY

DAVID STOOD BY THE DOWNSTAIRS EXIT ON THE EMPTY BUCKLED sidewalk and looked out at a world that did not sleep. It was humid. Haze burned in the bright lights; the smog was heavy, even at night.

The old Elaki female was gone from her post by the back door. David wondered where she went at night.

There'd been a message waiting for him at the morgue. Stephen Arnold had landed at Saigo International and was coming directly to PD headquarters to give a statement. It was understood that he wanted to talk to the detective in charge.

At home the girls would be sleeping, the night sky black and infinite and full of stars. So unlike the hazy, light-fogged sky of the city. He had not seen his daughters in forty-eight hours. He had the sudden nagging feeling that there was something he had forgotten, some school program he had missed.

There were noises from the garage. The voices had serious overtones—none of the jokey relief of men and women coming off shift. David leaned up against the side of the building.

Stephen Arnold, flanked by two large, uniformed officers, made his way across the sidewalk that led from the garage to the side door. Arnold moved steadily but slowly, like a man walking on the bottom of the ocean. Drugged or in shock, David thought. Possibly both.

One of the uniforms looked up and down the street, but neither noticed David, camouflaged by the shadows. If the cho invaders wanted this Arnold, they would get him. David thought of safe houses and witness seclusion.

Arnold disappeared under the overhang. David heard the side door open and close. He waited and watched, but there was no sign that Arnold had been followed. David went inside through the back door, going slowly up the stairs to the bullpen of task force desks.

Arnold was crying when David opened the door of the inter-rogation room. It was a small room, stark, furnished with a green slate table and two folding chairs. There was a pitcher of water and two glasses on the table, next to an old model Miranda-Pro.

Arnold was a tall man, thin. Younger and better-looking than David had imagined. He seemed too young to have a grown daugh-ter and grandchildren.

Either that, David thought, or I'm getting older.

Arnold had brown hair, parted on the side. His face was long and narrow. He had blue eyes, with wrinkles at the corners, and his face was brown and weathered—wet now, with tear tracks. He spent a lot of time outdoors for an academic. Another surprise. Arnold wore a blue cotton dress shirt, collar open, khaki pants, and work boots. The odor of cigarettes clung to him.

"Dr. Arnold?" David said.

Arnold fished a crumpled plaid handkerchief from his pants pocket, dislodging a handful of quarters that spilled onto the floor. David bent down and picked them up, pretending not to see the one that rolled out of reach beneath the chair.

Arnold blew his nose and stuffed the handkerchief back in his pocket. David offered the quarters. Arnold took them absently, clutched them in his fist, then opened his fingers. He looked at the quarters and frowned, then looked at David. He put the quarters into his other palm and extended a hand.

Arnold's grip was firm, his palm cold and dry.

"I'm Detective Silver," David said. "You a coffee drinker? I've got some going, should be ready in a minute." David smiled. "We use the coffee to make prisoners confess. Talk or drink."

"Coffee would be good," Arnold said.

"Please," David said gently. "Go ahead and sit down."

Arnold looked behind his legs at the chair, as if he needed to get his bearings. He sat down and crossed his legs.

"Dr. Arnold, let me start by saying how sorry I am about your daughter. And your son-in-law."

Arnold nodded. "But the boys. They're okay."

"Yes," David said.

"I talked to them."

"Yes."

"On the phone." Arnold paused. "They cried."

"Dr. Arnold, we can cut this short here tonight. Would you like to go to a friend's house or a hotel? Somewhere you can get some rest?"

Arnold's voice was soft. A country boy, David decided, though the accents were faint. A country boy a long time ago. David would not have figured him for the School of Diplomacy.

"I want to see my little girl," Arnold said. He opened and closed his left fist, clutching the quarters.

"Of course." David had called Miriam. Clean her up, he had said. Give me time, she had said. "I'll take you down in a few minutes. Dr. Arnold, what exactly did the Minneapolis police tell you?"

Arnold leaned back in the chair. "Said somebody broke in the house." His fingers stroked the package of cigarettes in his shirt pocket, then moved away.

"It's okay," David said. "You can smoke in here."

Arnold smiled suddenly. "You sure? I got no desire to be covered in foam by a smoker's *friend.*"

"Neutral territory," David said. "Go on ahead."

Arnold took a cigarette from the almost-new package. His finger scraped the top foil, activating the memory chip.

"The Surgeon General . . ."

"Shit," Arnold muttered.

" . . . wants you to know that smoking not only gives you lung and heart disease, but can also cause cancer and respiratory illness in those around you—especially children. Think about it. If you're pregnant, please don't smoke. It's the law."

Arnold put the pack carefully back in his pocket. "I talked to Sergeant Montvilier in Minneapolis. You know him?"

"Talked to him on the phone a few times."

Arnold nodded. He picked a shred of tobacco from his tongue. "He told me it was a burglary. And whoever broke in killed Charlotte and Mark." Arnold's eyes looked glazed behind the smoke. "Montvilier didn't know details." His voice sounded flat, matter-of-fact. "Did they rape her?"

"No. Your daughter wasn't sexually molested."

Arnold's shoulder jerked and he looked at David. He dropped the burning cigarette to the floor, seemed unaware that he'd lost it. He took a deep breath. Then another.

"Dr. Arnold? Are you all right?"

Arnold nodded. "What . . ." His voice was thick. He cleared his throat.

David leaned down and picked up the cigarette. He looked around the room for an ashtray.

"Let me get you that coffee," David said. "Cream? Sugar?"

"Black, please."

David took the burning cigarette out of the room. He took his time with the coffee, filling cups absently, giving Arnold a moment. Arnold thought she'd been raped. He seemed to have no understanding of the crime. Coffee slopped over one of the cups, burning David's thumb.

Why had Mark McCallum been clutching his father-in-law's itinerary? An accusation? To protect his father-in-law? To say that's what the killers were there for?

David took a small sip of his coffee. It was acrid, tasting of ashes. He glanced at his watch. Arnold had had long enough.

Arnold was staring at the wall when David went in, and he didn't look up. His cheeks were wet, and there were deep circles beneath the red, bleary eyes. David thought of Wendy McCallum, and how she had blushed when she talked about Arnold.

Something there?

"Black." David handed Arnold the cup. "Careful now, it's hot."

Arnold took a small sip. David watched for the usual grimace that greeted departmental coffee. Arnold's face stayed blank.

"Dr. Arnold, did Charlotte or Mark seem worried, unusually? Were there odd phone calls, strange people hanging around?"

Arnold shook his head. "My son-in-law was his usual gloomy self. My daughter was . . . fine, I think. Everything was as normal as it ever is. With the boys and three working adults—the usual chaos. And Sitter? They said he's dead, too? Has his Mother-One been notified?"

"Yes," David said.

"How did they do it? How did this *bastard* kill her?"

"She was shot."

"*She* was shot. Mark?"

"Drowned."

"*Drowned?* How?"

"They filled the tub with water and held him under."

"*What?* They—this makes no sense. What kind of—" The thought hit him. Suddenly and hard. "Not thieves."

"No."

"Invaders. Cho invaders. *Cho invaders?*"

"That's how it looks."

Arnold's hands began to shake and coffee slopped onto his fingers. His hand jerked, and the coffee went over his wrist and onto the floor. He cried out, face dark red, eyes squinted in pain.

David moved quickly. He grabbed Arnold's hand and jammed

it down into the water pitcher. Ice chips and water sloshed over the side, and Arnold's shirt sleeve turned dark blue.

Arnold bellowed and swept his arm sideways, tearing his hand from David's grip and knocking the water pitcher sideways. It hit the floor and spun into the wall.

Arnold grabbed David by the collar and jerked him close. "Did they *cut* her?"

David's throat closed, throbbing. He reached for Arnold's hands, heard with relief the door thrust open and slam against the wall.

Arnold backed him into the corner, squeezing. David felt helpless against the man's sudden, adrenaline-hyped strength. Mel loomed behind Arnold and got him in a lock, pinning his arms behind his back. Arnold had a fistful of David's shirt, and the material gave, ripping from neck to waist. One of the buttons snapped and flew across the room, clattering on the linoleum.

Arnold was breathing hard and wheezy, sweat and tears running down his bloodred face. The veins in his neck were taut and throbbing.

"Did they cut her vocal cords?" The words came out hard, between clenched teeth.

David swallowed and it hurt. His breath came hard and fast and he was trembling. He touched the collar of his shirt and it pulled loose, hanging limply in his hands. Another shirt.

"David?" Mel said. "You okay?"

David nodded. "Fine." His voice was hoarse. "I'm fine."

Arnold gulped air. "Did they?"

"Yes, Dr. Arnold, they did." David's voice was soft. "And your son-in-law died with your itinerary chip in his fist. Maybe you can tell me why that is?"

Arnold sagged like a rag doll, dragging Mel to the floor.

TWENTY-ONE

STEPHEN ARNOLD SLUMPED IN THE CHAIR. HE WAS SMOKING HARD, one cigarette after another.

The medic grimaced. "Put your cigarette in the other hand. I can't look at your burn with a cigarette in your fist."

Arnold tossed the cigarette to the floor with a sudden jerk of his fingers. David flinched. Mel ground the burning cigarette out with the toe of his shoe.

"Needs a sedative," Mel said.

Arnold made a face. "I don't want a sedative."

Mel flicked a finger at David. "I meant *him*."

David's throat was sore. He watched the medic hold Arnold's hand up to the light. The wide web of skin between the thumb and index finger had blistered and turned white. It didn't seem to be causing Arnold any pain.

David frowned. It would.

"This is connected to my work." Arnold looked at David. Coldly. "I don't expect you to go along with that. You folks have done nothing but ignore the political implications of these cho invasions."

"You're wrong, Dr. Arnold. I think it's likely you were the target. You just didn't happen to be home."

"Should have been." Arnold was awkward with his left hand. He brought a new cigarette to his lips, lit it, inhaled.

Mel shrugged. "Who knew you were leaving?"

"It was a last-minute thing. I hadn't planned to go to the conference, but a colleague of mine, Paul LeMatt, decided to go, and I wanted to meet with him."

"When did you make your decision?"

"Just . . . really, two days before I went."

"That would be when?"

"Let's see. I left Tuesday morning. I called the airport Sunday night. And one of my colleagues, to see if she would take my classes."

"And that would be?"

Arnold looked at David. "The Elaki. Angel Eyes."

David looked at Mel.

"You know her?" Arnold asked.

Mel grimaced. "I seen her on TV."

"I saw an Elaki out there," Arnold said, waving a hand at the door.

Mel stuck a finger in his ear and scratched. "So?"

"Izicho?"

Mel looked at David. "This guy's a diplomat?"

Arnold stretched his legs and looked up at the ceiling. "I am something like an expert. On cho invasions, and Izicho." He narrowed his eyes and looked at David. "I want to know exactly what happened to my daughter. You understand? My imagination is filling in detail after detail. Nothing could come close to what I'm imagining."

David took a breath. He wasn't sure that Arnold was right. He glanced at the medic. "Sedative?"

"Done." The medic packed his bag, leaving a crumpled pile of wrappers on the table. Arnold held his bandaged hand in the air.

"Hurt?" the medic asked.

Arnold ignored him. The medic shrugged and left.

Mel examined the end of his finger. "Dr. Arnold, we'd like your theories on why your son-in-law died with your itinerary chip in his fist."

Arnold narrowed his eyes behind a wisp of smoke. "Mark," he said. "Give him a name."

"They put him in the bathtub. Filled it up and held him under. He died with it in his fist."

David watched Arnold's face. In a small corner of his mind he felt cruel. But fascinated.

"He died with it in his hand," Arnold repeated.

"His *fist*," Mel said. "Why do you think that is?"

"Why do you think?"

"I was asking you."

"To keep it from them. They might not know he had it. He must have thought they were after me, and took it. Except . . ."

"Except what?" David asked. He tried to gentle his voice, but it was hoarse.

"Except why would he be worrying about *me*, when Charlotte . . . He had Charlotte to look after."

"Where was the chip?" David asked. "Where did you leave it?"

"It was one of those kind with the magnets," Arnold said. "I left it stuck to the front of the refrigerator. Like I always did." He stubbed his cigarette out. "Detective Silver?"

"Yes, Dr. Arnold."

"Tell me what happened to my daughter."

"We're still piecing it together. It looks like she and your son-in . . . Mark . . . were getting ready for bed. The doorbell rang. Somehow, the killers gained entry." David paused. "Your daughter was shot and killed. Your . . . Mark was drowned. The Elaki was in your grandsons' room. He was shot and died instantly."

Arnold nodded slowly. "Were they tortured? Did you find burn marks, missing fingers . . ."

David did not look at Mel. "Their vocal cords were cut. Vocal chamber pierced on the Elaki. Other than that . . . I haven't had autopsy reports."

"Was it Elaki? That did it?"

"As I said, Dr. Arnold, we're waiting for results."

"You know," Arnold said. "You just won't say. Which answers my question, doesn't it?"

"Dr. Arnold, why would the Izicho want to kill you?"

"Because of my work."

"Teaching?"

Arnold grimaced. "I've been researching the politics of Elaki revolutionaries. The Guardians. And so I've collected a great deal of information on the historical working of the Izicho. The old Izicho. In particular, whether or not they've really changed all that much. From the bad old days."

"And have they?" David asked.

Arnold frowned. "Until these invasions started, it was really hard to say. There were stories, of course. They have incredible autonomy, so they're wide open to abuse. There's always rumors, but nothing I could honestly pin down. Of course, their methods of working aren't . . ." He grimaced. "I was going to say constitutional. But the kind of things the Guardians, Angel, would recount." He shook his head. "I did a number of Elaki interviews. I could never corroborate anything until the invasions. Historically, yes. There was a bad element in power when Angel was young. But nothing recent." He flicked ash from his cigarette. "Until this."

"You don't got any doubts?" Mel said. "No question in your mind who's doing it?"

"Of course I have doubts. It could be an offshoot, some kind of new bunch with Izicho ties."

"That doesn't really explain why you're a target," David said.

"It would if the Izicho are behind it." Arnold had a satisfied but hard smile on his face.

David cocked his head sideways. "Were your publications so dangerous?"

Arnold leaned back in his chair. "There's a possibility, given the circumstances, that our government might refuse to allow anyone who is Izicho, or who has Izicho ties, to emigrate to Earth. If it can be documented that the organization is persecuting Elaki who embrace the ideals of our own government . . . We may establish policies to keep them out."

David frowned. Dahmi had attended meetings, that was all. Except that she was wealthy. Were there connections here that he did not understand?

"Did you know an Elaki Mother-One named Dahmi? I understand she attended lectures." David got up, opened a file on the table, and picked out a picture. He handed it to Arnold.

Arnold frowned. "I don't . . . I don't think so. It's hard for me to tell."

"They all look alike," Mel said sourly.

Arnold looked at him coldly. "Not to me they don't." He tapped the picture with a fingernail. "I don't know if I've seen her or not."

David took the picture and slid it back into the file. "Dr. Arnold, I've arranged protection—"

"No. *Hell,* no. I don't want it."

David stared at him.

"I want to see my little . . . Charlotte. And then I'm going home."

Mel sighed. "Dr. Arnold, you do that, they'll kill you."

Arnold was stony-faced. "I'm going to see my grandsons. And then I'm going home. Is it—"

"It's cleaned up," David said. "For the most part. But it will be a couple of days before you can go home. Let us—"

"I want to see Charlotte."

"You go visiting those grandsons," Mel said, "you could be putting them in danger."

Arnold stood up. "Can I go now?"

David nodded. "Don't go out of town, unless you let us know."

"And Charlotte?"

David nodded again. "Right now, if you'd like." He wasn't looking forward to it.

TWENTY-TWO

THE CONFERENCE ROOM HAD—MIRACULOUS THIS—A TINY WIN-dow, the panes reinforced with wire mesh. David wondered how long since it had been cleaned. He leaned close, squinting. She was out there, the old Elaki, teetering on the sidewalk. He turned back around to face the conference table. Ash—the smallest of the Elaki-Three—was unbending paper clips, then hooking them together.

Captain Halliday scratched the back of his neck. "So the consensus is, then, that the Guardians took Dahmi from the hospital, and are hiding her."

David's stomach had that tight, burning sensation that was becoming too familiar.

"But if they wish to protect," String said. "Why not take her before?"

"Before what?" Mel asked.

"Before she kill the young ones."

Walker teetered backward. "Likely did not know she was going to do this thing. Only find out after happen."

David looked at Della. "You get anywhere, piecing together her last few days?"

Della shook her head. "Still don't know what spooked her."

David looked at Pete. "Any ideas on where she got the gun?"

"Any *criminal* could get one." He shrugged. "It doesn't explain where she got it. No luck so far."

"Are political assassinations, these killings," Ash said. "Elaki targets should be warned. Arnold Doctor should be in the protection."

"He don't want it," Mel said.

David looked back out the window. It was hot today. It couldn't be good for the Elaki, as old and frail as she looked, to be standing for hours in the heat. What made her do it?

"David?" Halliday said.

92

"I'm sorry?"

"I said Ogden wants to go with this. He wants to hold a press conference, and say these killings are political."

"And?"

"Do you have any objection?"

"I don't care what he does."

Halliday sighed. "Do you agree? That they're politically motivated?"

David shrugged. "I'm not putting anything in writing. But the McCallum killing seals it. Arnold, for one, is a worthy target. But, it's the same old story. Go public too early, we could wind up looking stupid later on."

"Or keep it quiet, and look like we're burying it."

David nodded. He looked back out the window.

Halliday watched him for a long drawn-out moment. "Anything you want to discuss?"

David shook his head.

Halliday glanced around the room. "Anyone else?"

No one said anything.

"Meeting's over," Halliday said. He crooked a finger at David, then Mel. "In my office, guys."

David waited until everyone began filing out. He edged close to Ash. "What do you think? You think these killings are political?"

Ash slid backward, and dropped the string of paper clips he held. "Is too much coincidence, Detective. Victims involved with Guardians. All with Guardians. Only question—"

"Yes?"

"I might speculate that such as these would go for the Angel Eyes. More prime target."

David frowned. "That could backfire. Make him a martyr."

"Please to explain?"

"A martyr, a figure of sympathy, a . . . never mind. You see that Elaki out there?"

Ash rippled his bottom fringe and swerved downward and sideways to look out the window David had to crane his neck to see out of.

"You know that Elaki?" David asked. "Any idea why she stands there all the time?"

"No ssssir."

David stretched and rubbed the back of his neck, moving back in front of the window. The old Elaki was swaying rhythmically. David frowned. This had gone on long enough.

TWENTY-THREE

DAVID WAS REMINDED OF A HORSE HE'D TRIED TO APPROACH when he was a little boy. The horse had been pastured, and he'd climbed up on the bottom slat of the wood fence, and leaned over the top. He couldn't have been more than six years old. His father had given him a piece of carrot, showing him how to hold it out on the flat of his hand.

The horse had tossed his head and trotted steadily toward the fence, lips peeling back from strong yellow teeth. It had taken all David's courage to keep that hand out, waiting for the touch of wet, velvety lips.

David watched the Elaki with the same sense of nervous fascination.

People gave her a respectful berth without seeming to notice her. Her lime scent was strong in the heat, mingling with the odor of exhaust and hot oily pavement. String had told him at least once that to speak first to such an elder was a terrible breach of etiquette.

David stopped, close enough to touch. The Elaki wobbled back and forth on her bottom fringe, and he expected her to crumple to the sidewalk at any moment.

A woman in overalls and a ball cap, the back of her hair cut in a divot, glanced at David, frowned, and looked away. A hundred yards down the road, a boy glanced over his shoulder as he walked behind a man with a briefcase. The boy, David decided, was after the briefcase.

David stayed put.

The sun was high. He felt sweat break out on the back of his neck. Did Elaki sweat?

The Elaki turned slowly, sunlight glinting in her scales. Her inner belly coloring was splotchy and yellowish. She had raw patches where scales had dropped off and not grown back.

David took a breath. There were scars on her belly, near the breathing slits, a fine white web of scars that looked like lace. He had seen scars like that before. On Angel Eyes.

One of the Elaki's eye stalks was cloudy and unfocused. The other swiveled his way.

"Ah." The Elaki emitted a long, whistling noise.

Elaki stress, David thought. He considered turning around and dashing back to his office.

"I beg your pardon," David said.

"At last." The Elaki spoke slowly, voice faint.

"Every day I see you stand here," David said. "I was wondering if you need help."

"You are police official?"

"Detective Silver. David Silver."

"It has taken much time. I need to speak with a police official. A *human* police official. A detective is this thing?"

"Yes," David said.

"I am missing someone who should be here is not to be found. Are you the finder?"

"Let's go up to my office," David said. "Get you out of the sun. Let you sit down."

The Elaki arched her back. "Elaki do not sit."

"Come inside anyway," David said.

They took the elevator. Stairs were awkward for Elaki. David wasn't sure the elder could handle stairs.

She moved like she had a palsy—shedding scales, quivering and skittering on her belly scales. The elevator was slow. The Elaki stayed to one side, and everyone else boarding kept their distance, crowding David to the back. He took slow, even breaths. Someone on the elevator was wearing perfume that smelled like grape soda. David realized he hadn't had lunch.

The door slid open, and the Elaki moved serenely through the precinct, canted to one side, stiff but graceful. David glanced into the captain's office as he walked by. He saw Mel through the glass partition, and remembered that he was supposed to be there, too.

The Elaki stopped moving and focused an eye stalk. She twitched. David saw that she was leaning toward Ash, Walker, and Thinker, who stood at their station, conferring in muted voices.

"Izicho," she said. Coldly.

"No," said David. "Police officers."

"Elaki police officers are Izicho."

"These are human-type police officers."

The eye stalk swiveled his way. "*These* are humans? Detective?"

Walker hissed. "Not *Izicho*."

The old Elaki moved with sudden, disturbing intensity. "Young one," she said, voice stronger than David had heard it. "You are out of your manners."

Walker skittered backward. David stopped and watched. As did everyone else in the bullpen.

"Young one," the Elaki said again. "You are disgraced."

Ash and Thinker moved away from Walker. Ash turned his back. As did Thinker.

"Beg pardon." Walker swayed from side to side.

"Remove."

Walker made an odd noise, and slid from the room.

"I had a math teacher like you once," David muttered.

"Please to repeat."

"I said please, um, stand here, where you'll be comfortable. Where I hope you'll be comfortable. Can I get you anything?"

"Sushi?"

"Um, no, sorry. We don't have that. Coffee?"

"Cinnamon coffee? Elaki coffee?"

"Just regular. But we've got cream and sugar."

"Some cream please," the Elaki said.

"No coffee?"

"Cream."

Della was watching from her desk. "You want me to get it?" She was grinning.

"Please," David said.

"It's nondairy cream," Della said to the Elaki. Her voice was sweet and respectful. "That's all we got."

"That will be most pleasant," the Elaki said. David had the feeling she was humoring them.

He sat on the edge of his desk, noticing how dusty it was, the surface littered with computer printouts, file folders, and two cups half full of cold, old coffee. One of the cups had lipstick on the rim. David glanced at Della, but her back was to him.

David sat up straighter. He was not at eye level with the old Elaki, but she didn't hover over him quite as much as she would if he'd taken the chair. He pictured Angel Eyes, bending at the middle. Angel Eyes. Did she know where Dahmi was?

"What exactly are you missing?" David said.

"My pouchling."

David felt his stomach tense. "You have pouchlings?"

"Only the one."

"How long?"

"How long I have the pouchling?"

"How long has your young one been missing?"

"Hard to say. Is full grown and is . . ." The Elaki hesitated. "Is Izicho. But not here for work. Coming here to escape the chemaki."

"Ma'am?" Della handed the Elaki a brown paper cup.

David scooted to the edge of the desk and leaned surreptitiously forward till he could see into the cup. It was half full of nondairy creamer. The Elaki took a delicate pinch of the powdery white cream, the lace work of scars flexing. She had much the same attitude, David thought, as he had when one of his daughters invited him to a pretend tea party.

More regal, David thought, but gracious.

"Please to understand my pouchling is grown. Male, name of Calii. Calii, you should be informed, is Izicho. To my shame."

David cocked his head sideways, wondering what she meant.

"He did not come home to me when he was summoned. This not happen right. Something be very wrong. Cannot find Calii. Calii is gone missing."

David wondered how he would word this in the computer file. If he did a file. He folded his arms.

"When was the last time you saw him? You did say him?"

"But yes." The Elaki was silent for a long moment. "How you count this? Would be the years. Eight of the years."

"But—" David frowned. Elaki had not been on Earth more than four years. "*Where* did you see him?"

"Home. Home planet."

"What planet is he on now?"

"If I know, I not be here. He should be on home planet. But not answer my death summons. I dying. He not come. Last communication he come here. He not return. I do not understand, so I do *not* die. I come looking."

It was good Elaki did not marry, David thought. What a Mother-One-in-law she would be. David cleared his throat.

"Let me make sure I have this right. Your son—your pouchling. You haven't seen him for eight years. You thought you were dying."

"I *was* dying."

"And you summoned him. Right so far?"

"But yes."

"And he didn't come."

"No."

"So you were worried, and have been looking for him."

"Yes."

"Why here? Earth?"

"He was to come here. On point of departure. But word is did not arrive. Is some confusion. Regulations say he leave, but not come."

"He left your home planet, but didn't arrive on Earth?"

"Good boy."

David glanced over his shoulder at Della. She gave him a blank, innocent look.

"Why did you come to Earth looking for him?" David asked.

"Because him not home."

"How long has he been gone?"

"That is . . . let me to think on you terms. Please a moment." The Elaki quivered on her bottom fringe, incapable of stillness. "Tuesday-day of the month fourteen, last season."

David swallowed. "Of . . . of this year?"

"But yes." The Elaki sounded weary, impatient. "I have wait much time to tell you of this. How much wait until you find?"

"Your son, your pouchling, is Izicho?"

"Yes. This matters?"

"I don't know. You never know what details will come in handy."

"Ah. The scatter-fact approach. Most appealing to human. Does this method yield?"

"Sometimes," David said. "Ma'am . . . um, what is your name?"

"You may call me—"

"Patience?" David asked.

"That would be acceptable."

David gritted his teeth. "I need your Elaki name. Please."

"It is Yahray."

"Yahray," David repeated.

"Yahray."

David nodded. "Yes. Tell me, ma'am. What kind of relationship did you have with Calii?"

The Elaki made a noise. She spoke slowly. *"He-was-my-pouchling."*

"Yes," David said. "But you haven't seen him for eight years—is that right?"

The Elaki's midsection sagged. "That is correct, Detective David."

"That's a long time," David said gently. "Did you have a falling out?"

"Falling out of what?"

David glanced around the precinct. Where was String? Ash still had his back turned. Thinker—ever savvy—was out of sight. David crooked his finger. Ash did not appear to understand the gesture.

He tried again. "Why haven't you seen Calii for so long? Are there bad feelings between you?"

"Ah. Yes, I fear the politics would intrude. My pouchling most brilliant, and raised just so. And will still become Izicho."

"Are you a Guardian, Yahray?"

The Elaki spoke softly. "But yes. I was the most active political. My Calii was brought up in the middle of the exciting times. He is too young to have the bad memories."

David glanced at the scars on her midsection.

"I most distressed when he become Izicho. The betrayal, you call it?"

David nodded.

"What does this mean, this movement of the head?"

"It means yes."

"Say yes, then."

"Is it possible, Yahray, that Calii does not want to be found?"

David caught a movement from the corner of his eye. String. Thank God. His Elaki partner, ragged-looking as ever, moved silently toward them.

The old Elaki stiffened beneath her scales. David expected her to know, but she did not. String stopped, but said nothing. There was a long, tense silence.

"Good of the day," Yahray said, at last, "Forgive my impertinence. But you *are* Izicho."

String swept sideways, and teetered on his fringe. "I am Izicho, most Mother-One. Forgive *my* impertinence. I believe I know of you. You are Yahray?"

"Do not tell me what I know, young one."

Young one? David gave String a second look.

"I do not wish to extrude," String said. "Is there assistance required?"

"This human does not understand. Calii—my only pouchling— summoned to final rites for Mother-One. Did not appear. The human does not understand the significance."

String waved a fin. "It is to be unthinkable."

"In spite of—" David glanced at Yahray. "Major differences?"

"Unthinkable," String said.

"Have you no Mother-One?" the Elaki asked him. "Pardon the personal, do humans really come from eggs?"

"Yes and no," David said.

"No wonder the confusion."

David put his chin in his hands. Captain Halliday was watching from his office.

"I need some time to look into this," David said. "Where can I reach you?"

The old Elaki raised a fin. "Out there."

David looked at String. "Think we could find her a hotel?"

TWENTY-FOUR

DAVID SHUT HIS EYES, JUST FOR A MOMENT, THINKING ABOUT private moments and how often cops were involved—uninvited but involved.

"All beautiful buildings are for funeral homes," String said. "This is why?"

Mel shrugged.

David shifted his weight. He was perched on a high wood stool that would be uncomfortable before too much longer. Mel leaned against the wall, his arms tightly folded. He yawned, jaw cracking.

"This sucks," he said. "Arnold didn't do nothing. You think he had anything to do with this?"

"Something isn't right about it," David said. "The whole setup."

"You really think *Arnold* had anything to do with it?"

"Likely?" David shook his head. "I think he was the target. But I also think he couldn't stand his son-in-law."

"Yeah, but what about Charlotte?"

"Could have been a mistake. Maybe she wasn't supposed to be there. The grandsons were taken care of—stashed out of the way. And he turned us down flat on the protection."

String stood silently, looking through the two-way into the next room.

"Something on your mind, Gumby?"

String twitched an eye prong. "Please to explain. This is not home movies? This is not the real memory?"

"Nah." Mel studied his fingernails. "It's a form of grief counseling. You get a hologram of your . . . the person that died. They put it together from questionnaires and stuff. It helps the bereaved accept the death."

"Why would they *not* accept it?"

"Well, it could be a sudden thing. Say some lady's sister dies of some disease or something. This gives her a chance to say good-bye."

"Why does she not just say good-bye when the sister becomes ill?"

"Gumby, you wear me out. She didn't *know* her sister would die."

"But surely the medicals would warn her. What disease did the sister have?"

"There *wasn't* a disease. There wasn't a sister. And you—"

"Humans are unreasonable," String said. "To need this help to accept what *is*. Better just to grieve."

"It is grief," Mel said.

"It puts me in mind of a female Izicho I did the training with when I was but most young. She was odd in that . . ." String's voice trailed off.

Mel looked at David, then back to String. "And so?"

String stayed silent, his body turned to one side.

Mel leaned close to David and spoke in low tones. "He ain't told me a whole story or done a magic trick since he caught us by the van in the parking garage."

"Count your blessings," David said.

The door to the next room opened, a wedge of thickly carpeted hallway in their range of vision through the two-way.

"Heads up," Mel said.

Stephen Arnold was formally dressed in a dark grey suit. His shoes were polished and glinting, and he wore a thin black stripe down his white shirt. His hair had been mussed by the wind. He smoothed it back. One piece stuck up at the top, making him look vulnerable.

The funeral director was waving his hands. "No, sir. The insurance company covers all of this. Your particular policy was what I call generous."

Arnold said something David could not hear.

The director lowered his voice. "That's not usually done. The expense would be prohibitive—and to tell you the truth, it's not recommended." The director held out a hand and turned the palm up. "Some experiences aren't keepers. You have to move along afterward." He glanced self-consciously into the two-way.

"Aw," Mel said. "Quit *looking* at us. This guy. Does it every single time. Must be he does it on purpose."

David felt the first twinge of an ache in the small of his back.

In the next room, Arnold looked around, arms tight against his sides. The room was small, the couch an old Duncan Fyfe, tautly stuffed. The end tables were mahogany, simple lines, Queen Anne.

The walls were papered and set off with white wood molding. Arnold perched on the edge of the couch, then glanced at the two floral wingback chairs. He got up and moved from the couch to a chair.

Arnold crossed his legs. David adjusted the volume until he could hear him clear his throat. David heard his own door open. The funeral director stuck his head in.

"Ready in here?" He spoke in a loud, hoarse whisper.

"It's a go," David said. He sniffed. The director was wearing a heavy dose of shaving lotion that smelled like vanilla. His face was florid, well scrubbed.

"You wearing vanilla extract?" Mel asked.

"Male Bonding."

"What?"

"The scent."

"Smells like vanilla to me."

The funeral director grimaced. "Any minute now."

"Dad?" The voice was young, female, coming from the next room.

The director ducked out the door, and David looked through the two-way.

Charlotte stood in the room in front of her father.

"Charlotte." Arnold stood up and reached a hand to his daughter. His fingers, flesh and blood, passed through the hologram that registered on his skin as so many dots of light.

Arnold sat down very suddenly, grasping the knee of his pants leg in a wad.

"Dad, I'm so glad to see you! I knew you'd come."

"Course," Arnold cleared his throat. "Of course."

David was surprised at how pretty Charlotte was. There was something there, some quality the portraits had not caught.

"I wish things weren't . . . well, *you* know. The way they are."

Arnold nodded. He blew his nose on a handkerchief.

"Daddy, do you remember Cleopatra?"

A brown and white border collie appeared beside Charlotte. The dog barked, pink tongue lolling. Charlotte bent down and picked up the dog, holding her belly side up like a baby. " 'Member how I used to carry her like this?"

"Yes," Arnold said hoarsely. He nodded vigorously.

"You always told me it was bad for her back. Oh, and Daddy! How about this day? You remember?"

Charlotte was younger suddenly, her hair long and straight. She was slender, her nose freckled. And she looked worried.

"Remember how I was so nervous about defending my disser-
tation before the committee?" She held up a foil-wrapped package
of chocolates. "And you said eat chocolate, Charlotte, you'll feel
better. And you sang that *stupid* song. About sex, chocolate, and
females." Charlotte tilted her head sideways, her laugh deep and
gusty. "That song ran through my head the whole time, Daddy.
It drove me nuts!"

Arnold's smile was painful.

"How about this one?" Charlotte was plump-tummied and tan,
hair slicked back. She stood at the edge of a swimming pool, the
blue water shimmering with sunlight.

"I'm going to *dive,* Daddy!"

Charlotte was suddenly an adult again. "I don't know why."
She shrugged, face full of good humor. "These are the ones that
stuck in my mind." Her smile faded.

David felt sweat prickle his palms.

"Here it comes," Mel said.

David nodded. The psychiatrist had particularly warned them
about the next section, which she herself had prepared and spliced
in, according to the class four court order they had obtained. Class
four was mild. There would be no sudden accusations, no surprise
reenactments of the death scene. Which was just as well, David
thought. Arnold didn't deserve it. He didn't deserve any of this.
It was interesting, though, that Mark was in none of the happy
memories.

Something somewhere didn't sit right.

Charlotte's lip trembled. "Why did this have to happen to me,
Daddy?"

Arnold wiped his eyes with a handkerchief that was crumpled
in his fist.

"Please, just tell me what I did."

Arnold was shaking his head. "My fault," he whispered.

Mel leaned forward.

"It was me they were after. It should have been me."

David let air escape from between his teeth. No apologies. No
confessions. Arnold's pain-wracked face convinced him. Whatever was tainted here wasn't Stephen Arnold.

"Take care of the boys for me, Daddy."

Arnold was nodding.

"Take care of my babies." She turned away, then looked over
her shoulder. "Still one more," she whispered, a half smile on her

face. "The best one,'cause she was there. You remember, Daddy?
The night you and me—and Mom was there, too? The night I
thought the moon was close enough to get to. I thought if we
could just walk far enough, we could go and get it." Charlotte's
voice softened. "I wish you could come with me, Daddy. Like we
did that night." She smiled at him over her shoulder. "Going to
find the moon. All kids get that notion, sometime or other. When
mine do, will you take them looking, Dad?"

"Yes, Charlotte. Yes."

And she was gone. David caught a glimpse of a man and a
woman walking over a hill, a heavily diapered toddler between
them clutching both their hands, taking large and uncertain steps
up a grass-covered hill.

TWENTY-FIVE

THE FUNERAL WAS A BAD ONE.

Ogden had alerted the press pack—he would be there and he would make a statement.

He was magnificent, as always. His suit was sober and expensive, and his shoulders broad. He took up a lot of room. A cluster of cops stayed close.

"Oh, la," Mel said. "Take a look at the queen bee."

"These are not normal police," String said. "Watch them. They are . . . they are *protecting*."

David folded his arms, one shoulder higher than the other. He spotted Wendy McCallum. She wore a dark grey dress and a hat. Hats were popular again. She looked pretty in it—feminine and dignified.

She was flanked by two small boys. David recognized George and Mickey, Charlotte's children. Mark's too, he reminded himself. Somehow it was Charlotte who stuck in his mind.

The boys' hair had been wet down and combed back, making them look fresh and young. They wore suits and shiny black shoes, new.

A knot of reporters stopped the three of them, clumping around Wendy McCallum, who edged backward. David got a quick glimpse of her white, panic-stricken face before she was swallowed up.

David turned to Mel. "Who's doing crowd control?"

"Hell, I don't . . . looks like Van Meter over there."

"He's doing a lousy job. Go over and see what you can do." David moved quickly, heading for Wendy McCallum.

Her hands were tightly entwined in the small fingers of her grandsons, but she was answering questions with becoming dignity. It was the boys that worried him. Their eyes were huge and dark. They looked dazed.

David stuck his left elbow into the ribs of the man closest, then

106

felt a prick of guilt when he saw it was Arnie Bledsoe—definitely a nice guy. David worked his way to Wendy McCallum's side.

"Commander Ogden is arriving," David said. He pointed at random to the right. He didn't know the man getting out of the station wagon, but it wasn't Ogden. Ogden had already arrived, and he favored limousines.

The reporters ebbed away. Wendy McCallum took a deep breath.

"Detective Silver. Thank you very much." She bent close to the boys. "George? Mickey? This is Detective Silver."

George extended a hand. David leaned down and shook it. George frowned at his brother.

"Shake," he whispered.

Mickey gave David his hand. It was ice-cold.

Wendy McCallum was looking toward the street. "Law is parking the car," she said. "*Why* are all these people here?"

"Curious," David said. "And Ogden's called a press conference."

Wendy McCallum frowned. "Is there news?" She glanced at the boys.

"No," David said. "When there's news, I'll come and tell you myself."

"Thank you. I appreciate how kind you are."

"He's our departmental sweetheart." Mel was loud, as always, but he smiled at Wendy McCallum and shook her hand. "I'm Burnett. Me and David work together." Mel glanced toward the crowd. "It's time you went in, Mrs. McCallum. I'm supposed to tell you your husband is already inside, waiting. We'll keep the news folks out of the church for you, but the grave site will be something else." Mel reached down absently, ruffling the hair of the littlest boy.

George gave him a stern look, and smoothed his brother's hair back in place.

Mel nudged David. "It speaks."

Ogden stood on the steps of the church, pausing dramatically halfway up. He turned and faced the cameras. It was cloudy and overcast, and someone was shining a light. David frowned. The light was held by a cop. Good job for a cop, David thought. No point in the man wasting time trying to actually catch these killers.

"Jesus Christ, he's wearing makeup." Mel grinned. "Let's go see what it says. Maybe he's solved the case."

Ogden was looking concerned, but competent. He raised his right hand. "There is no doubt now that these killings are political."

Mel groaned. "Here come de FBI. Thanks, Ogden, I love you, too." Mel blew a kiss.

Ogden straightened his back. "I myself have received no less than three death threats in the last two months." He swept a hand toward the men and women clustered around him. "And can go nowhere, without this security force." He smiled bravely. "Whether I like it or not."

"Surely got more than three," Mel said. "I sent him one myself."

David clenched his fist.

"We *are* close to naming names," Ogden said.

A grating female voice rose in the air. "Are these killings done by the Elaki Izicho?"

Enid West, David thought.

Ogden paused. He gazed off to the horizon for a moment, then looked Enid West in the eyes.

"I cannot directly comment on that question at this point in time."

"But you don't rule it out?"

"No, Ms. West." Ogden looked solemn. "I don't rule it out."

David stepped forward, and Mel grabbed his arm suddenly, his grip tight and painful.

"Stay out of it," Mel said. "It won't do no good. Plus, one phone call, and he'll have your career."

"Welcome to it."

Mel let go of David's arm, and glanced over his shoulder at the crowd. "Where's Gumby, anyway?"

"Missing," David said. "As usual."

"He's getting damn hard to trust," Mel said. "I wish I knew why I still trust him."

A fine drizzle, barely more than mist, came in on the breeze. David hunched his shoulders and turned away from Ogden. It was then that he saw her—getting out of a limousine where she had been sitting—so human—beside Stephen Arnold. Must be a shortage of Elaki limos, David thought. If there was such a thing. Arnold held the door, and Angel Eyes touched him lightly with her fin as she rolled out.

David frowned.

"Blah de blah," Mel said. He was still turned toward Ogden. "You listening to this? David, you—what?" Mel caught sight of

Angel Eyes and Arnold. "Oh, ho. Make a nice couple, don't you think?"

"They work together," David said flatly.

Mel grinned. "You take me too seriously, sweetheart."

David watched Angel. She was wearing a black jacket with satin lapels—expertly cut to hang properly on an Elaki frame. The jacket had no sleeves, but billowed out on each side, something like a cape. Arnold stayed very close to her. The press pack was getting restless. They picked up Angel's scent, and moved, as one, in her direction.

Angel paused. She seemed oblivious, but David detected the stiffening beneath the scales. She could not be unaware that she had upstaged Ogden. He considered applauding.

She turned and saw him. Their gaze locked and she made a very small movement with her left fin. David nodded. She swept sideways and faced the press.

David grinned. He wished he could hear what she was saying. But the look on Ogden's face was enough. And she had been perfect. Good timing, good entrance. He'd make a point of catching her later, on Enid West's broadcast.

TWENTY-SIX

IT WAS STRANGE TO BE HOME. DAVID PARKED THE CAR IN THE barn, stopped to pet the calf, then looked around warily. No new animals. No ostrich.

Unless it was in the house.

David slid the barn door shut, noticing a mud-spattered Jeep parked behind the house. He stopped midstride, then went in through the back door.

They were sitting at the table, Rose and Haas, drinking coffee and talking fast. It seemed so natural, the two of them there, heads bent together. It was as if the last few months had never been.

"Haas?" David caught his breath.

Haas had lost weight, too much weight. There were deep circles of old dark pain beneath his eyes, and the blond hair was thinner. The deeply burnished tan on his forearms had faded, leaving the skin milky colored and splotchy.

"*David.*" Haas turned in his chair, a smile of pure pleasure on his face.

David felt a twinge of guilt. Why did the line "how the mighty have fallen" have to pop into his head?

Haas was moving slowly. But he was moving.

"You walking?" David asked.

"Show him," Rose said. Her eyes were red; she'd been crying.

Haas lifted the bottoms of his jeans, showing ankles of flesh-colored plastic. "Artificial." He touched both thighs. "From here to here."

No wonder he walked funny. Haas shook David's hand, but there was something dark in his face that hadn't been there before. Something bitter.

"Couldn't you wait? Couldn't they fix it?"

Rose turned and looked at him. "*David.*"

"No, it is okay. You see, David." Haas smiled apologetically. "It was not to be. I am at bottom of list. *No* medical priority. For each week nerves not repaired—less chance of ever working right, you see? And the farther down my chances go, the less priority I have. And I wind up back at bottom of list again. It is the old catch, you see. I have not the medical priority, they will delay the fix. And when they delay the fix, my odds go to no priority." Haas sat back in the chair. "I cannot wait in these beds forever. In the *warehouse* hospital is a terrible place." He smiled at Rose. "I am grateful to you, Rose, that you would try to adopt me." He grinned at David. "It would be hard to be calling you Papa, even to get to the top of the lists."

David grimaced. "I thought right up till the last minute there it was going to get approved."

"Medical priority," Rose said. "The only cop perk."

"They'll bury me free, too," David said.

"Speaking of which." Rose looked at him. "How was the funeral?"

David loosened his tie. "Sad." Haas was sitting in his chair, so he hung his jacket on the back of Lisa's chair, which, of the children's, was the least sticky.

He poured coffee. "Haas?"

"Please."

"Rose?"

"Warm it up."

"You've been gone a long time." David took a sip of coffee. "We didn't hear from you. We were worried."

"*You* were worried. Rose was not."

"Why do you say that?" Rose asked.

Haas grinned at her. "Because I know you, Rose. You were not worried, you were angry. I think angry is better." Haas looked at David. "For her, it is more natural."

David's coffee went down the wrong pipe. He choked and coughed, and Rose slapped him on the back. Hard. David sat and stretched his legs, back pressed against the lapels of his best suit coat.

"Ogden was there," he said. "At the funeral."

Rose groaned.

"What is the Ogden?" Haas asked.

Rose pursed her lips. "Commander Ogden is now officially in charge of the investigation. I told you about it. The cho killings?"

"I have read of this." Haas narrowed his eyes. "This Ogden. He is like the Barton Cavanelli?"

"No," Rose said. "Not like that at all."

David stared into space. They were cryptic as always.

"More like a Jeanette Hisle. You remember her?"

"But yes." Haas glanced at David. "When Rose is leaving Drug Enforcement Agency, and we first work together for animal activists. The time we rescue the gorilla. Remember, Rose?"

She nodded.

"Jeanette was Rose's commanding officer in the DEA. Always holding the press conference. She would jeopardize personnel and job—jeopardize *Rose*—if she can make the DEA look good, even though what she does is pulling the plug on what Rose is doing."

"You never told me that." David looked from Rose to Haas.

"But yes. Rose was almost hit when we were in England."

"England?"

"After the gorillas," Rose said.

"But you weren't with the DEA then," David said.

"I know. But there were still several contracts out on me. Three majors. Lots of little ones that didn't count, but three that did."

"*Three?*" David said.

"Not unusual for visible agents."

"Jeanette exposed her when she should not," Haas explained. "Then claimed her *own* life was in danger."

"Like anybody that wanted her fat ass couldn't have it," Rose said. "She never went anywhere without protection."

"Rose, did you never show him the T-shirt?"

David looked at her. "What T-shirt?"

"Is black, with red target on it. A good-bye gift from colleagues."

David frowned. "This Jeanette sounds a lot like Ogden."

"Bureaucrats," Rose said.

"The man's got me stumped," David told her. "We've known from day one that these killings are probably political. But the biggies haven't wanted to step on any Elaki toes—bottom fringes—whatever. And the Izicho is a tense subject. Now all of a sudden Ogden takes over, and the first thing he does is hold a conference and say he's investigating the investigators—then he hints it's been the Izicho all along. What's he up to?"

"Covering his ass, for one," Rose said.

Haas nodded. "The change of command, and then he immediately supports what everyone already knows."

"I'm sure he's brave and no nonsense about it," Rose said.

"You say he cannot accuse the Izicho?" Haas asked.

David shrugged. "It would surprise me to see the department going up against the Elaki establishment."

"Maybe," Rose said. "Maybe he'll wave his hands and find a scapegoat. He pounding your ass? Telephone calls, pressure, looking over your shoulder?"

David frowned. "No."

Rose smiled, but it was nasty. "Then he already knows who did it."

"The only way he could *know,* or think he knows, would be if it is Izicho."

Rose frowned. "Halliday understand what's going on?"

"Seems to. Up to a point."

Rose looked at Haas.

Haas turned to David. "Watch your back, my friend. And consult with Rosey. She is most good on handling the bureaucrat."

"Oh, yeah?"

"Hold up a mirror," Rose said. "Turn their own methods back onto them."

"Rosey, you remember—"

David yawned. "Where are the girls?"

Rose gave him a frown that he knew meant she was annoyed. "Kendra is sleeping over. Mattie and Lisa are in their room."

David set his coffee cup down on the table, and went down the hall to the children's room. He heard a dog whimper, and toenails scratch the wood door.

He knocked. "Open up in the name of the law."

"Daddy?"

"You betcha."

David heard the sound of small fingers fumbling a knob. The door opened a crack and Mattie peeped at him.

"Don't let the animals out."

"If they want out," David said, "let them out."

The door swung open and Hilde burst from the room. She jumped and raked David's pants with her toenails, then sniffed and licked his fingers. Haas's laugh, deep and resonant, sounded from the kitchen. Hilde cocked her head. Her ears pricked forward and she pushed off David's legs and ran down the hall, tail wagging.

Mattie grabbed David, her arms reaching just below his waist. *"Daddy."*

David picked her up. She seemed heavier. He held her in the air, legs dangling.

"You *grew*," David said. Mattie grinned and kicked her feet. She was hard to hold that way, but David hung on. "I went to work, and you grew!"

"Don't go to work so long, or I get *sooo* big."

David hugged her and set her down. The floor was covered with plastic animals, clumped in various tableaus, as if they had gathered for group portraits. Some of them were posed in front of a box that was filled with shredded paper—a food trough, David guessed. Others were tied together with string. Some were on their sides—dead or asleep, David didn't know.

He glanced around the room, looking for Lisa. He almost missed her, asleep on the bed behind three precarious piles of clean laundry.

Mattie sat back in the floor. "No *please*," she said, voice deep and mournful. "I do not wish to marry you. I will have my baby alone."

David frowned and glanced over his shoulder at his youngest daughter, then looked back to Lisa. Her face was flushed, her mouth open. He could see the gap where a new front tooth was slowly growing back. There was dirt on her cheek. She looked like she'd been crying.

David touched her forehead. Warmish. Lisa opened her eyes—soft brown eyes, swollen and red-rimmed. She sat up and looked at him.

He sat down beside her on the bed. "Hey, kiddo."

She looked at him and blinked. "Hi, Daddy."

He put an arm around her shoulders. "Something wrong? You have a bad day?"

"I don't get to go on the honor roll field trip this year."

"How come?"

She shrugged. "Only ones going are Elaki. Daddy, don't you think it's funny that none of *us* made it, and all of them did?"

"Who is us?"

"You know. Hot dogs."

"Lisa." His voice was harsh, and she shrank away from him.

"That's what they call us."

David touched her cheek. Should he go up to the school and talk to somebody? There was a new principal this year. When would he go?

"Where were you going this year?" David asked.

"Washington. We were going to see the old FBI building."

David grimaced. It felt like betrayal that she even wanted to go.

"Hey," Lisa said suddenly. "Those are *my* animals."

"You don't play with 'em," Mattie said.

David heard the phone ringing. Rose appeared in the hallway. "Mel." She sounded distracted.

"Feel Lisa's head. See if you think she's running a fever." David brushed close to Rose in the doorway, and she looked up and smiled. "Hello, stranger." He squeezed her fingers.

Haas was standing at the back door. He turned when he saw David, gave him the ever-ready smile, and moved toward the living room. His walk was slow and jerky. David could not help comparing him with the old Haas—the tan, muscular build, the almost tangible emanation of physical self-confidence.

David picked up the phone. "Yeah, Mel?"

"David, I got String right here. He says he needs us tonight."

"For what?"

"He won't, uh, specify."

"Mel, what is this?"

Mel sounded preoccupied and serious for once. "I don't know what it is, partner, but I think you better come."

"I haven't had dinner at home with my family for five weeks."

"So eat first. We'll pick you up, give you some time."

"I *haven't*—" David saw Rose going through the hallway. She was wearing tight blue jeans and a white shirt, and her hair was down and curly, like he liked it.

"I don't want to hear it," she shouted back down the hallway. "Another cross word, and you're dead meat."

"David?" Mel said. "Haven't what?"

"Okay. Pick me up."

Rose smiled at David and headed to the living room. Haas was standing, but he looked ill.

"I best go," he said.

"Stay for dinner."

Haas shook his head. "I have just come to town today. I have not even been home yet." He nodded at David and touched Rose's cheek. "I will call you."

David put an arm around Rose.

"He's changed," she said, watching Haas limp away. "I wonder if she's coming down with something."

"Who?"

"Lisa. Your daughter."

David made a sympathetic noise. He'd been away from home too much. His daughters had gotten taller, and he was out of the habit of Rose's grasshopper mode of conversation. David moved his hand down to the waistband of her jeans.

"What's this?" he said. "No panties today?"

"I got panties on."

"Uh-uh."

"Do too." She cocked her head sideways and looked at him. "Prove it."

TWENTY-SEVEN

DAVID CARRIED HIS TENNIS SHOES INTO THE LIVING ROOM. MEL and String stood in the doorway, talking to the girls.

"Let them in," David said to his daughters.

Lisa opened the door. Mattie went straight to String.

"Are you hungry?" she asked. "We hadn't had supper, and you could eat with us. Homeboy food."

Mel grinned. "Yeah, she and Lisa were explaining how you and Rose were in the bedroom with the door locked, and wouldn't come out and cook supper. You did say you hadn't, uh, had dinner at home in a while?"

David sat down on the couch and laced his tennis shoes.

Rose walked into the room. "Hello, String. Dammit, Mel, can't you give him any peace?"

"No, but—"

David looked at him.

Mel cleared his throat. "Sorry, Rose. But we got to work, no kidding."

"Please to hurry," String said. He was waving a fin over Mattie's head, making her hair stand up with static electricity. "We have long drive."

"Where we going?" David asked. He heard a spit and a hiss and looked over his shoulder. Alex, asleep on the back of the couch, had suddenly spotted String.

"It's a surprise," Mel said.

"Nice kitty animal," String said. "Bring jacket," he told David. "It is to be cold tonight."

"Heater in the van screwed up again?" Mel asked.

"We will be outside much."

David pulled his socks tight. The closet door opened and closed, and Mattie appeared, draped in his favorite leather jacket.

"Thank you," David said. He kissed her on the top of her head, and winced when the shock of static electricity zinged his lips.

"Ow, Daddy."

"Be good for Mommy." He beckoned to Lisa. "The FBI," he said softly, "isn't all it's cracked up to be."

She nodded, corners of her mouth turned down. "Kiss me good night when you come home, Daddy. Even if I'm asleep."

TWENTY-EIGHT

IT WAS DARK SO FAR OUT OF TOWN, NO STREETLIGHTS. HARD TO
see which way the narrow road snaked. David's eyes drifted shut.
He opened them wide, blinked, and shook his head. He'd been
off the road grid for forty-five minutes. He wasn't used to the
fatiguing monotony of driving without tracks.

They'd been on the move since seven. The last hour had been
an eternity on a skinny mountain road that dropped steeply to the
left as they climbed. String, driving two car lengths ahead in the
van, signaled, and David followed him onto a gravel road that
was little better than a track.

"Gravel is contraindicated," the car said, in soft, masculine
tones, "considering the condition of these tires."

David pushed his foot hard against the accelerator. The tires
crunched and scattered rock. He checked his rearview mirror. Dark
behind; dark ahead, the red glow of String's taillights leading the
way. Tall, narrow trees were illuminated by the headlights.

Mel opened his eyes. He rubbed his face with his palm, and
sat forward.

"Whoa," He looked out the window. "What the hell *is* this?
Gravel?"

"Yeah."

"Gravel, huh. How long I been sleeping?"

" 'Bout an hour and a half."

Mel stared out the window. "I bet there's not a hot cup of coffee
within twenty miles of here."

"Thank you, Mel. Until now, I hadn't thought about it."

Mel folded his arms. "I'm cold. You cold?"

David shrugged.

"Getting chilly."

David squinted and leaned forward, straining to see out the
windshield. The van veered right, and pulled into a flattened circle
of hard-packed dirt that clouded up under the tires, looking smoky

in the headlights. David pulled in behind the van. He looked at Mel.

"Good thing we trust this guy, huh, David? Otherwise I might, you know, be kind of nervous." Mel glanced through the window. "Way the hell out here." He took his gun from under his coat pocket, switched off the safety, waited till the green light glowed. "Out here in the dark and all." He tucked the gun into the back of his waistband.

"Don't blow your butt off," David said mildly. His own gun was uncomfortable but secure, just beneath his armpit. He left the safety on.

"What are you complaining? Long's I cover your ass, too."

The van door slid open, groaning in the track. String trundled from the side of the van, and skittered into the glare of David's headlights. String's left eye stalk drooped. He swayed back and forth, waiting.

"Come on, David." Mel opened the door, then shut it. Gently.

David got out of the car.

It was chilly. He reached into the back seat for his leather jacket, thought of Mattie wearing it over her head when she brought it to him, and smiled. The breeze touched his back through the thin cotton shirt. He looked over his shoulder, snatched up the jacket, and told the car to lock.

"Come please, Detectives."

David folded his arms, one shoulder higher than the other. "It's time you explained what's up here, String."

"There is not the time—"

"Make time," David said.

Mel looked from David to String, and narrowed his eyes.

String turned to one side, then back again. "You have the suspicions. You have checked the navigator in my van. You change it. Why?"

Mel shrugged. "We only—"

"Mel was covering your tracks," David said.

"Tracks?"

"The Elaki-Three," Mel said. "Particularly that Walker. She came down to check where you'd been. I messed it up, so she wouldn't know."

"Ah. The Polish restaurants. This was you?"

Mel nodded.

"Why you do this?"

Mel looked at David, then back to String. Neither said a word.

"Is bad," String said. "This problem between us. Hard to do the work." String turned and paused at the edge of the woods. He beckoned them on.

Mel looked at David, shrugged, and followed.

The path was narrow, covered with pine needles, spongy under their feet. String waved a large black flashlight, cop issue, and David and Mel moved close to the light.

String spoke, voice low. "It is as you say, Detective Mel. Must prove Izicho not involved."

David stumbled. "Shit."

String paused, then went forward again, more slowly.

"How does walking in the moonlight prove squat, Gumby?" Mel said.

"There is no moonlight."

Mel glanced at David. "Incredible powers of observation. Is this guy born to the job, or what?"

"There is meeting tonight," String said. "Illieus. Society inside the society. The group inside the group. We are cadre. Of dedicated ones."

"Dedicated to what?" David asked. The wind was beginning to blow, and the branches of the trees creaked and swayed.

String stopped. "We Izicho."

"Hot damn," Mel said, and whistled. "The Izicho version of the Bunkhouse Boys."

"These Izicho," David said, frowning. "They working during what Angel calls the bad old days?"

"Oh, it's *Angel* now," Mel said.

String stopped, then went on. "No. All of these much younger. Become Izicho after."

"After?"

"After the purge. Bad time, and shame. Is past."

"Yourself included?"

"Include myself."

"Angel Eyes thinks the bad old days are back," David said.

String turned to David, skittering sideways. "Do not you trust her, Detective David. No matter how you believe what of who. She is old. She is dangerous. Do not trust the Angel."

String moved away. His light bobbed, lonely in the night. David and Mel followed slowly. David heard rustling noises off the path.

"Insects," he told Mel.

"Yeah?" Mel's voice dropped to a whisper. "Got some pretty big bugs out here."

An owl hooted. David glanced over his shoulder. He started to zip his jacket, thought of the gun, and left the jacket open and loose.

String hissed suddenly, and stopped. Through the trees, David could see the orange flicker of fire.

"Did you, um, let your buddies know we were tagging along?" Mel asked.

"Has been cleared with the few. The major few. Best though to stay close, and, ah . . . follow the leader?"

"Just don't start throwing us in trees."

The fire flared high and hot, thin dry branches snapping in the teeth of the flames. Someone had been tending it. Not that David could see anybody now. He glanced around the clearing and found the darkness heavy with presence. There were shapes in the shadows, shapes that encircled the fire.

Ten of them, he decided. Between ten and fifteen Elaki, silent and unmoving.

Mel bent close to String. "What's the significance of the bonfire?"

"Warmth," String said. "Cold night, do you not think?" He raised his voice. "Please to come close, and begin."

The Elaki moved quietly, like leaves blowing, no talk. David's muscles tensed as the tall, dark shapes rolled close. The wind picked up, gentle still, but noisy in the trees. String staggered backward, rippling.

David heard him mutter something. Gabilla?

The Elaki encircled them, visible now in the flicker of firelight. David and Mel stood close together, almost back-to-back.

"Fucking weird," Mel said, under his breath.

David's heartbeat picked up. He looked at String, who stayed in the circle, close enough to touch. It made him feel better. Let him know who was on whose team.

Someone spoke, a female Elaki, her voice intense. David scanned the circle of Elaki until he spotted her. She was brown-black on the outside, pink in the middle. Her eye prongs were large and symmetrical, and her scales shone, except for a bald patch on her left side.

"I must thank you for coming," she said. Even in the mild breeze, she tilted sideways. "Please pardon the outdoors meeting. It is very like a home meditation. Conducive to decision making.

You have this, in your own organization?"

"We sit at a big table," Mel said, "and meditate over coffee and doughnuts."

"Ah," she said. "I will please come to point. You are nose talker—humans who do the investigation of what be called the cho invasion?"

David nodded.

The Elaki looked to String.

"He mean yes," String said.

"Is it of you opinion," the female continued, "that the cho killers are Izicho?"

"I can't comment on that," David said. He folded his arms and frowned, very aware of the gun beneath his arm. He wished the Elaki would back away, just a few feet farther out.

The female turned to String. "He mean yes by this also?"

"I mean no comment," David said. "I'm here because String brought me. I'm here out of courtesy"—he nodded his head—"to my partner. You said you would come to the point?"

The Elaki hissed and skittered backward.

"He is most correct," String said. "And the human is impatient. I too am waiting."

"You have new human habits," the Elaki female said.

"No need to insult," another Elaki said. This one sounded older, male, tired. "Much indication show these crimes committed by Izicho. We ourself to check for not be sure when initial occur. But is not truth. We agree the crimes model for old methods use in bad days, by bad segments of Izicho. We here represent hierarchy, and we know is not to be."

"What's he saying?" Mel asked. "He saying they didn't do it?"

"But yes," String said.

Mel folded his arms. "Who then?"

The female Elaki moved sideways, out of the way of the male behind her. He was pale grey, with a splotchy coloring that David had not seen before.

"Ah," the old Elaki said. "Do not know. Targets are Guardians. Significant. And yet . . ."

"Yeah?" Mel asked. "Yet what?"

"Could be group with scores to settle? A human thing?"

"The crimes were committed by Elaki," David said. "The physical evidence is overwhelming."

The Elaki female waved a fin. "Accepted. But crime not committed by Izicho."

"We have done to investigate also," the male continued. "To bring in youthful, unbiased help from home planet."

David frowned. "And?"

"And is most to perplex. Young Izicho . . . they do not come. They leave home planet. But do not arrive."

David frowned. And thought, suddenly, of the old Elaki female whose adult pouchling had disappeared. Adult Izicho pouchling.

"We have for you the documentation of disappeared Izicho. We wish to know where they go. What happen. We believe if can understand this, we can understand possible connection to crimes. Crimes we do not commit, no matter what the Angel Eyes say."

David heard hisses. He glanced around the circle of Elaki.

"She is most dangerous," the female said. "Truly, an old victim, most logical that she would be blame Izicho. She has suffered most of anyone."

David nodded, thinking of the torture scars. These Elaki seemed almost morbidly distressed by her suffering. Their concern surprised him.

Mel scratched his left armpit. "Thing is," he said loudly, "telling us you didn't do it. It don't prove nothing."

David grimaced. They could have nodded their heads, said thanks very much for the input, and gone home.

"Is most of a good point," the older Elaki said. "And we have made the arranges. We have called upon young Izicho from home planet. We would wish for you to watch this young one, and follow through with him the lure."

"You mean he's bait?" Mel said.

The old Elaki waved a fin. "Perhap we can learn what be to happen to the young colleagues. Perhap be connection. To invasion murders."

"Does this Izicho Elaki know what she . . . he—"

"He," the old Elaki said.

"Does he know what he's up against?"

"He know," String said. "We most fair to use one from personal connection. No stranger at risk."

"Your . . . pouchling?" Mel glanced from String to David.

"Pouchling from my pouch-sib," String said.

David scratched his chin, new beard rough on his fingertips. "Nephew?"

String teetered forward on his bottom fringe. "No. But some like that. Young relative."

"You have no idea what he'll be walking into," Mel said.

"He will be protected."

"I'll watch him every minute," David said.

"Yes. Watch, but stay off. You must do the job and learn. Protection otherwise provided."

"You guys hang too close," Mel said, "it may foul things up."

"No Izicho. No. Have selected human protector."

David had a sudden, odd feeling. "Who?"

String swiveled an eye stalk toward him. "Have all agreed." He waved a fin toward the other Elaki. "Have selected Rose Silver."

David took a breath, opened his mouth, and closed it.

Mel laughed and nudged David, hard, in the ribs. "Hope you guys got finances," he said. "She charges an arm and a leg."

TWENTY-NINE

IT WAS WARM INSIDE THE DOUGHNUT SHOP. THE TILE FLOOR WAS white and clean, the brightness hard on tired eyes. Even in the middle of the night, the place was full.

David took a sip of coffee that was hot enough to hurt going down.

String chewed a jelly doughnut. Raspberry filling and powdered sugar had showered his midsection, but he was restful for once, no skittering back and forth on his fringe scales.

"What you say, String?" Mel ate a glazed doughnut in two bites, then took a gulp from a box of orange juice. "You rather be outside meditating?"

String reached for another doughnut. David watched to see what the filling was this time. It looked like lemon pudding.

"You wish a jelly doughnut?" String waved a fin at David. "Good homeboy food."

David shook his head. "Plain cake doughnuts, or nothing."

Mel pursed his lips. "Austere."

"This is bad for nutrition," String said. He waved the doughnut, sprinkling confectioners sugar on the tabletop.

David glanced around to the other tables. People were careful not to stare, but this was a rural area, and they didn't see too many Elaki so far off the path.

David leaned back and closed his eyes to slits. The doughnut was warm, yeasty, sweet. He swallowed, thinking suddenly of Dahmi.

Where had she gotten the gun?

Someone like Dahmi wouldn't be likely to latch on to a weapon like that, not a six-millimeter Glock automatic pistol. Not with ablative sheath bullets. Had one of the Guardians given it to her? Angel herself? But if they had, wouldn't they have protected her— kept her safe from cho invasions, so she wouldn't feel so alone, so desperate she was driven to kill her babies?

Where was she now? Suppose the Guardians didn't have her. Was it the cho killers who'd taken her from the hospital?

David rubbed his face with his hand.

" 'Nother doughnut?" Mel asked.

"No." David looked at his watch. One A.M. Too late to talk to those kids Angel had mentioned. He'd get to them first thing in the morning.

"You are to be annoyed?" String asked. "Detective David?"

David looked up. "I'm sorry?"

"You are not happy with me," String said.

"Next time you take me to a secret meeting in the dead of the night in the middle of the woods—I'd like some idea of what's on the agenda."

"Yeah, no need to scare the crap out of us," Mel said.

String turned to him. "But, Detective Mel. Did you not find the conditions conducive to clear thought? Stimulation?"

"Damn right stimulation," Mel said. "Don't go stimulating me like that no more,'less you warn me first."

"You talked to Rose yet?" David asked.

Mel grinned.

String cocked an eye stalk in David's direction. "No. Awaited until approval all around."

"I guess it's all right," David said.

"I mean from Illieus."

"The Bunkhouse Boys," Mel said. "You sure you want her? Things tend to get violent, when you pull Rose in."

"Is already violent," String said. "I am most responsible for this young relative. And fond, also, Biachi most good. Must be Rose Silver. She is the , , , the . . . what you say? Man for the job."

Mel smashed his orange juice box with his fist, scattering sticky drops. The box made a crackling noise and stretched back into its original shape. Mel slammed it again.

"String, give me some background on the Guardians," David said. "Angel Eyes in particular."

String swayed from side to side. "I know of Elaki. Male. Name of Bahran."

"He's telling stories again." Mel scooted back in his chair and stuck his legs out.

"Bahran wishes a certain chemaki. And chemaki has suffered the loss of a male, and needs new member. The lost male—he has disappear. So Bahran take him place. But the missing one come back. He has been hurt and cripple. No vision and limited movement. Yes?"

David crossed his legs and scratched the back of his head. He looked at Mel.

"Hang on, David. Usually, you know, he works up to some kind of point."

"This is a chemaki most concern. Many male members, only one female—unusual. Now they feel must accept the missing one back, but have too much males. Very out of balance and members unhappy. Bahran asked to find other grouping."

"Broke his heart, I bet," Mel said. "You guys got hearts?"

"But Bahran wish to remain," String said. "So he removes eye stalks, and so loses vision, and asks also to come back. And because he now unlike to form new chemaki, old one feel responsible and take him."

"Son of a bitch," Mel said. "An Elaki love triangle. Quadrangle. Pentagon? How many were there?"

"What's this got to do with Angel?" David asked.

"This is determination, Detective David. A willingness to do anything, you see? To accomplish the end. The Angel Eyes very dangerous."

"Because she's tenacious?"

"She hate Izicho unlimits."

"I'd hold a grudge, too, you guys tortured me like you did her."

String picked up a jelly doughnut. "Much more than this, Detective Mel." He set the doughnut back on the table. "Izicho kill pouchlings of Angel Eyes. Two baby ones."

Mel whistled. David took a slow, steady breath. He looked at String.

"She start the Guardian, understand. Most active; most ruthless. Even then, at begin, dangerous to deal with. And those many bad old days. Many what you call the . . . the atrocity. On both side, the atrocity."

"Cho invasions?"

"But yes. Friendship groupings, chemakis, sibs, pouchmates, pouchling and Mother-One. Pierce vocal chamber of victim, all times. Anyone to do with Guardians, to know Guardians, or to have habits of Guardians. Most bad times, this is dark. Squads go out, two to three in squad. And do this killing."

"And the Guardians fought back?"

"Fought back hard and vicious," String said. "I not in the world, you understand. Angel Eyes very young, but already leader. And target. It is the death of the pouchlings that turn it around. Everything else? Explain away quit. You protest? You victim. But this gives publicity and many revulsions. It make her most dangerous. You see that?"

David thought of Angel Eyes on the news broadcast, calm and sympathetic, asking people not to judge a desperate Mother-One. He pictured her in the gardens of Edmund University, talking about Dahmi. Had she been crying, or was it his imagination? How did an Elaki show grief?

"String," David said. "Do Elaki ever cry?"

"Cry?" String ate a small bite of jelly doughnut. "No, Detective David. Only the human makes tears."

THIRTY

THE CAMPUS WAS HUSHED, THE BUILDINGS DARK. ONLY THE STU-
dent center was lit. David put a hand on his hip and arched
his back. He had not gone home. He had gone straight to the
office with String and Mel, working through reports that would
be garbled by Della's computer program, going over the details
of Dahmi's last days.

Another night of no sleep. No wonder he felt like shit.

He shivered. Overhead, streetlights were blinking out, as grey
light seeped into the darkness. David crossed Grosevenor Drive,
onto the campus proper.

They still didn't know where she'd gotten the gun.

David remembered Lisa suddenly, her downturned face, and
her plea for him to kiss her good night no matter how late he
got home. He looked around for a pay phone, then checked his
watch. If Tate Donovan and Dreamer had eight o'clock classes,
he'd have to catch them now.

A steady stream of students burst through the doors of the dor-
mitory, all of them moving fast. Some of the kids were dressed,
some were in T-shirts and sweats, some in nightgowns—all had
that bewildered air of leaving in a hurry. Many of them held their
hands over their nose and mouth, a few were coughing. A girl in
jeans was running, the birdcage she carried swaying.

"Shit fuck," she muttered. A parakeet swayed back and forth
on a swing inside the cage. David half expected it to fall off.

He looked at the windows and rooftop, expecting smoke. There
was none. No alarm was ringing. Just students, coming steadily
through the double doors.

Two of them, at least, were keeping their heads. David spotted
them by the left side of the building. One, a tall, whippy Elaki,
hovered behind a large bush, watching in silence. He wore a black
beret like the Israelis did these days, though his sloped at an angle

behind his eye prongs. Beside him was a boy—three hundred pounds if he was an ounce—blond crew, arms folded. He had a watchful expression, an intelligent face.

Some kind of prank, David decided. And these two were the perps. He expected them to be laughing, but the pair seemed serious. Oddly serious.

David approached slowly. The Elaki noticed him first. He could see the stiffening muscles when Blond Crew became aware, but the kid did not look at David. Not even when David came very close.

"Excuse me?"

The Elaki swiveled an eye stalk. Blond Crew turned. He had honest blue eyes, a tan, lightly freckled face, and a serious smile that was not without charm.

"Morning," Blond Crew said. "I help you, sir?"

Sir. David flipped his ID.

The Elaki slid sideways on his fringe.

"Yes, Detective?" Blond Crew gave him an intelligent, appraising look.

"I'm looking for Dreamer and Tate Donovan."

Crew's eyes widened. "That's *us*," he said ingenuously. "Is anything the matter?"

David smiled knowingly, then glanced toward the front of the building, where students were talking in groups. A campus security car, lights flashing, pulled up in the circle drive. David got the strong impression that Dreamer and Donovan would very much like to leave. But Donovan kept a steady, innocent gaze, good eye contact, and David was impressed.

He waved an arm, casually, toward the knots of students grouped on the lawn.

"What's up here?" Work it right, he thought, and they'd be relieved to get onto the subject of Dahmi.

Donovan smiled.

"There is of the building a very bad smell." The Elaki raised a fin tip. "Very bad; most bad. People run away."

"*Elaki* run away?" Donovan laughed.

Dreamer's belly rippled. "Elaki slide away."

David was envious of their camaraderie, remembering the uncomplicated, tight friendships he'd had at that age. Gregorio Alonso and Bennie Howitzer were long gone. Bad ends. He looked at these boys, Elaki and human, and wondered where they would be in twenty years. He glanced at the security guard who was heading their way. Jail, possibly.

The campus cop was tall, with a red, well-scrubbed face, and a self-conscious pride in the belt that held up his pants and sagged with equipment. Nightstick, electronic cuffs, prod, flashlight, beeper—surely this couldn't be standard issue?

The campus cop's jaw was tight. His name tag said Smed, Ben.

"Morning," he said, voice pleasant.

He was very young, David thought. Not much older than Blond Crew and his bud.

Smed nodded to the Elaki. "Sir."

David frowned. He flipped his ID. Again. "I have no idea what's up here." David waved an arm. "I'm questioning these gentlemen on another matter entirely."

"I see," Smed said.

David smiled blandly. "If you'll excuse us?"

Smed ducked his head and headed toward the front entrance of the dorm. Dreamer looked at Donovan.

"He knows," David said.

"Beg pardon?" Donovan was all smiles.

David scratched his cheek. "I understand you boys know Dahmi/Packer?"

"Packer?" Donovan frowned. "Yes, sir. We knew her. Is she—"

"Is she what?" David asked.

"Is she okay?"

"When's the last time you saw her?"

Donovan scratched behind his ear. "We saw her just before it happened. At the Wednesday night series. Right?"

The Elaki moved to one side. "That is the yes. She come most Wednesday-day night lecture."

"You talk to her?" David asked.

"Dreamer, did she go over to Brownie's with us that time?"

"Yes. She go. She not eat, but she go. She stand near for the table most usual we talk."

"What did you talk about?" David asked.

"The lecture," Donovan said. "We're studying the Guardians. They're the—"

"I know who they are." David smiled coldly. I live in the world, he thought.

"Professor Angel was one, back, you know, back when. On her planet. Did you know that?"

"How interesting. Tell me, did Dahmi seem upset that night? Nervous?"

Donovan folded his arms and shook his head, gaze steady. A nearly psychopathic liar, David decided. Not that he was necessarily lying right now.

"Not so you'd notice, no, sir. We just talked about the usual stuff. The lecture. And Professor Angel."

"She excited," the Elaki said.

Donovan looked at him.

"Hard for *you* to tell on Elaki," Dreamer said. "You a nose talker."

Donovan grinned. "And you're a goddamn bellybrain Elaki. Watch your mouth slit, or I'll leave you out in a storm."

The Elaki turned his eye stalks to David. "She leave early." He had relaxed as soon as David moved to the subject of Dahmi. "And three times she ask of me the hour of the day."

"And that was unusual?"

"She have pouchlings. But not usual want the time so much. I think maybe some special thing Wednesday-day night."

"Was she worried?" David asked.

The Elaki slid sideways. "I do not have the knowledge."

"At the time, did it strike you that way? That she might be worried or afraid?"

"No, no. I think then she be excited. Have somewhere to go. That make her high up feel funny."

High up feel funny? David frowned. Too bad String wasn't around to translate. But it didn't sound like Dahmi had run across whatever frightened her so badly she killed her pouchlings. It did sound like she had an appointment. He'd give a lot to know who with.

"Did she leave earlier than usual?" David asked.

Donovan frowned. "Not sure."

"She leave," Dreamer said.

"Do you know where she went?"

"Nope."

"Do not."

"Okay, then. Here's my card. If you think of anything, remember anything—"

"We'll give you a call," Donovan said.

David turned away, then glanced back over his shoulder. "Either of you own a gun?"

"No." Donovan smiled sweetly, and the sun glinted down on his close-cropped hair. "Guns make me nervous."

"Not safe for Elaki," Dreamer said.

David nodded. A small movement caught his eye, and he stared over Donovan's shoulder, getting a side-angle view of an Elaki who David thought, just for a moment, was String. The Elaki was smaller than usual, but thick, kind of ratty-looking.

The Elaki moved away, but David had the feeling he had been there awhile; that he had been watching.

THIRTY-ONE

DAVID STARED INTO THE SMALL CERAMIC BOWL OF HOT AND SOUR soup. Whatever it was that had surfaced looked amazingly like a deflated scrotum. He fished it up with his spoon.

Della leaned forward. "Mushroom, hon. Don' you want it?"

He held the spoon out and she took the mushroom between her small, white teeth, crunching delicately. She glanced sideways as she chewed, scouting Mel's plate.

David tipped back the brown bottle of Thai beer, finishing it off. There was an ancient cigarette burn in the red plastic tablecloth, two or three inches from his plate. He glanced at his watch. Angel's lecture was an hour away. He looked at Mel, who was frowning, then across at String, who had rice scattered down his scale front. He decided to go by himself.

"You talk to Rose?"

String cocked an eye prong. "But yes. She most willing to help. Unsure if pouchling problem. Say she will work it out."

"Kendra can look after her sisters for a while," David said.

A small dark man in a shirt and slacks rolled a metal cart to the table. He handed Mel a bowl of red sea curry, Della a plate of pepper steak, and David a plate of pad ka prao. He set a stainless-steel bowl of sticky rice in the middle of the table, then looked at David.

"You need beer." It wasn't a question, but David nodded his head. The man looked at Della. "Sweet sour sauce?"

"Yeah, hon."

He looked at String. "Hot mustard."

"What about me?" Mel asked.

"You fine."

David helped himself to rice, then spooned chicken, onions, broccoli, and the intense brown sauce onto his plate. He bit into a thin, tender sliver of chicken and speared a strip of onion.

"Where's Pete?"

Della rolled her eyes and chewed a mouthful of rice. "He can't get those Elaki straight on their terminals. That little one, that Ash, his keeps screwing up. It won't accept his voice patterns." She ate a baby corn cob from Mel's plate. "Hey, but there's a two-inch printout on your desk, Silver."

"Of victim similarities?"

"Lot of it's background information. It's in the file, so you can scroll through if you want. But the graphs and comparisons—that's all in the printout."

"Just give me the rundown. Cut to the chase."

"Pete'll be disappointed."

"I'll look at it later."

The waiter took David's empty bottle and set a fresh beer on the right side of his plate.

"Okay. Similarities." Della chewed a piece of steak, then wiped her mouth delicately with the corner of a napkin. "They all got some connection to Angel's group. Those Guardians."

David raised his beer, then frowned and set it down. "What connection, exactly?"

"Well. Dahmi. She went to the lectures. Assuming she's part of it."

"She's part of it," David said. She was the key, if he could figure it out.

"Okay, and Arnold. He's actually doing research on the Izicho. Past and present. And he's on the faculty with *her.*"

"Angel."

"Yeah. Assuming Arnold was the target—and the reason the McCallums got whacked. And the Elaki. He worked with Arnold. Some kind of student at the School of Diplomacy."

Mel stabbed a large piece of shrimp a split second before Della got to it.

Della glanced over at David's plate. She fingered the collar of her shirt. "There's the other two. That Beston bunch. Whole Elaki chemaki and pouchling. Two of the Elaki males from the chemaki had direct connections to the Guardians. They were some kind of gofers for the organization. Like, you know, somebody who works in a political campaign.

"And that couple with the teenage girl and the . . . what you call them, Elaki exchange students? The girl and the Elaki attended lectures pretty regularly. Elaki were doing some research work on them."

"You know what's funny about this?" Mel said.

David chewed a chunk of broccoli. "What?"

"I mean the victims. Not exactly movers and shakers there, in the organization. Know?"

Della leaned back in her chair. She sucked a piece of ice up from her glass, then pushed it into the pouch of her cheek. "Yeah. But if they'd gone after the big guys, we'd of been onto the political thing first off."

"So?" Mel said.

"If they're trying to put the fear into people, then it makes sense." David spooned brown sauce onto his rice. "The hard-liners aren't going to be scared off. And if you off them, you create instant martyrs. People get mad, and the organization flourishes. Plus, you get heat, because the big ones have the influence."

Mel chewed another bite of shrimp. "If I were them, I'd go after Angel."

Della shook her head. "Did you hear anything he just said?"

"Be worth it," Mel said. " 'Cause she's got a heck of influence. Best she gets out the way."

"If you're looking for repression, and you go after the little people," Della said, "then they get scared. They feel vulnerable. And you got no grass roots support."

String waved a fin. "Angel too hard to get. Protection big. Still has Weid. Constant companion."

"Weid?" Mel said.

"Elaki like a man/hench. Loyal companion guard the body. He be with her since early most days. They try to kill her, but Weid kill them."

"Describe him," David said.

"Umm, Small height—like human. Thick, for Elaki. Many scales missing patch. Bent up the eye prongs."

David cocked his head sideways. Had Weid been the Elaki who was hanging around the dorm, watching him question Donovan and Dreamer?

String cocked an eye prong. "He has what you call the sexual aura."

Mel waved his fork. "Ought to be able to spot him right off." He swallowed. "But, you know, just out of curiosity, what is it exactly gives an Elaki his sexual aura?"

"Ah," String said. "You see—"

David checked his watch. "Got a lecture." He took one last drink of beer, wiped his mouth, and grabbed his jacket. Della was inching a fork toward his chicken before he'd pushed his chair in.

The waiter stopped him on the way out the door, offering a basket of fortune cookies. He took one from the bottom of the pile and broke it open as he went through the bead-covered door into the chill, black night. He crammed the broken cookie into his mouth and unraveled the white strip of paper. There was just enough light in the parking lot to read the fortune, printed in large black type.

**WHAT BEGINS AS FLIRTATION
COULD BECOME SERIOUS.**

David tucked the fortune into his jacket pocket.

THIRTY-TWO

DAVID STOOD IN THE BALCONY OF THE WARD BENDEN LECTURE hall. A draft of air came from his left, strong enough to ruffle his hair. He stayed back in the shadows, watching. The room beneath was warmly lit, the oak parquet floor waxed and gleaming, and the rows of folding chairs full. An Elaki, late and hurried, glided across the floor on his bottom fringe. David thought of ice skating.

The wall behind Angel Eyes was a bank of windows, floor to ceiling, and the night pressed close and black. David shivered, thinking of snipers. Angel stood before a microphone, her contralto voice enveloping her audience, most of whom were Elaki.

David leaned forward. Something or someone was moving, just outside the window. Someone with a light. Impossible to see much from inside. David watched, muscles tensing, as the pinpoint came closer. The light moved close to the door and disappeared. The door opened quietly, and an Elaki slid in.

Weid. David smiled with the side of his mouth, wondering about Elaki sexual auras.

The audience didn't notice Weid. There were few fidgets, none of the humans coughed, no one whispered or left early. David could not distinguish the words, but he was affected by the rhythm of speech, the cadences that were alternately soothing and invigorating.

Then it stopped. There was a silence, then the humans applauded, self-consciously. Chairs scraped the floor. One human (One *human*? David asked himself) moved hesitantly toward Angel, but was swept aside as three Elaki slid across the polished parquet floor.

Weid appeared behind Angel. David saw Angel move sideways and lift a fin. Weid moved back and away.

Know each other well, David thought.

He turned and went down the stairs. Elaki were leaving, others talking in groups. The Elaki were tall, making it hard for David to see.

A large noisy group was forming, and David saw Donovan and Dreamer. He moved to one side to watch. Angel Eyes was still talking to a steady stream of Elaki, though she was inching toward the door. She moved sideways, then stopped when she saw him.

Her eye stalks slanted in his direction, and the conversation stopped. The knot of Elaki encircling her turned and looked. For a moment it seemed that the room grew silent, though he later decided it had only seemed that way. His face felt warm. He folded his arms. He was aware that Weid had spotted him, and was studying.

The door opened and closed loudly, breaking the silence. There was movement from the left. An Elaki came quickly, rudely, through the crowd. She was intent on Angel Eyes, who seemed not to see the approach and was making her way to David.

Angel lifted a fin and David moved forward.

"No popcorn tonight?" There was something in her voice that sounded like a laugh.

David smiled. "I'd have brought some, if I'd known you were hungry."

"I *am* hungry. But I would guess you have the questions?"

David saw a flurry of movement to his left. The Elaki who had pushed so rudely through the crowd was almost upon them. Her pouches were loose. A Mother-One.

The Elaki stopped. David looked back, wondering why, after being so forceful, she did not come close. She turned her back, and threaded her way into the crowd. David frowned. She had seemed familiar.

"Detective?"

David looked back to Angel. "I'm sorry?"

"I just said . . . do you think we might talk over a meal? Have you eaten?"

"No," David lied. He was grateful he'd left Mel and String behind. Angel would best be handled gently.

"I know of a favorite place—"

"Angel?" Stephen Arnold caught sight of David and froze. "Hello, Detective." He turned to one side, standing slightly in front of David. "Angel, the kids." He inclined his head toward a knot of Elaki and humans, Donovan and Dreamer included. Weid stood to one side, close to the students, but separate. They were all watching. David wondered if he was imagining the hostility.

Could be the cop thing. Harassing the idol. Though in his opinion she hadn't seemed harassed until Arnold showed up.

"The kids asked me to use my influence." Arnold was smiling, but he looked exhausted. The skin on his face looked tight, and there were bags beneath his eyes. His shoulders were rounded, slumped over. "They're going over to Brownie's again tonight. They want to buy you a beer if you'll come. And, of course, they loved the lecture."

"Ah, Stephen." Angel sounded tired. Maybe, David thought, even annoyed. "I think *not* tonight." She waved a fin, almost touching Arnold, but not quite. "Why do you not go with them?"

"Maybe I will." Arnold's back was straight and stiff. He turned to David. "Anything to report, Detective?"

"Not just yet," David said. "Have you been all right?"

"My daughter freshly murdered and tortured, Detective? No. I haven't been all right. Do you know, Angel? That the police suspect *me* of having something to do with her killing?"

"But no, Stephen." Angel's voice softened as she turned an eye stalk to David. "I must be sure you are mistaken on this."

"My main concern is for *your* safety, Dr. Arnold. I think you're wrong not to accept our protection. Unless you know something I don't?"

"I *know* that I'd be damn glad for whoever murdered my baby to come after me. I can handle myself. I'd just like a chance to handle them."

"*No*, Stephen." Angel turned to David. "Detective Silver is most correct. You should be careful. We could not afford to lose you now."

Arnold put a hand on her back scales, just where her body flared. David noticed the quiver, quickly suppressed, before Angel moved almost imperceptibly, just out of reach.

She doesn't like to be touched, David thought.

"Not to worry, Angel. Everything I have is backed up. All my notes, everything. The study's complete. The conclusion—first draft is done, and I'm revising. The gist of it's there." Arnold nodded curtly at David. "I'll leave you to your interrogation."

"Actually," David said, "we're just having dinner."

Arnold narrowed his eyes, then turned and walked away. David wondered why he had said what he did.

THIRTY-THREE

ANGEL HAD FOLDED IN THE MIDDLE AND TUCKED HERSELF INTO his car without hesitation.

"I like this, David." She peered at the lights and dials on his dashboard. "I have had the secret desire to ride in the police car. Much is the gadgetry."

"You need to ride in a cruiser."

"You have pouchlings, David?"

"Three."

"So many." She sounded wistful. "Are they the golden hair blue eyes?"

"What, with me for a father?" David shook his head. The car took a turn he did not expect, and his hands slid on the steering wheel. "My wife is dark, too. Brown-eyed, curly-haired brunettes. All three."

"Is your wife also the police officer?"

"No." David frowned, wondering how best to describe Rose. As always, she defied description.

"What does she do? She is like Elaki Mother-One, then? All time for the children?"

"Nooo. Rose is a sort of free-lance troubleshooter. She works with animals a lot."

"I see. If you have animal misbehavior, she will train."

David turned left onto Merton Avenue. Angel had programmed the car. He didn't like the section they were heading into.

"No, she doesn't train animals," David said. "She protects them."

Angel was quiet and David glanced sideways. The Elaki's belly rippled—a genuine Elaki laugh.

David cocked his head sideways. "Why is that funny?"

Angel turned to him, and leaned back into the seat.

Caught you, David thought.

"Please excuse," she said. "It just seem to be the funny. Animals call you wife for help. But how?"

"You should answer our phone for a week." David laughed, but felt a little bit traitorous. He glanced out the rearview mirror. Where *was* this place?

Angel leaned close, pointing out the windshield. "It is there, see? Is Café Pierre."

The Café Pierre occupied the bottom half of an old, white brick building built into the jutting triangle of the street corner. It was one of those odd places of peculiar and definite ambiance that seemed to attract Elaki.

The shutters were freshly lacquered in black, and there were lush red geraniums in the window boxes on the second floor. David would have expected tables outside. There were none. But then, Elaki would not care to dine al fresco. Not when a good strong wind could blow them next door.

"Okay." David told the car to park. He crossed the street beside Angel, watching for traffic. She seemed oblivious to cars, preoccupied. She swarmed gracefully up the front stoop of the restaurant.

"Is charming place," she told him.

A huge glass window on the side wall was dust-streaked and cracked in the top left corner. BAR was stenciled in large white letters. A red-checked curtain, thin and dusty, hung in the bottom third of the window. The door was two-thirds glass, with a wood bottom panel. RESTAURANT was stenciled across the top of the door, with PIERRE a few inches down in ornate script.

David followed Angel in. He looked around and blinked. An odd place. A period place.

The floor was ancient patterned linoleum, none too clean. A mahogany wood bar ran the length of the back wall, and on the shelf behind it were glass bottles of liquor. David looked closely. They were filled to varying degrees with amber and clear liquid, but they had to be fake. Liquor hadn't been available in bottles for years.

There were fresh flowers behind the bar—black roses. Another vase sat on the wood ledge that separated the dining room.

"Good evening," a man said, his voice low, depressed.

David gave him a second look. He stood beside the bar, arm resting on the surface. His trousers were loose cotton, black, banded tightly at the ankles over large, oversize leather work shoes. His pullover sweater was hunter-green, old and nubby, and the shirt beneath was black like the pants, and buttoned all the way up to a tight collar. He wore a shabby black blazer, the lapels wide.

His face was harsh and hawk-nosed, and he didn't smile. His hair was dark, short, and greased back over a round skull. His eyebrows were dark. He looked past David and Angel Eyes, into the night.

"What do you think?" Angel said.

"Smells good," David said. It did. Garlic, gravy, wine.

The man looked at David, eyes flat and uninterested. "Order the beef bourguignonne." His voice was rough, accented. David couldn't place it.

"My table open?" Angel asked.

The man nodded, but did not look their way.

"*Who* is that?" David asked, voice low.

"That is Pierre," Angel said, moving quickly away. David followed her to the back of the café.

The tables were mahogany, solid and round, perched on pedestals, so there was plenty of room for legs. The tabletops were high, like bar tables, able to accommodate Elaki, who would stand, and people, who could sit on tall, slat-back chairs with wide, padded armrests. Elaki and human could dine eye to eye prong.

The tablecloths were thin, striped, some of them had holes. They reminded David of dish towels his mother had used in their kitchen, before his father disappeared. Died.

He glanced up at the ceiling. Plaster? It was cracked from one corner all the way to the center, where a globe light hung from a nest of red ceramic flowers. Why did it make him think of genitals? From somewhere came a burst of music. Country blues.

"Ah," Angel said. "The classic. Patseeee Cline."

"Who?" David said.

"She was singer. Before you time, David."

"How do you know her?"

"I know the *music,* David."

David glanced over his shoulder. "I'd have expected something classical. Or jazz, maybe."

"Pierre play what he like. What he like different, no pattern type. Most of it very good, but not my personal taste the calliope music."

"Mine either," David said. But it might be kind of fun if the kids were along. Then it would be legal to enjoy it.

He looked around the room. The clientele was about half and half—Elaki and human, but no mixing between tables. He and Angel attracted stares. Some of the people were dressed up, others, nearly threadbare. They were no more than two miles from the disadvantaged area of Little Saigo.

The menu cards were old, well fingered, and David had doubts that their choices would register. There were three entrees—boeuf bourguignonne, brochettes de moules, and larves de hanneton en papillote.

Angel glanced at him. "Difficult to decide, yes, David?"

"Ummm." He pressed for the beef.

Angel looked up. "Did you order as he say?"

David nodded. He didn't recognize anything else. He watched as she bent down and made her choice. Larves de hanneton en papillotte. He wondered what it was. Larves—did that mean snail? He'd had snails and liked them okay.

Pierre had said the beef. David looked at the back of the menu.

"There is nothing else to order," Angel said. "Pierre decides side dishes and drinks." She swiveled an eye stalk in his direction. "He has the good instinct. You can trust."

"Interesting attitude," David said.

"Pierre is most unusual human. Not"—Angel tilted sideways—"that I am the perfect judge. He like to cook and feed, and like to sell to Elaki because Elaki have no taste prejudice. Will eat any nutritious, well-prepared meal. Pierre is true gourmet."

David looked at the front of the small café. Pierre still stood beside the bar, unsmiling.

"You are flattered, David," Angel said. "Pierre does not speak to many."

David smiled. "He spoke to you."

"But yes."

It snagged him, for a moment, the way she said it. It wasn't conceit, he decided, so much as admitting reality. She was Angel. Angel Eyes. Of course Pierre talked to her.

Angel waved a fin. "Do you believe that SSStephen Arnold is in danger from Izicho?"

David sat back in his chair. "I think he's in danger, yes."

"Most careful, you," Angel Eyes said.

Their food came—brought by a thin girl with short, lank blond hair and large brown eyes. She wore blue jeans that sagged over her bony hips, and a black sweater with holes in the sleeve. A dirty apron was tied around her waist. She wore long earrings, but no makeup, gave David a hesitant smile, but flinched when Angel looked her way. The boeuf bourguignonne, smelling like heaven, came in a brown tureen accompanied by a plate of noodles. Beside the beef were spears of fresh asparagus. David wished he hadn't already had dinner.

David glanced across the table at Angel's plate. "What is that?"

"Larves de hanneton en papillote," the girl said.

Yes, David thought. But what was it?

"How do you prepare it?" he asked.

The girl put a cutting board on the table and set a long crusty baguette on top.

"Salt and pepper them," the girl said, wiping her hands on the apron. "Roll them in flour and bread crumbs, wrap them, buttered. He bakes them in ashes."

David sighed. "What are *them*?"

"Grubs."

"Grubs of what?"

"Beetles," Angel told him. "Want to try?"

"No," David said. "But thanks." It was good Pierre liked cooking for Elaki. Someone should.

The beef was the best—and the richest—he had ever tasted. Tender brown chunks in red Burgundy gravy. The asparagus was pickled and tangy. He ate it with his fingers, and tore off hunks of bread, and was well on the way to finishing his second big meal of the evening.

David took a large swallow of wine. Angel did not seem affected by the alcohol. A shame it didn't work on her like it did on String.

David chewed a noodle. Slowly. Shoving food in was beginning to hurt. He would definitely call a halt to the bread. He raised his wine glass, then put it down.

Angel ate slowly but steadily, one fin splayed into fingerlike extrusions. Silverware was one human habit she had not acquired.

"Suppose the Izicho aren't responsible for these cho murders, Angel." David opened his hands. "I don't mean *believe* it. Just suppose it, for the sake of argument. If they weren't responsible, who would be?"

Angel waved a fin, dropping a buttered crumb onto the striped tablecloth. "Is no one else, David Detective Silver. Talk frankly?"

He nodded.

She glanced sideways, then back to his face. Her eye stalks were rigid. "No other grouping has the reason to hurt. No other grouping the power of position."

"Why?" David said. "Why concentrate their efforts here and now? What's the catalyst?"

Angel leaned sideways. "I must tell you now is the very critical moment. Mainline Elaki, mainline Izicho—go together, you see? And they feel the threat of the Earth habit. Here . . ." She snagged a wrapped beetle grub and ate it. "Here there is not the habit of social force. The pressure of the others, the social group, the community of peers that regulate the society. Yes, some places, we have found like things. Some of the oriental groupings, and in—I believe it is Haiti? The smaller places. But not to the extent of home. And this give Elaki much freedom and little structure. The Elaki who are coming in—they are the creators. And the criminals, yes, I do admit this. And because of the one, the Izicho answer is to suppress the other. Suppress all. This work against philosophy of Guardian. Guardian feel the society pressure not worth the squelch of us. Too much oneness in Elaki, can you understand this? Face Elaki with problem—will go stand in a bog all night. Become one?" Angel waved a fin, and went rigid. "This mean *do nothing,* accept a what you call, oh, status quo. Stagnant, David, still waters of sludge. This is Elaki mental state, so too often."

"But not you," David said.

"Not me ever. But Izicho want to scare. Keep Guardian from getting strong hold, here, where the ideas most acceptable."

"Won't that backfire, though?"

The waitress appeared with ceramic mugs of coffee. David's was rich brown, cream no sugar, Angel's black. He wondered how they knew he liked his coffee that way.

It was strong, but not bitter. A clear taste, rich, no odd notes of aftertaste. He could drink this coffee all night.

"It backfire?" Angel said.

David wiped his mouth with a black cloth napkin. "Do them more harm than good. Killing families, torturing them. What's more likely to happen is the Izicho will get thrown out."

"They very close to human government figures. Do you not know this? Study own history, David."

"Not if it happens in people's faces. Not like this." He grimaced. "Enid West won't allow it. There's already been one backlash."

"Ah, yes," Angel said. "The experiments. The drug the Elaki have. This Black Diamond."

"There was a lot of anti-Elaki sentiment over that."

"You must understand mentality. It is fear reaction, these Izicho. *Fear,* not logic. If ruled by logic, would not have happened, the past . . . the past atrocities." Angel leaned sideways. She had stopped eating, and she slid a fin across the side of the coffee cup. "This place, you know. It remind me. I was young Elaki, when began Guardians. Did you know I was there? Early times?"

David nodded his head.

"Yes. I be there." She was oddly still now, the stillness David associated with Elaki meditation—the state of being one Angel scoffed at. "Full of ideas then, and excitement. I think time of much happiness. I think then it be possible to make the big change, you see, and so full then of the way it could be. We meet together for food and hot drink and . . . is hard to explain."

David nodded gently. They were revolutionaries—young, excited, idealistic, changing the world to suit their vision of what was good. A moment of happiness, before the scars that would come. He glanced at the white web work on her midsection, and wondered how she had held under torture. He wondered how he would hold.

"There is much we do not know then," Angel said. "About how scared Elaki Izicho can react. About how our own selves react." She turned toward David. "There are betrayals," she said. "In our own group. It is such a thing that takes my pouchlings."

David felt a tickle of coldness at the base of his spine.

"I had little baby ones. Two pouchlings, male and female. This you knew?"

He nodded. Her voice had gone so soft he had to lean across the table to hear.

"What happened?"

"Is cho invasion," Angel said. "I not home with them. Off. Off to make a little inconvenient mess. How childlike and pointless that now seem. And while I gone, the Izicho come. My little baby ones tortured. A chemaki male and female, there to watch and protect . . ." She leaned close. "Literally, David Silver. They are torn to pieces."

David swallowed. He thought of her on television, asking for understanding for Dahmi. Did she know where Dahmi was? Did she have her safely tucked away? It was almost more than he could ask. Almost.

"Where is Dahmi?" David said.

Angel Eyes was very still. She did not have the nervous movements he knew so well. Just stillness. She turned her eye stalks and watched him. Her eyes looked moist, but he knew better. He knew Elaki did not cry.

"I do not know where Dahmi be. I worry for her, most often."

"Angel, isn't it possible that these cho murders are the work of some fanatic, offshoot group of crazies?"

"Elaki do not have this, the mental illness crazies. We do not have such fragility of psyche. It is our luck. Be careful not to project this human trait to us. It will lead you wrong."

David sat back. "Maybe if there—"

Her sudden, high-pitched whistle of distress brought him up out of his chair, and he was by her side in a moment. She curved over, supporting herself on the tabletop. Her cup of coffee went sideways, spilling onto her plate, a brown swirl of liquid making a mush of well-seasoned grubs and bread crumbs.

"What is it?" he said. "How can I help?"

He was aware of Elaki turning their backs, and people craning to see.

"Is pain, old pain. Physical problem." Her voice was brittle. If she'd had teeth, she'd be gritting them. "Old problem be later okay, *must* go now."

"I'll drive you home."

She could barely move. He tugged gently, feeling a ripple of something—revulsion?—beneath her scales. Again, he knew she did not like to be touched. He was careful, gentle. She clamped a fin around his arm and he pulled. She was lightweight, sliding in fits and starts on the snake-belly scales of her bottom fringe.

Pierre watched them, eyes sharp and knowing.

"I'll drive you to a hospital," David said.

"*No.* Not necessary. Old problem, need rest and must have Elaki vehicle. Cannot afford pleasure of police car."

"Of course," David said. His face was red. He should have known without being told.

Pierre nodded when David asked for a car. The man moved quickly, with grace, no panic, and little real interest. Just competence. David and Angel moved out to the front stoop to wait, to avoid the eyes of the humans, and the backsides of the Elaki.

The car came quickly. A red van.

"You sure you'll be okay? I hate to send you off like this."

She was shedding scales. "It is old problem. From bad old days—"

David was embarrassed. It seemed bad form somehow, to bring up torture. Socially unacceptable.

"Is not offshoot group doing cho, my David."

My David, he thought.

"I know these Izicho, I better than anyone. The cho killers are Izicho. I have not the hesitation of knowledge. My own hopes are stone. Have been too long in the years. For so long, I do not have the *care,* only now . . . now . . . I feel the care, again. I do not like it. It feels like being afraid." She went rigid under her scales. "I know the smell and the feel and the taste of it." She hissed. "I know the habits of the beasts."

THIRTY-FOUR

DAVID PEERED INTO THE ELAKI DOCUMENTATION CENTER. IT WAS a clean, tunnellike building that consisted mainly of a narrow walkway bordered by crushed red rock. Elaki design. Elaki milled in what passed for a line, skittering on their fringe scales, some of them hissing.

Waiting in line, David decided, was a new and unappreciated concept.

He moved away from the window slit, stuck his hands in his pockets, and staggered off. The market cacophony of noise and color would hit hard after the cocoonlike confines of the documentation center. David scratched the heavy growth of beard on his cheek. He smelled bad. The nano odors he'd acquired made him nauseous, but God knows he was a convincing drunk. Nobody would smell this bad on purpose.

He wandered down the crushed gravel walkway that led from the EDC to the market. Long narrow stalls, painted translucent colors, emitted spicy cinnamon food smells—cinnamon coffee, cinnamon tacos. The walkways were narrow and people bent backward to stay out of his way. Most stalls had a flag out front, so the Elaki could judge the strength of the wind. Newly arriving Elaki were hyper on the subject of Earth's killer winds.

The stalls sold junk. Large belts, vests, real human artifacts that could be worn. Earth vids were everywhere, claiming to explain humans and human behavior. The stall proprietors were Elaki, but they used people for the scut work. Teenagers roamed the street, ignoring each other and waiting.

Mel stopped at a window and looked in.

"Here, David, you should look at this." Mel's voice was loud in David's earpiece. "Be sure and stand downwind, okay?"

David looked around the marketplace, saw Mel standing in front of a stall several yards away. He waited for Mel to leave before he worked his way over. The star display was a harness and anchor, dangling from a metal hook. A tiny screen showed an Elaki wearing the harness as he slid down a "typical" Earth street. A sudden wind took hold of the Elaki, who quickly pulled a ripcord and "dropped anchor." The wind became fierce. Another, unluckier Elaki was picked up and carried away, hissing and squirming.

"See the vid?" Mel was saying. "Our hero in harness. Stays put while his buddy gets the mother of all blow jobs."

"Does not work," String said. He bent close to a water fountain—something he could never resist. The water arced high in a cold, steady stream, splattering drops on the Elaki's eye prongs. David realized that he would have to stand on his tiptoes to get a drink. None of the newer fountains were made for people.

David heard String mutter to a wall clock, asking for the time. He checked his watch. Two minutes after the hour.

"Biachi to arrive in seven of the minutes," String said. "Rose is here? I do not see her."

"Said she'd be here, she's here," Mel said.

David frowned. He hadn't seen her either.

"What of the pouchlings?"

"They'll look after themselves awhile." David was muttering the way he'd seen drunks mutter, as they wandered the streets alone. "Big sister in charge. We got a friend coming over around dinnertime. He'll see they get fed and looked after till one of us gets back."

"It is time for the scatter," String said. He flashed a signal to Walker, who signaled Ash and Thinker. The Elaki-Three fanned out.

It was bright out, sunny. Wind chimes made of doll-like people clanked and tinged at every slap of breeze. The wind wasn't strong—just enough to make String falter now and then, before it died down.

A boy walked the top ledge of the brick wall. He held a basket of popcorn balls, strung together with edible plastic. He jumped down and moved to the center of the sidewalk, two feet from the mouth of the tunnel that would disgorge newly arrived Elaki into Earth society.

Thirty-seven Elaki were due in at 1:07. Elaki proprietors kept an eye prong on the streets, and their human employees edged ever closer to the documentation center. Everyone was waiting—stall keepers, guides. Cops.

In the last thirteen months, twenty-seven Izicho officers had left the Elaki home planet. All had been seen leaving. Each one had supposedly been processed through the EDC. None had been seen since, including Calii, Yahray's long-lost son.

David wanted an overview. He wanted to know how much involvement there was on the street, how thoroughly orchestrated the action.

Walker and Ash and Thinker were stationed inside the EDC where they could blend with other Elaki, stay out of trouble, and watch. They would see that Biachi, code-named the Little Nipper (by Mel), made it through. All three were under orders to stay out of the way under any and all circumstances. Rose would pick Biachi up on his way out of the tunnel. The rest of the team had a section of the market to watch.

Rose would stay with Biachi. No one else was supposed to get close.

"Heads up." David heard the captain's voice in his earpiece. "Little Nipper's coming through."

David shoved the sleeves up on the ratty sweater he wore, and took a swig of tea from the box of alcohol. He let some of the liquid dribble down his unshaven chin.

Mel paused by a fountain of water that cascaded into a pool. He climbed up on the stone wall at the water's edge and held up his arms. He wore a rumpled plaid suit, and David knew from riding over with him that he smelled like onions.

"Sinners!" he shouted. None of the humans paid any attention, but several Elaki looked up. "Fornicators! Elaki abominations! Chemaki boffing adulterers! Let the one true God show you the way."

A very small Elaki male pouchling slid close and gazed raptly up at Mel. The young one waved a fin, demanding one of the vid cards Mel held.

"Beat it, kid," David heard Mel say, sotto voce in the mike. "This stuff'll warp your mind."

The Elaki skittered backward and away. David ducked his head, swigging warm tea. The nano odors were getting stronger in the sun. He noticed one of the Elaki stall owners watching him. The owner moved back and forth on his bottom fringe. Unlike everyone else, he did not watch the EDC. He watched the crowd. He watched David.

David wiped his mouth with the back of his hand. He belched. The Elaki hissed and turned away.

The first swell of Elaki newcomers swarmed out of the tunnel.
David watched from the corner of his eye. He spotted String's
nephew immediately. He hadn't expected to see a family resem-
blance—the Little Nipper wasn't direct lineage—but he was the
image of String. His left eye prong was crumpled and drooping
and there were bald patches on his scales. He was small, slight,
and hesitant as he rolled into the marketplace.

He was immediately approached by three teenage boys, who
smiled and ducked their heads ingratiatingly, like bashful sharks.

"Got him," David said. "Proceeding southwest toward the harness—"

"Got him, no," String said. "Ah, here. This one."

This one was a surprise. Tall, even for an Elaki, jet-black.
Thickset, symmetrical. Handsome devil, David thought. For an
Elaki.

"Spitting image of you, String." Mel's voice was loud in
David's ear.

The Little Nipper looked around carefully. Young, David decided. He held a satchel, and his eye stalks moved back and forth,
focusing over David's head, then looking back.

"Smart kid," Mel said in his ear. "Be a good cop when he gets
some subtlety."

"Here it comes." The captain this time. David paid attention.

A thin girl, dark hair cut short and teased into a ruff from forehead to neckline, stood close to String's nephew. She moved her
hands, pointing toward the stall where the Elaki owner had been
out watching the crowd. Then she pointed to the stall next door.

The Elaki slid backward, but stopped, flanked suddenly by two
other Elaki who seemed to come from nowhere. They all spoke—
David hoped Della was picking it up on the mikes. The Little
Nipper followed the girl, an Elaki on either side. Firm and friendly
persuasion.

A young girl, black hair pulled back in a ponytail, hands in
her pockets, went into the stall behind them. Fresh-faced and
waifish, the girl wore faded blue jeans, and her sweater had a
hole in the back.

Rose, David realized suddenly.

Mel was singing—"Shall We Gather at the River." A signal.
David stood up so he could see who was watching him. The same
Elaki stall owner who'd stared at him before. David scratched his
crotch, eyes narrowed into thoughtful slits, and the Elaki hissed
and went back in his stall.

The dark young nephew disappeared from view. String went to the next stall and bought Elaki cinnamon coffee. David would not have minded a cup. String must be nervous, David decided. He had passed up the tacos.

A new wave of Elaki burst from the documentation center. The pattern was the same. A young, waifish human, smiling big and talking fast, made the initial approach, followed up by two largish Elaki, flanking the newcomer, guiding them into the stalls. David watched carefully. Not all the Elaki were hit, just the more hesitant, the more prosperous. But almost every stall had its mark.

Captain Halliday's voice was a harsh murmur in his ear. Everyone was freaking—trying to keep watch and see what was up with the strong-arm sales technique. The Little Nipper was the only Izicho due in. Maybe this approach wasn't the one they were looking for.

David chewed his lip. It could never be easy.

He stood up and stretched, colliding with a newly arrived Elaki who was holding a ball of popcorn and backing away from a girl who pointed to a stall down the walkway.

"Please to . . . oh, my . . . *gabilla.* Please to excuse you," the Elaki said, skittering away.

David glared at the girl, who made an obscene gesture and took off after the escaping Elaki.

Another Elaki, a large one, stopped to look at him. David stared back. The Elaki's belly rippled.

"Greeting," he said. He sounded different from the others. Relaxed, but excited. He opened a plastic pail and took out a lump of plastic. He stared at David while he molded the soft material, rippling it with his fins.

An artist, David decided. He'd heard they were coming in droves. He wondered what artistic temperament would be like, filtered through the Elaki psyche.

David stumbled away, glancing through a translucent window. The small, ratty Elaki had been herded inside by the teenage girl. He clutched his popcorn ball while the girl left him to the devices of a boy who looked enough like her to be a brother. The boy handed the Elaki a vest, and an ashtray with a bell. The Elaki backed away, rigid beneath his scales, and his eye stalks twitched. A large Elaki moved close enough to touch, edging the newcomer through the narrow aisleway, while a man behind a counter smiled, nodded, and tallied up purchases.

Mel was singing again.

"Aw shit." The captain's voice. "David, watch your back."

David glanced over his shoulder. The shopkeeper who had been watching was back in the street, talking to a uniform. Saigo City PD to the rescue. Time to clear the human undesirables out of the marketplace. The Elaki waved a fin in David's direction. David wondered if he'd gone a little too far with the crotch routine.

He ambled into the shop where the small, ratty Elaki held a mounting armload of purchases. David moved around the Elaki and headed toward the back. Surely there was a back door somewhere.

The man behind the counter frowned. "Beat it, nose talker."

"Who you calling nose talker?" David stumbled toward the Elaki, making the teenage boy move away. He looked over his shoulder. There was a door behind the counter—an Elaki door, tall, slender, and slightly ajar. With any luck it would lead to the alley in back.

He headed toward it, then stopped, glancing back at the small Elaki, backed up against the counter, caught between the teenage boy and the larger Elaki. His fin was still wrapped around the sticky ball of popcorn.

If ever an Elaki needed rescuing, David thought.

"Where's bafroom?" David teetered sideways. "There bafroom in here for people?" He blinked. "Got go, bad."

The teenage boy was skinny, but wiry and strong, and the shove he gave David sent him crashing against the counter.

Good thing I *don't* have to go to the bathroom, David thought.

"Go on," the kid said. "Outta here. *Jesus,* you stink."

"Take 'em off me," David said. He launched himself against the boy, knocking him backward into a display of harnesses. David heard glass break. He grimaced. If IAD got wind of this, he'd be in deep. They could dock his pay.

"That bafroom?" David veered sideways, heading for the metal door.

The Elaki tourist inched sideways toward the front of the shop. *Hurry up,* David thought.

One of the large Elaki blocked the little one before he could get away.

"Hey," David said. He stepped between the two Elaki, grabbing the big one by the head.

The man moved from behind the counter and grabbed David's shoulders, and the teenager punched David hard, in the stomach.

He shut his eyes and doubled forward, making sure he landed on the Elaki bullies. It was sheer luck that he was able to bring the counterman and the teenager with him. More breakage. And he was feeling sick. He swallowed hard, and wondered if he would throw up on the counterman.

That would be good to key into a report. Assaulted perp with vomit.

David scrambled to his feet.

The boy was coming up just behind him. David kicked him hard, in the ribs, and the kid fell backward. The cop was coming through the door, the Elaki stall owner right behind her, hissing.

"Shit," David said. He ran for the door behind the counter, squeezed through. He heard shouts as he pulled the door shut behind him.

David moaned and took a deep breath. It was dark, hot, and narrow, and he couldn't see a damn thing. His stomach hurt, and the nano odors didn't help. It would take him a month to work up a smell this bad in real life.

"Lights," he croaked, stumbling forward. Nothing happened. He touched wall on both sides and moved ahead, sweating. The old familiar panic made his chest feel tight.

His eyes began to adjust and he moved quickly through the senseless and obtuse turns Elaki incorporated into their architecture. A strip of daylight lit the bottom of a door a few feet ahead. He went for it, the tunnellike corridor veering left.

The door was locked from the inside, held together by wire and bolted with a metal bar. David's fingers felt thick and clumsy, and the wire made his fingertips sore. The metal bar was heavy, and he let it drop to the floor, wincing when it clanged.

David stopped and listened. No sound of anyone behind him. Would he follow somebody who smelled like he did into a dark corridor? He eased the back door open and peeped out.

The cop had her back to him. She was waiting by a different door, the door that would be the logical choice if Elaki architecture made any sense. She spoke in low, insistent tones—calling for backup. There were sweat stains spreading across the back of her uniform shirt, running down the spine.

David held his breath and moved slowly into the alley. He ducked behind a Dumpster. The ground was hard-packed dirt and the smell of rotting vegetables was strong. So was the smell of raw sewage, baking in the sun. Another overflow of effluence—breaking out in an ever-growing area around Little Saigo.

At least she wouldn't find him by his smell.

David waited until he was a hundred yards away before he picked his pace up to a slow jog. The alley was empty, except for the palpable activity of insects and rodents going about their business, just out of sight.

"Silver, report in. Silver?"

"Moving through the alley," David said in a harsh whisper. He was out of breath. "Where's the Nipper?"

"Hasn't come out of the shop," Halliday said. "But we got scams out the wazoo here."

David nodded to himself, watching for movement. His foot slipped out from under him, and he fell on one knee.

"Shit."

"What is it?"

"Dog shit," David said. He wiped his shoe sideways in the dirt.

Somebody was laughing in his ear. "You okay, Silver?"

David heard a door creak, and voices.

He turned off the earpiece, and crouched beside a stack of nano boxes. Be nice if there was time to make one shape around him.

The door opened. David ducked lower.

He heard a bark and a snarl and the hairs stirred on the back of his neck. He moved his head up no more than a quarter inch. Just enough.

Biachi, another Elaki he couldn't see, and a dog. Not just any dog. This was a new hybrid, with the look of a small, lean lion. It was black and rigid with tension, and saliva gathered along the hard, slender jawline. The dog stayed within inches of Biachi, and David knew the Elaki could feel the dog's warm, humid breath.

David's legs felt weak. The dog could find him in a second.

The dog stayed focused on Biachi, looking as if it were held by an invisible leash. Someone was talking. Another Elaki, just out of sight. The voice was soothing, speaking in the Home-tongue that Elaki never used in front of humans. David tried to pick up phrases, but there was nothing his mind could latch on to except the reassuring roughness in the tone of voice.

Biachi was extraordinarily still.

He'd been hurt, David realized. The Elaki's tender midsection had been ripped open, and was leaking thick, yellow fluid. The edges of the wound were raggedly torn, and the inner tissue was swelling and turning grey. Biachi tilted sideways, and David could see the tip of the fin the other Elaki put out to steady him.

"Guard down," the Elaki said suddenly.

The dog backed up a step and pretended to sit, haunches two inches off the ground. The dog's head moved sideways, watching. David ducked backward.

He moved slowly and carefully, holding his breath. His hands were cold, but sweaty, and he took his gun from the holster tucked inside the armpit of the loose green sweater. He rested his fingertips on the butt of the gun, pressing so the sweat would not make them slip off. As soon as the light glowed green, he leaned forward, poking his head around the corner.

Biachi was disappearing around a jog in the alley, the Elaki leading him just out of sight. The dog followed them, then stopped, and headed back toward David.

"Fuck," David said softly.

The dog tensed, sniffed, then trotted behind the Dumpster.

David heard a creak. The door from the shop moved slowly open. David could see the dog's hindquarters. The animal tensed, but stayed silent, hackles rising. He and the dog watched the door open slowly.

David saw a slender arm, well muscled beneath the ragged sweater, then a woman with dark curly hair. Rose. Sweat streamed down David's temples. He gripped the gun and took aim. Rose slipped into the alley.

David's hands were shaking. He heard the dog's toenails scrabble in the dirt, then it leaped, a black streak. The dog came fast, knocking Rose sideways into the side of the building just as David got off a shot.

He missed. David rose from his crouch, gun up.

Pain was unexpected and intense—like being hit from behind by a truck. David opened his mouth but made no sound. His muscles spasmed, his nerves overloaded. He hit the ground hard, helpless to break the fall. His last impression was blurred, but he saw a uniform and black leather, just before the savage kick landed in his side. He was too far gone to notice when it connected.

THIRTY-FIVE

CONVERSATION LACED WITH STATIC. POLICE RADIO. THE SOUNDS were familiar, comforting. David ached—his back sore, his head pounding. Something smelled awful. He realized with a sense of outraged humiliation that the smell came from him.

Nano odor. Undercover drunk.

He heard a woman laugh, the deeper tones of a man talking. He tried to touch a tender spot on his ribs, but couldn't. David took a deep breath and opened his eyes. He was handcuffed—facedown in a squad car.

The cruiser had its lights on, flashing stripes of blue light on the torn, nubby upholstery. David squinted and groaned. His head hurt and he felt a swell of nausea.

"Sweetie's waking up."

The woman's voice. He remembered the uniform who had stalked him through the Elaki market. She had stunned him, using a setting just short of lethal.

"Sweetie, you puke in my squad car, and I'm going to use that prod on your privates."

David rolled sideways.

She was a big girl, blond and heavyset, features broad but not unattractive. She stood with her legs apart, belt heavy with equipment, and he noticed that her eyes were small. Not overly bright.

One of the bad ones. David had seen them before—women cops who had to prove how tough they were, escalating situations that could and should be defused. They made for bad cops.

He thought of Rose, suddenly. Hitting the wall sideways under the weight of the dog. He'd had a clear shot and missed. His hands had been shaking.

"Get the cuffs off." His voice was groggy, but hard. The sun had gone down, gone down a lot. What was he still doing in the back of the squad car?

"Not too likely, buddy."

The cop had a partner—a big guy, barrel-chested and going to fat. Here were a couple of cops who spent their breaks at the doughnut shop. The partner had gnarled red hair, kinky, a pale, pudgy complexion showing a five o'clock shadow, brown eyes under a thick, heavy brow. "Not till you explain this." He held David's gun upside down in a baggie. "This here's a *cop's* gun, slimeball."

It explained the brute force, anyway. He'd had the gun out, ready to fire.

"It's a cop gun because I'm a *cop,* dickhead."

The blow came from the blonde—he hadn't been watching her. David brought his knees up and gritted his teeth. He knew better. There were cops like this in every department in every city and pushing them was brainless. A simple maxim that every cop and lawyer knew, that prisoners had whatever rights the arresting officers gave them.

"David Silver," he said through clenched teeth. "Detective David Silver, Homicide Task Force. You assholes have screwed up an undercover operation *get the cuffs off now.*"

The blonde lowered her flashlight and looked sideways at her partner.

"Bullshitting," the guy said lamely. The gun sagged in his hand.

"I don't think so," the blonde said.

"What do we do?"

David had a frisson, wondering if they would do something really stupid. But they wouldn't. Not with the car witnessing, the streetlights recording. He was being paranoid.

"We take off the cuffs," the blonde said.

David sighed.

He rolled back on his belly, so she could get her thumbprint on the release. It was close in the back of the squad car. Hot. Her knee pressed against his leg, her hands working under his wrists. He had the impression she was holding her breath.

The cuffs clicked open.

The cop scrambled out of the car, but not before he noted her name tag. Gaskin. Officer Gaskin. And beside her on the sidewalk, with the expression of a dog who has made yet another mess on the carpet, was Officer Bertelli.

Two fine specimens, David thought.

They stood close together, Gaskin with her arms folded. Neither of them, David realized, was going to apologize.

"You guys are so far off procedure I'm not even going to list the infractions."

"S'not *our* fault," Bertelli said. "Can't say you're not convincing. You stink like hell."

Gaskin tilted her head sideways. "I think we can make a case."

"If I file a grievance, that'll mean hours of computer work." David gave them a small smile. Bertelli smiled back. "Then there's all that bullshit with IAD—" David waved a hand. He shrugged. "So what I'm going to do is wait a week."

Bertelli froze. Gaskin folded her arms.

"Then I'm going to make a call. That's all it'll take, you know. One call."

What struck him particularly was how unhappy they looked. Not just because they were in trouble now, and knew it, though that was there too. They were like children, undisciplined and allowed to run wild, and unsure why they didn't enjoy it more.

"There was a woman," David said. "And a dog." He took another breath and clenched his fist. If he passed out there was no telling what these two would do. He rubbed the back of his neck. "In the alley, around the corner from where you attacked—"

"Apprehended."

"Took me into custody. You must have seen or heard *something.*"

Gaskin looked at Bertelli and shook her head.

"I don't believe you."

"I left you there." Gaskin bit her lip. "As soon as I zapped you and you were down. I left you and ran back to find Bertelli."

"You didn't see anything?"

Her face was blank. "No."

David leaned his head back against the car. "Why didn't you just *call* him?"

"I did. I had been, but he didn't answer and I was worried about him."

David looked at Bertelli. "So where were you?"

"Out front of the store."

Where the taco stand was, David thought. Elaki coffee. Popcorn balls.

"My radio wasn't working right," Bertelli said.

David scratched his chin. He wished he didn't believe them. He wished their story of goofy incompetence didn't ring true.

Where was Rose now?

David felt dizzy suddenly. He leaned against the squad car and took a deep breath.

"You okay?" Gaskin asked.

"Never better," he said through clenched teeth. "Just explain one thing, Gaskin. Why the hell are you just sitting here now?"

"Roadblock, Detective," Gaskin said. "All available units, SEP."

Special emergency procedure. David rubbed his face in his hands, then looked up. They were at the corner of Bran and United. All cars had been frozen in their tracks. Anybody moving would stick out.

"How long's this been going on?"

"Two hours. They got a cop . . ." Gaskin faltered.

David sat down on the street beside the squad car and put his head in his hands. "Yeah, right. They got a cop missing."

THIRTY-SIX

CAPTAIN HALLIDAY STEADIED THE COFFEE CUP IN DAVID'S HAND. "You sure you're okay?"

"He don't smell okay," Mel said. He'd taken off the plaid sport coat and rolled up the sleeves of the ill-fitting polyester shirt.

"No sign of either of them?" David asked. It was dusk now. The bad smells in the alley had taken on a sweetish whang that made his stomach churn.

Mel was chewing gum. He shook his head. "Everything went to shit about the same time. We lost track of Rose and the Nipper when we lost track of you."

David studied the limp corpse of the dog. The eyes looked like black marbles; the jaw was open wide. The dog's throat had been torn open, and blood and tissue stiffened in the coarse black fur. Even now, David was taken aback by his wife's savagery.

Mel bent down and peeled a triangle of black cloth from the dog's bloody yellow teeth. David frowned. Rose had been wearing a black sweater.

Halliday glanced at David. "She's probably okay, David."

Mel shrugged. "Either way"—he looked down at the dog—"the People for the Ethical Treatment of Animals are going to toss her ass."

"Those two cops," Halliday said.

"Gaskin and Bertelli?" David looked over the captain's shoulder and watched a cockroach zip up the brick wall.

"I can file a grievance," Halliday told him.

"Why should *they* cause *me* trouble? I got cho killers to deal with."

"They're bad cops," Halliday said.

"Make phone calls," David said. "Unofficial. I don't want reprimands, I want to give them real trouble. I want to make their life hell for a while."

Mel stuck a finger in his ear. "Not pissed are you, David? Get thrown up on a few times, you get hard about it. Gaskin, you know. She's probably just getting her period."

David stared at him.

Mel took the gum out of his mouth, stuck it absently on the brick wall, and smiled. David took a swallow of coffee. Elaki coffee, cinnamon coffee, superior to any coffee made by mere humans. He resented and craved it.

"She hasn't called in," David said flatly. "Nobody's seen her."

The captain squatted beside him, nodding patiently.

David stared at the puddle of blood, drying in the dirt, still sticky. "Animal blood."

"Oh, sure." Mel leaned up against the wall, scraping his foot along the brick. "Doggie blood, you know, it's different. Your human blood looks more highly evolved."

"The lab's on it," Halliday said quietly. "But look at the splash patterns. It's mostly from the dog."

"Mostly," Mel said.

"You're a lot of help," David said.

"Yeah? You're not. How's about we go find her, instead of farting around here? Unless." Mel wrinkled his nose. " 'Less you want to go somewhere for a shower."

The door from the market stall opened and String rolled into the alley.

"She has called in," he said, skirting the body of the dog.

Halliday stood up. "She got Biachi? Where are they? What happened?"

"Message cryptic," String said. "Just says for husband to meet at home for dinner."

"They're okay, then," David said.

"You think Biachi well?"

"Far be it from Rose to let us know," Mel said.

David shrugged. "Let's go and see."

"Yeah, maybe she'll surprise us. Maybe she'll cook."

THIRTY-SEVEN

IT WAS DARK WHEN THEY GOT TO THE FARM. THE OUTDOOR SECU-
rity lights were up and every room in the house was lit. David's
girls ran through the cold, dew-wet grass, chasing the calf from
one end of the yard to the other. David stopped the car halfway
up the drive.

Haas's Jeep, side door hanging open, was parked next to the
house. Mattie ran straight for it, then veered left suddenly, out of
harm's way.

"Thought she was going right into that goddamn door." Mel
took a deep breath. "Police work's okay, David, but you got to
be an action junkie to have three kids."

Kendra, Lisa, and Mattie bunched around the door of the cruiser, attracted, as always, by an official squad car. Mel flipped the
side door open. The calf bawled and zigged sideways, trotting
across the yard.

"Uncle Mel." Lisa put her hands on her hips. "Now we'll never
catch him."

"Hey, kid." Mel opened the back door for String, but kept his
eyes on Lisa. "That any way to say hello to your favorite uncle?"

"Good a way as any. *Phew.* What is it? *Daddy?*"

"Hi, girls," David said.

His daughters ran screaming from the car.

"Going to have to get it fumigated," Mel said.

String thumped out onto the lawn, shedding scales on the grass.
David saw movement from the corner of his eye. Something large
came from behind the Jeep.

"Oh, no," he said.

String hissed and scrambled up onto his fringe. "The *beast*!
Behind you, Detective David."

Mel backed up a step. "Is that—"

"Ostrich," David said.

The ostrich moved past Mel and stretched its neck out toward
String. It opened its hard beak, showing a thick black tongue.

String seemed to swell and get larger. He hissed.

"Gahwon!" Mel waved his arms. "Outta here!"

"*Beware,* Detective Mel."

The ostrich twisted its head sideways toward Mel, squawked, and ambled off. David rubbed his temples. Girlish screams made him wince. His headache was getting worse.

String slid across the grass to the house. He folded suddenly, leaning sideways to the ground. He backed up and stopped by the open Jeep, caressing the front seat with an extension of his left fin.

David caught up with him just as he held up a fin smeared with gluish yellow blood.

"It is Elaki in trouble," String said. "Elaki hurt. Biachi hurt." He moved swiftly toward the house.

The Elaki was folded backward over the couch, sagging so loosely that David thought it must be dead. Rose stood behind the couch supporting the Elaki's head. Her hands were torn and raw, though David could see the tears had been cleaned and sealed.

"Biachi?" String said softly.

The Elaki did not respond.

"David," Rose said.

Her sweater was torn and stiff with dried mud. Her cheek was deeply bruised, most of her hair had come loose from the clip that held it back, and her face looked drawn and thin.

Haas was bent awkwardly over Biachi, and David smelled the harsh, clean odor of liquid antibiotic. Haas peeled a wet towel off the Elaki's midsection. David winced. The wound he had seen earlier had swelled and torn wider, and grey-yellow flesh bulged from the edges.

String moved close to Haas. "Is sign of the hot microbe spread?"

Haas turned sideways. His hair stuck up. He was muddy, like Rose, and well splotched with yellow. Elaki blood, David thought. Haas hadn't been watching the kids all day. He'd been backup for Rose.

He looked it.

"I have never seen such infection," Haas said, voice hushed. "It is virulent and very fast."

David looked at Rose. "Why didn't you take him to Bellmini?"

She raised an eyebrow. "Same place you left Dahmi?" She glanced at Haas, then back to David. "Kids okay?"

He nodded.

"My God, what a day." She arched her back. "Anybody see an ostrich out there?"

"What is it that happens?" String said.

"Dog." Rose frowned and glanced at David.

He met her look steadily. "It's not like you had a choice."

"How would you know?"

"Who do you think fired the shot?"

"That was you? Where'd you go? You know you almost hit me?"

"It's the thought that counts."

Rose looked at String. "I'm sorry about this. Biachi shouldn't have gotten hurt. I didn't plan on the fucking dog."

"Hands okay?" David asked.

She shrugged.

"Bad technique, to rip a dog's throat." Haas sounded irritable. "I have told her. Fold head back and snap the neck."

"Somebody want to tell me what *did* happen?" Mel asked.

"Could we *please* not have this hopping from subject to subject?" Haas was pale. He looked tired, and there were grooves from his nose to his lip. "I am veterinarian, not Elaki doctor." He looked at String. "This unconsciousness is very deep. I am not sure of the proper vital signs. We must get—"

"Elaki, yes," String said. "Aslanti, medical."

"I'll get her," Mel said. "You stick here and look after Gumby Junior."

"I come," String said. "Call van to meet at hospital. The medical must not be cramped into back of squad car."

"You romantic devil," Mel said. "Sure you don't want to reconsider? You could fold up in the back seat together. Maybe shed a few scales." Mel headed for the door, then glanced over his shoulder at Rose. "See you, kiddo. Get your story polished while I'm gone. And no exaggerating how many people you killed."

String slid out on the porch after Mel. The screen door slammed. David heard a loud, prolonged hiss.

"Go *on,* you," Mel shouted. "Stupid bird."

"You think we should get the girls in," Rose asked.

"Leave well enough alone," David said.

She nodded. She looked tired. "It's a long story."

He inclined his head toward the Elaki. "You want me to hold his head for a while? Give you a break?"

"Maybe," she said. "Maybe you better take a shower first."

"Burn the clothes," Haas added.

THIRTY-EIGHT

THE NIGHT HAD GONE COLD AND CRISP, AND DAVID SHIVERED, HIS hair still damp from the shower. He handed around blankets, ever the considerate host. Rose was on the porch swing, one leg hooked over the side. Haas was on the other end, and Kendra and Lisa were sprawled between them. Haas and the girls were asleep. The perfect family grouping, David thought.

Haas had deep circles under his eyes. David draped a blanket over him.

"You cold?" he asked Mel.

"Nah. But you'd better cover up the munchkin here." Mel patted Mattie, who was curled up in his lap.

David spread a blanket over his youngest. Her hair was curly on one side, straight on the other. The wires or whatever it was they were using weren't working out. David pulled the blanket up till only the top of her head and the tip of her nose were exposed.

The wicker chair creaked as he settled in. The living-room curtains were open, the lights inside bright. David could see String and Aslanti bent over Biachi. Aslanti had brought a cot that made the S shape favored by sick Elaki. She was treating String like a particularly stupid trainee. String was cowed in a way David had never seen.

"What we need," David said, "is coffee. Elaki coffee. With cinnamon."

"Don't look at me." Mel patted Mattie's back. "I'm pinned down. Kid's getting big here."

Rose stretched her legs and settled them in David's lap.

Mel pointed a finger at her. "Let's hear it. And no exaggerating."

Rose pushed hair off her shoulders. "They kill them," she said flatly. "That's what's been happening to your Izicho."

David glanced at Mel.

Rose stared out into the darkness. "They hustle them into a

169

shop, like it's that extortion scam. But then they take them right out the back."

"Is it the same people?" Mel asked. "I mean they're doing it all over the place. Hustling the rubes right from the EDC into the shops. Intimidating them into spending. Plus then, they push them into going to hotels these shopkeepers are connected too."

The front screen opened and String slid slowly onto the porch. The Elaki moved to one side, poised on the edge of his fringe.

"Don't sweat it, Gumby," Mel said. "I ain't seen the bird in a while."

"How's the kid?" Rose asked.

"I believe he will recover," String said. "Aslanti is to finish the clearing. I am hearing the conversation, and must comment. This crime, this pressure of Elaki from EDC. It is Elaki to Elaki the victim. Is this you impression also?"

"Looks like it," David said. "With special treatment for Izicho."

"They took him to three different places," Rose said. "There was one Elaki in particular who stayed with him. Plus the dog."

"Why'd they sick the dog on him?" Mel asked.

"The kid broke. String, did he know I was watching out for him?"

"He knew he was to be protected."

"Um. He got scared, and split for the alley. That's my fault, I didn't expect him to freak, so I wasn't close. He made it out, but they called the damn dog on him. By the time I got there he'd been mauled. They hustled him back in one shop, then went back out through another." She shook her head. "It's a goddamn maze back there. Anyway, I got closer, and saw them take him back through the alley again, and load him into the van."

"I am too slow," Haas said. He sat up and rubbed his legs. "I am supposed to drive close, but did not get there in time for this."

Rose shrugged. "We followed them to Little Saigo. Picked them up again inside, down in the tunnels."

David shivered. He'd grown up in the tunnels, living in the dark underground community.

"They go all the way down," Haas said.

David leaned forward. "To the pump?"

"Yeah," Rose said. "The sump pump. Not working, as usual, but it smelled to high heaven."

"Then what?" Mel said.

"They were going to throw him in."

"Throw him in what?" String asked.

"Down into the pump mechanism. Into raw sewage."

"What is the sewage?" String cocked an eye stalk. "This is human waste?"

"Yes," David said. "What did you do, Rose? What happened to the perps?"

Rose glanced at Haas. "They left Biachi with a couple of Elaki. The one in charge, a kind of thick, ratty-looking one—I think he wanted to hang around for the finale, but something happened. There was some kind of message that came through, and he left. That's when we went in after Biachi. I'm *sorry*, David. They had him up, and almost over. We left it as long as we could."

"Too long," Haas said.

Rose nodded. "Yeah."

"You didn't call it in? You didn't ask for backup?" David gritted his teeth. "What happened to the Elaki that were left?"

"Have you ever wrestled an Elaki?" Rose said. "It's like tangling with a giant squid or something."

David closed his eyes.

"There wasn't time to call for backup," Rose said. "We'd stopped for that, Biachi would be soup. But I didn't kill them, David."

"Then what?" Mel said.

"They are dead," Haas said. "We have them pinned and trussed, but alive. Maybe hurt some." He glanced at Rose. "But alive. And then, not alive."

Mel looked at David. "You understanding any of this?"

"I am understanding it," String said. "Do you know that Guardians"—he looked at Mel—"will self kill to protect integrity of organization?"

"And you just left them?" David asked.

"We had to get Biachi out," Haas said. "This is Little Saigo, David. I do not need to tell you that police need police to get out of tunnels. Better to get out quiet."

"I hid the bodies," Rose said. "In case you want them."

"In case—"

"That was thoughtful," Mel said.

David closed his eyes. He was tired. Very tired. And he would have to go to Little Saigo now—tonight. The last place he wanted to be. He stood up and stretched, then opened the screen door to look into the living room.

Aslanti was bending over Biachi, her silhouette quivering on the wall.

"He all right?" David asked.

"He look all right?" The Elaki turned, flexed the muscles under her scales. "He will recover most well. Not as bad as look to the human. Proper medication has been administered. Now the requirement is rest. Will take him to hospital."

David nodded. "I'll arrange for protection. You want me to get an ambulance?"

"Can use van."

David closed the door. "String, Aslanti is ready to go back. Call Della, and arrange some kind of guard to stay—"

"The hell he will." Rose got out of the swing roughly, jarring Haas and the girls. She went into the living room, found Aslanti, and folded her arms.

"He stays here."

Aslanti teetered backward on her fringe. "I cannot have the responsibility."

Rose cocked her head sideways. "Who *asked* you? He's my responsibility. He stays with me till I know he's safe."

"Who you?"

"What's it to you?"

"Rose," David said.

"Don't get in my way, David."

He hated it when she said that.

Rose looked at Aslanti. "He's not your responsibility, he's mine. Not yours either." She glanced at David. "Dahmi went to Bellmini under security. Dahmi's gone. I'm one person, and I have to sleep sometimes. Be a lot easier if he's right underfoot."

Haas's voice drifted in from the porch. "No good to argue, David."

David looked over his shoulder. String was peering into the open window. Cool night air ruffled his scales. David glanced down at Biachi. Surely it was too cold in here for an injured Elaki.

"He is recovering?" String said. "He is most quiet and still. This is good."

Aslanti skittered sideways. "His abilities of concentration excellent for young one. Much is the discipline." She waved a fin at String. "A pouchling of the chemaki?"

String leaned backward. "Am not chemaki active. Pouchling of pouch-sib."

"Ah," said Aslanti. "I myself am not chemaki active. It is difficult to arrange, in consideration of the work."

There was a long moment of silence. Mel looked at David, raised his eyebrows, but for once kept his mouth shut.

"He will be safety first here," String said.

Aslanti became still. "Best at hospital, for the safe side. Pouchling of pouch-sib. Must take care."

"No," Rose said.

David knew his face was turning red. But he would let String call it.

"I do not like this feel," Aslanti said. "Am I the body technician only?"

Rose leaned against the wall. "How much do we owe you, sweetheart?"

David glanced at Rose and then Mel. There were times he couldn't tell them apart.

THIRTY-NINE

THE LIGHTS OF THE HOMICIDE VAN PULSED IN THE DARKNESS. FOUR
A.M. was a down time even in Little Saigo. David chewed his
lip, keeping an eye on the ready team. They had overestablished
their presence, in his opinion—too much gear, protective padding,
weapons in view. It would be an outrageous display in any other
part of town.

David watched a mother line her children up to watch. He
thought of his own daughters, tucked at last into bed under the
watchful eye of Haas.

Rose was leaning against the entrance to the tunnel. She was
still, except for her little finger, tapping a hard and irregular staccato against her thigh.

"Come on, Gumby, not tonight."

Mel's voice. Loud. David turned to look.

String held a three-foot length of rope. "You must cut in half
and I will make it restored. It is the trick of magic."

"Aw, gee, and I don't got a knife."

David noticed the children, eyes round and watchful.

"Rose. Got a knife?"

She handed him a small, razor-edged flick knife, highly
illegal.

David wondered when she had quit carrying the benevolent
Swiss army knife that was equipped with a gentle blade and tiny
scissors. He turned sideways, trying to block the blade from the
view of the children. Likely, he thought, some of them carried
similar knives.

The blade snipped through the rope as easily as he could break
a toothpick.

"Can't *see*," one of the children said.

David stepped back out of the way. Someone—he couldn't see
who—aimed one of the spotlights at String. The Elaki held up
both ends of the rope and waved them at the children.

174

"This a new exercise in community relations, David?" Captain Halliday had his hands in his pockets, a quirky half smile on his face.

"Beats armed robots and SWAT snipes," David said.

A cheer went up, and two of the smallest children clapped. String held the rope high, intact now, and though there were groans from the cynical, no one moved away.

"Please to request the bucket? Is available?"

"What you going to do, Elaki-man?"

"David?" Halliday said. "What we got here?"

David turned his back on String and walked toward Rose.

Halliday made a noise. "Should of figured, with Rose in on it. We got bodies, right?"

Rose folded her arms. "Captain."

"Rose." He jammed his hands deeper into his pockets. "I understand we have you to thank for keeping String's nephew alive."

Rose shrugged.

"You have the guys that did it?"

"Elaki guys," Rose said. "Two of them."

"Dead, I suppose?"

"Suicides."

The captain raised one eyebrow. "A tendency people often have when they run into you, Rose."

"Don't take *my* word for it, Captain."

Halliday was nodding, looking back over his shoulder. "Let's get a look."

Rose glanced at David. "You don't need to go down with us, David. You can—"

"I'm going," David said flatly.

Rose lifted her chin and turned her back. David crooked a finger at Mel.

String turned a bucket upside down.

"Show must go on," Mel said. "Want we should leave him?"

David glanced at the absorbed faces of the children. "Leave him."

The tunnel entrance was wide, clear, and empty. The floor sloped downward immediately, and the passageway narrowed, lit by tubing that ran along the ceiling.

Little Saigo. Proposed as an underground community for the elite, and abandoned when the idea didn't catch on, and the cost of blasting through solid rock sank the overly optimistic contractor. Halfway constructed, several levels deep, construction tunnels and

entrances winding their way in and out of solid rock and dirt—
Little Saigo became a magnet for those without choices. Rent free,
no government interference, it had been something of a haven
until, inevitably, the predators arrived.

There were two major forces in Little Saigo. Residents aligned
with Maid Marion or the tunnel rats in a system that was intensely
feudal. Both groups coexisted uneasily, territory divvied up, and
each looked after their own for a price.

In the dark and desperate years after his father's disappearance,
David and his mother had been allied with Maid Marion. David
wondered how Marion was. She was old now, blind, but still
the ultimate grandmother—strong, wise, ruthless, and enormously
maternal. Police business would play her no favors. He wouldn't
seek her out.

He had the impression of movement, here and there, at offshoots
and junctures. No doubt they were observed from time to time,
though whenever he turned to look there was no one there. David
zipped his jacket. The tunnels stayed a chilly fifty-three degrees,
like caves. David wondered if Rose was cold. Her arms were bare
and muscular, the summer tan beginning to fade.

She turned sharply, veering left into a wormhole—one of the
access tunnels left by the construction workers. David clenched
his teeth. As a child, he had moved in and out of the tunnels like
a small rat. It hadn't been the narrow corridors and small spaces
that scared him then—just the possibility of what he might find,
or be found by.

Sweat started in the small of his back. He took slow, steady
breaths.

Mel glanced back at him. "Hang on, David."

The way narrowed and David had to stoop. The walls were
close enough that his jacket scraped rock on both sides. He was
hot suddenly, and wanted out of the jacket, but the passageway
was too constricted. Rock slid beneath his feet, and the air clouded
with the dust they were kicking up. There was a bad smell here,
faint, but noticeable. They were getting close to the pump.

The tunnel closed tighter, slope sudden and sharp. The air
warmed up, and the smell was strong. David had to tilt sideways.
He took small steps. If he fell, the walls would hold him in place.
He didn't like being in a place so tight you couldn't fall.

The farther down they went the warmer it got. David's back
was itchy with sweat and heat. The pump was back in operation.
Pulse and vibration resonated through the rock like surf at the

beach. David sagged against the wall. He closed his eyes, thinking
of the press of solid rock miles over his head.

He needed air. Air and light and open space.

Total darkness ahead. The noise from the pump was louder, and
the smell made him gag. He stumbled forward, trying to catch up.
The passage jogged and he hit solid rock. His breath came out
like a sob.

David braced his arms on the rough rock walls and went forward, feeling his way. There, ahead, a glow of light. The pump
was loud here. He felt the vibration in his bones.

The passage ended in a large, open chamber, with a pit that
dropped down from the center. A column of steel, ten feet thick,
plunged from the levels above, then disappeared into the depths.
It hissed and groaned like a gigantic lung.

The chamber was lit over the pump, the walkways around hidden in shadow. The floor was hard-packed dirt and rock. The
barricade of wire mesh that encircled the pump had been torn
open and thrust aside. David went to the edge.

It was something like a well, a deep cylinder in the earth dropping God knew how far to collect and be pumped out for treatment.
Current accusations said the sewage went directly into local water
tables.

Halliday had tied a handkerchief around his nose, and Mel was
looking ill. The noise of the pumps made it impossible to talk and
be heard. Rose beckoned, then disappeared behind a rock fall.
David followed.

The Elaki, cushioned by loose rock and mounds of shed scales,
had been tied together and neatly stacked. They were male, or
females who had not borne young. They were grey and flaccid,
naked and raw without their scales, like plucked birds. David
was taken aback. Did Elaki always lose their scales so soon after
death?

He knelt close to the bodies. He saw cuts and swells of flesh,
but no wounds that struck him as mortal. The eye stalks had shut
and filmed over, and the belly slits had spilled a yellow-pink fluid.
David thought of poison. He poked the smaller Elaki. A movement
sent him reeling backward, and he slipped from his haunches to
the floor.

Not one rat, but a mass. Huge and fat, red-eyed and moving slowly. What he'd taken for rubble was a living mass of
rodents and cockroaches, so huge and bloated they could barely move.

David scrambled up and backed away. Rose watched him, her eyes glassy. He thought of her down in this pump room, scrabbling in the dirt for her life.

David sidestepped the shiny, black-brown wave of roaches. Some were as long as his hand. They were feeding regularly and happily, and not on sewage. David looked at Mel, who held a handkerchief to his nose. Rose stared off into space, her arms folded.

David pointed to the mass of rats. She nodded, a shudder rippling across her shoulders.

"Why?" he mouthed.

Mel brought his light, shining it into the dark, shadowy corner. Scales and vertebra and more rats.

Twenty-seven Izicho missing. David glanced down at a rat that was so fat its stomach dragged across the rocky dirt. He thought of the old Elaki female who had stood day after day in front of his office, waiting for someone to find her son.

FORTY

DAVID SAT IN HALLIDAY'S OFFICE, PICTURING THE MOVING MOUND of rats and cockroaches. He closed his eyes and rubbed the back of his neck. He'd wanted to take Rose home himself, but he'd done good to convince the captain to let her go tonight and make a formal statement in the morning.

Mel shoved a bag of brownies under David's nose. "Have one."

David stuck his hand in the bag. The brownies were iced, chewy, full of nuts. A little bit stale, but who was he to complain?

"Where'd you get these?"

Mel grinned slowly. "Found them sitting on Della's desk."

David snatched his hand away.

"Coward."

The brownies were small. David took two more.

"Heads up," Mel said. "Eh, String." The Elaki was moving slowly, midsection sagging. "You get Aslanti squared away? How'd it go?"

String faltered. "Aslanti, medical does not like me. A sentiment I share in she direction."

"Sure," Mel said. "That's why she drove eighty miles in the middle of the night to look at your nephew."

"Is her calling," String said. "Human doctor would not do also?"

"Would not's about the size of it," Mel muttered. "Maybe you should have showed her a couple magic tricks." Mel winked at David. "I got a few tricks I like to show my sweethearts. Like you say she's got a flower in her shirt pocket, and she says no I don't. So you bet her she does, and you stick your hand in there, and by golly—"

"I talked to Rose a couple minutes ago," David said. "Biachi is resting."

"Not awakened?"

David shook his head.

"Best to rest," String said.

David offered the bag of brownies. "Have one, String. Chewy chocolate cake things."

"Ah, chocolate. Most prized among human females."

"Shit," Mel said. "Hide the bag."

David looked up. Pete had come into the bullpen. He stopped by Della's desk.

David slid the bag behind his back just as Pete stuck his head in the door.

"Hey, Pete," Mel said. "Been waiting to hear what you guys have come up with."

"The forensics team is still down there." He leaned against the wall. "But Della and I are doing records with the Elaki-Three. We've been spinning the implication wheel."

"Yeah?"

"You know these leaks? The sewer leaks from Little Saigo? We called up the EPA analysis, and we got *fragments*. It's a protein soup—part Elaki, part shit."

"Why didn't anybody let us know?" David asked.

"They did. They filed memos. Probably stacked in somebody's reader right now."

Mel looked at the ceiling and forced air between his teeth. "We going to catch hell on this one. How many bodies you think been dumped down there?"

"Who the hell knows?" Pete said. "But no question somebody's been dumping Elaki down there and doing it wholesale."

"The jewelry," David said.

Pete looked at him. "Jewelry?"

"String, do Elaki always shed their scales when they die?"

"Depend. After some kind of death, or certain period of time. Depend on what stage of molt Elaki scale cycle in."

"I saw an article," David said. "In that local magazine *Saigo City!*. And they had a piece on some woman from Little Saigo."

"Little Saigo?" Mel said. "In a chamber of commerce promo rag?"

"She was selling jewelry made of Elaki scales."

"Most bad taste," String muttered.

"I was just wondering," David said. "Where she got all the scales. Pete, call the magazine and find her. Bring her in."

"Nastier and nastier," Pete said. "Listen, you guys seen—"

The telephone rang.

"Homicide," Mel said. "*What*. Yeah? Sleeping like a baby.

Thanks, Vanelli. Nah, hell, don't disturb him. We'll be right down."

David looked at Mel. "Got one?"

"You bet."

"Which?"

Mel frowned. "They forgot to tell me."

"You forgot to ask." David stood up and grabbed the jacket from the back of his chair. The empty brownie bag fell to the floor, scattering crumbs of chocolate.

Pete picked up the bag and looked inside. He was quiet for a long moment. "Do I have to be the one to tell her?"

"Blame it on String. He said the magic words, and we made them disappear." Mel followed David out the door.

"Make me disappear," Pete muttered. "Hey, where you guys going?"

"Basement. Bunco."

"Is dangerous?" String asked, sliding close to Pete. "Coming between the female and her chocolate?"

FORTY-ONE

A ROW OF HOLDING CELLS LINED THE FAR WALL OF THE BUNCO bullpen. The first three were locked up tight. Biachi had gone through three market stalls after he'd been picked up in the EDC. Halliday had pulled in one human employee of each stall. More justice, David supposed, in picking up the Elaki owners. But Elaki were hard to arrest, and David and Mel had no idea how they would react as prisoners.

There would be a number of extortion charges, after the day's work in the market. Halliday had gifted the collars to bunco, so long as it was understood that homicide had dibs on the perps who snaked in and around the extortion sideline as a cover for Izicho murder.

Few of the merchants would be involved in the deaths. One, David figured. Maybe two. *Which* one or two was the problem. David headed across the squad room, String rolling along behind him.

Vanelli looked up from her desk and waved at David. She scooted her chair back and grinned, face enormously round. She stood up, a supple and graceful fat woman, balancing on very high heels.

"Where's Mel?" she asked.

"Went to take a look on the observation deck," David said. "Wanted to see which one was asleep."

Vanelli pointed to the door on the far left.

"That one," she said. "Name of Jon Cryor."

David nodded, wishing he'd forgone the last brownie. He was feeling queasy again.

"You ask them a lot of questions? Let them get a feel on what's up?"

Vanelli nodded. Her neck overflowed her shirt collar. "All about extortion, intimidation. You know the drill."

"Nothing about murder?"

"Nope. The other two are pacing and screaming for lawyers. Cryor's sound asleep."

"But *why* does the human sleep?"

David smiled and waved String toward the holding cell. "Because he's the one who's relieved." He looked over his shoulder at Vanelli. "My ID code work on one of yours?"

"I think so. If it doesn't, give a holler." She settled back down in her chair.

"I do not follow the logic," String said, tagging close to David's heels.

David paused outside the grey-metal door and dropped his voice to a whisper. "The other guys are upset, but it's all routine. They've been brought up on extortion, and they know the drill. This guy's involved in murder. He's been lying awake at night, sweating that he'll get caught. He's short on sleep, and guilty as hell, but when he does get caught, it's for bunco and nothing else. He's relieved, he's tired, he falls asleep."

"Ah. And this is how you decide which is one?"

"This is how we decide."

David punched his ID into the knob and let his thumbprint register. He waited for the metallic click of the lock release, then cautiously opened the door.

The holding cell was small, six by six, furnished solely with a white metal bench that was anchored to the wall. Cryor was tall, thin, unshaven. Wispy blond hairs sprouted from his chin. Too bad, David thought, juries couldn't see these guys before their lawyers cleaned them up.

Cryor was tucked into the corner, head against the wall, hands folded under the side of his face, like a child at prayer. The smell of his sweat was faint, but unmistakable. David had interrogated worse. Cryor's black T-shirt had ridden up on his back, exposing sallow, pitted skin. His jeans sagged, and the ridge of his black cotton underwear showed over the waistband of his pants.

"Mr. Cryor?"

Cryor opened his eyes and focused on String.

"Jesus." Cryor sat up and rubbed his eyes, rattling the handcuffs that encircled his wrists. He started to stand, then settled back on the bench. He waited, eyes flicking back and forth between David and String.

"Am I getting bail?" Cryor licked dry, chapped lips.

"You haven't been formally charged," David said.

"Oh, yeah. You got me a paralegal?"

"Mr. Cryor, it's four o'clock in the morning. It'll be a while before we can get someone in."

"Sure," Cryor said. "Makes sense."

David smiled. He was amazed at how often prisoners were reasonable, even pleasant. He raised a hand, waving it vaguely. "We could go ahead and talk now."

"Yeah. Get it moving." Cryor stood up and held out his cuffs, stretching the chains that were attached to a ring set in the wall.

"Thanks." David unlocked the cuffs, pulled them free of the chain, then put a hand on Cryor's elbow, guiding him out of the cell. He led him past Vanelli, toward the elevator.

"Ain't we talking down here?" Cryor glanced at Vanelli, and nodded hello.

"Hey, Cryor," she said amiably.

"Going to talk upstairs," David said. "I'm Detective Silver, by the way."

Cryor raised a hand toward Vanelli's desk. "Better get my file, then."

Vanelli grinned, picked the top folder off a thick pile, and handed it to David. David prodded Cryor and he shambled forward.

"You new in bunco?" Cryor asked.

They stopped in front of the elevator to wait.

"Homicide," David said. Cryor's eyes widened. David waved a hand at the elevator. "Homicide's upstairs. Third floor."

Cryor looked from String to David. The elevator door slid open. David took hold of the boy's bony elbow.

"Please," David said, nudging him in.

FORTY-TWO

CRYOR LOOKED ACROSS THE ROOM AT DAVID. HE SMILED, LIKE they all did when they were nervous.

"So what's up here, anyway?" Cryor licked his lips.

David settled into a chair and eased back, opening Cryor's file. "Murder."

Cryor flushed bright red.

Pathetic, David thought.

"What's he for?" Cryor raised his handcuffed wrists in String's direction.

"Him?" David looked up from the file. "That's Detective String. He works homicide too."

The door opened and Mel walked in.

"Hi!" Cryor said. Looking for friends.

Mel grinned. "How you doing?" He glanced at David. "This the guy?"

David nodded.

"They Mirandize him?"

"Did it down in bunco."

"We'll do it again."

"Why?" Cryor asked. He cleared his throat.

"Because when we get you to court, Mr. Cryor, we don't want any glitches. I like a clean collar."

Cryor sat up in his chair. "*Look,* you guys. This don't make sense. What am I being charged with? Why am I up here in *homicide*? Detective Vanelli's the one brought me in."

"Please," String said. "You have right—"

Cryor jerked backward, away from the Elaki. "I told you they did all this downstairs."

"The issue up here is murder," David said. "It changes things. You want a paralegal?"

"No, that would take all—what's this about?"

String pulled the Miranda-Pro close. "Please to put thumb here.

Press hard so machine may detect print."

David glanced through the file while String ran Cryor through the routine. Cryor was a small-time hustler. Nonviolent, until now anyway. He ducked and weaved, scraping. Prostitution without a license, several counts, sleeping in a public park, nonregistration of prostitution, illegal use of utilities. ID brokering. Illegal registration of firearms. David chewed his lip. No drug charges. No violent crimes. There was a note in the file, Vanelli's handwriting.

> *Kid dumped in mental institution, age fourteen, by parents who basically didn't want him. Juvie records indicate no real mental problems abnormal to age group. Runaway. Ward of court. On the streets since age 15.*

David chewed his bottom lip. He glanced at Cryor's pale skin, the weak chin, the oily, dark blond hair. How had he kept off the drugs? Cryor caught the look and stared at David, reminding him, somehow, of the calf Rose had brought home.

David's voice was soft. "Moving up to the big time, Jon?"

"What do you mean?" Cryor's voice rose in pitch.

He knows exactly what I mean, David thought.

Mel pulled a metal chair from under the table, turned it backward, and scooted no more than a few inches from Cryor's left side.

"Multiple counts of murder will put you away for the rest of your life, kid."

"I didn't *kill* anybody."

"Conspiracy," Mel said. "Same thing, Jon, in the eyes of the law."

"Who am I supposed to have killed?" Cryor's glance was drawn irresistibly to String. He looked away quickly, eyes downcast. "I don't know what you're talking about."

David sighed. Here was one that was going to be sweet.

"It just makes it worse," David said. "You have to know that going after Elaki is going to hit the fan. You'd do better to rob widows and orphans."

Mel shook his head. "You ever had the FBI up your nose? Or, God forbid, the CIA? Those guys won't bring you to trial, they'll just make you stop. Permanently. I seen 'em do it. String, you remember Ramie?" Mel shook his head. "How many times they shoot that guy?"

"It was most interesting," String said. "I was not aware the human could endure so much."

Cryor had a sullen look, his lips a tight line. He braced himself, tucking his feet around the chair legs. Mel was on the wrong tack, David decided. Cryor was going to shut down.

"Mr. Cryor," David said. "Homicide Task Force is going to stake jurisdiction on this. Nobody's going to hurt you. What will happen is we're going to charge you with conspiracy to multiple homicide. If you're convicted, you'll be locked up the rest of your life. But nobody will hurt you. As long as you're in my jurisdiction, I guarantee that."

Cryor had stopped listening as soon as David said "locked up." David thought of a fourteen-year-old boy, dumped in a state mental institution by parents who didn't want him.

Cryor grabbed the edge of the seat with his fingers. "I didn't do anything."

David cocked his head sideways. "Tell me who did."

Cryor wiggled his foot, stared at the floor. "Them guys." He sounded surly. "The Elaki, they go after each other. They do it to each other." He looked up at David. "They use us to make the contact, but *they* coach us on what to do, what buttons to push. They're mean bastards, too."

"Name names," Mel said.

"Give me a reason."

"No promises," David told him.

"You know the drill, Cryor," Mel said. "The more you help us, the more we help you."

"No jail time," Cryor said. "Please, guys."

David shook his head. "That's not going to happen. But what I can do is keep the time down. And I can influence how hard you do it. A cinder block cell—"

Cryor shuddered.

"Or a minimum security farm. That's dorms, and freedom of movement."

Cryor hung his head. David didn't want to send him to jail.

"I can ask the DA to recommend early release for community service," David said. "But no telling what the judge will do with it." He had seen one judge take such a written recommendation and make paper dolls of a guy wearing handcuffs. "None of this happens, unless you make me happy."

Cryor raised his hands. "I don't *know* all that much."

"Maybe you don't know what you know," Mel said.

"Mainly we were just ripping the bellybrains off." Cryor shrugged and glanced at String. "Sorry."

"Please. Continue."

"They get through that documentation thing. They're kind of disoriented, you know? Overwhelmed. And we go up, see, and tell them about bargains and stuff, and kind of herd them in. Get too close, you know? They're not used to people, and when we get too close it makes them nervous, and they back up. My main thing was getting them into the shop. It helps, you know, to be kind of nice. You know, figure what they want, appeal to their greed, or needs, or whatever. Like they're all afraid of wind, and I tell them how they can get a deal on one of those harness things. Tell them we got bad weather coming." He could not suppress the smile that spread across his face. "Elaki anchors."

"They do not work," String said.

Cryor shrugged.

"Go on," David said.

Cryor rubbed one thumb across the other. "One day my boss comes to me—"

"Your boss?" David asked.

"Yeah. He owns the store."

"Name," String said.

"Vinder, I think. I'm just supposed to call him *sir*. You know?"

David nodded.

"So he says to me that I got to get this certain Elaki guy in our shop. See, all the shops do it. They hustle these guys. But my guy says this certain Elaki has to come to our shop, and just him, and nobody else."

"Did he usually tell you which Elaki to hit on?" David asked.

"Nope." Cryor shook his head. "That's part of my thing. Picking them out. And this strikes me as funny, because I can tell as soon as I see this dude, Vinder's not making any money offen him."

"Why not?"

Cryor shrugged. "You can just tell, man. I'd of let him pass, if it was up to me. Some of 'em, you can just tell. They'd be trouble. But I go after him, and, dude, it's all I can do to get him *in* there. He's tough, and no way I'm scaring him just by getting in his face, you know? But I kind of made him curious, like, told him there was some trouble he was needed for. That the guy who ran the place asked me to get him. I could see he was suspicious, but he wanted to know what was up, see, so he went."

"Curiosity and a cat," String said.

"Yeah," Cryor brightened. "You heard about that?"

"Then what happened?" David said.

"It was weird. There was other Elaki there. And they just hustled this guy to the back of the shop and told me to beat it."

"They didn't try to sell him anything?"

"Nah. Weird."

"Didn't you wonder why?"

Cryor shrugged. "Long as I get paid, you know?"

"When was this?"

"I don't know. Kind of . . . well, it . . . first time was like more than a year ago. Maybe two, I don't remember."

David frowned. "Then what?"

"So it happens again. A bunch of times. Pick out this certain Elaki and dog him on in there, no matter what. They were all alike, too."

"In what way?"

"They were . . . I don't know. Not good marks. Too smart for my own good. And Vinder never made any money offen these guys."

"You said there were other Elaki in these shops?"

"Yeah. Two or three."

"Same ones?" Mel asked.

"Sometimes. They all—"

"Look alike. Yeah. Got any names?"

"No. No, sir." Cryor looked at David. He wiped his palms on the thighs of his pants, and the handcuffs jangled like a charm bracelet.

"But you would recognize?" String said. "The Elaki. If you shown a reasonable facsimile."

Cryor frowned.

"A picture," Mel said. There was a long silence. Mel looked at David and rolled his eyes. "Anything else you can tell us?"

"That's all I got."

David shook his head, slowly.

"It's *all* I got."

David crooked his finger at Mel. Mel scooted his chair across the floor, leaving a black scuff. David pointed to the file, and the firearms conviction. Mel glanced at Cryor. He scratched the back of his neck.

"Is it a good living?" Mel asked. "That prostitution?"

"Too much overhead," Cryor said.

Mel laughed. Cryor smiled faintly. He was sweating. He

jammed his toes tighter against the legs of the chair and stared at the floor.

"Lessee." Mel took the file from David's lap. "Prostitution without a license. Misdemeanor, misdemeanor. ID broker—made some money there, I bet you. Failure to . . . Uh-oh." Mel frowned. "Don't like this. Illegal registration of firearms."

"That was a mistake. A stupid paperwork mistake."

"You know"—Mel got up and perched on the edge of the table— "this lying gets to be a habit." He waved a hand and looked at String. "This is something you should know about people, see. They get in the habit of telling lies and just do it, like they was breathing. Now Jon here." He pointed at Cryor. "He so stupid, he don't know I can check this? Call up the arrest records, talk to the arresting officer? Illegal registration of firearms—you probably chipped that down from illegal sale of firearms."

"Possession."

"Come on, Cryor. *Selling.* You sell 'em now, don't you, kid?"

"I—"

"You sell guns and you sold them to these Elaki who strong-arm in the shops. And then they use your guns, Cryor, to *snuff* those poor suckers you go out and round up. You bring them to the shop, and you provide the gun to kill them with, and that—"

"No, no, I don't!"

"Maybe you do the killing, too."

"No, I don't, I'm no *killer.*"

"What the hey, *dude,* it's only Elaki, right? It's not like they're human."

"I *never killed them. Never.*"

"But you provided the guns," David said.

"*No.* That had nothing to do with this. That was just to Vinder, *one* time. One time he asked for a gun and I got it for him. He wanted it for protection. Something that the kickback wouldn't turn him into jelly, you know,'cause Elaki, they can't take it. But that's got nothing to do with this other stuff."

"What kind of gun was it, Jon." David's voice was gentle.

"Six-millimeter Glock. Small caliber, less kick."

"What kind of bullets?" David asked.

Cryor hung his head. "Ablative sheath. He asked for them."

David felt a tingle at the base of his spine. The same kind of gun Dahmi had. The same kind of bullets. He shifted in his chair and leaned forward.

"How do you know they didn't use your gun to off these Elaki you were rounding up for slaughter?"

"I didn't know they were killing them!"

"Yeah you did. When did you find it out?"

"I . . . 'long about the third guy." Cryor shook his head. "I had a bad feeling about that one, you know? You get a sense for it. And he gave them hell, wouldn't go back through the shop, fought like the dickens. Jesus, you should of seen him wrestle. This dude was strong, and he fought dirty."

"What happened to him?"

"Shot him with the gun you gave 'em," Mel said.

"No," Cryor said. He stared at a space just below David's shoulder. "He got out back, to the alley. They were yelling, calling me to help. But I didn't touch him, I just watched. And he makes it out to the alley."

"And what?"

"They let . . . they turned the dog on him."

"Dog?" David said. He knew Mel had glanced at him, but he kept his eyes on Cryor.

"Yeah. A dog." A drop of sweat ran down the bridge of Cryor's nose. His face was shiny red, oily. "One of these guys, he brings the dog when he comes."

"So what happened?"

"That motherfucker just tore him to pieces." Cryor looked at his hands. "Elaki, they . . . they bleed all yellow."

Mel was in his face suddenly, bending close and shouting. "You watched! You brought these guys in, Cryor, you led them to their deaths. You'll be locked up forever, man. Maximum security zoo."

"But you *said*—"

"Names," David said. "Of the Elaki. Names, ID them, testify in court. Do that and I talk to the DA. Cooperate one hundred percent."

"I only heard a name or two," Cryor said. "Sky. That's the one who brings the dog."

"And who?"

"Weid," Cryor said. "I think . . . yeah, it was Weid. He was like the big one in charge. They all kind of did what he said."

David looked at String. The Elaki was very still. "And you'd recognize him?" David asked.

Cryor frowned, then nodded. "Real patchy, like this guy." He pointed at String. "And pretty thick for Elaki."

"You sure you'd know him?" Mel asked.

"I'd know him. He's the one gave the kill order to the dog."

FORTY-THREE

DAVID CAME OUT OF THE CAPTAIN'S OFFICE RUBBING HIS TEMPLES.

"Silver." Della was sitting on the edge of his desk "We need to talk."

Brownies, David thought. "I'm kind of pushed."

"Not too pushed to talk to me." She raised a hand, jangling a bracelet made of Elaki scales.

"Where'd you get that?"

"David, will you listen? Ogden's raising hell about the reports."

David glanced back over his shoulder at the captain's office. "I know."

She sagged. "What we going to do?"

"Nothing."

"But—"

"I promised I'd see to it. That'll keep them off our backs awhile." He put a hand on her shoulder. "Bureaucracy meets bureaucracy. Stonewall."

Della folded her arms. "Sounds nice, Silver, but Ogden's got a team coming to 'help us out with our difficulties.'"

"What? Halliday didn't—"

"He doesn't know. I got tipped off by a friend of mine. No, don't ask, let's just say she's fed up doing guard duty for his eminence." She frowned. "What did Halliday say? We in trouble with him?"

"In so many words, he said make sure to cover our ass."

"In other words, he didn't want to know."

"Yeah. Ogden said anything about the reports before now?"

"Nah. Been expecting it, but no."

David frowned. "And now he suddenly wants more detail. Sounds like he's going to turn it over to the Feds."

"He's making noise about information content, you know? But I get the feeling he don't much care. Otherwise he'd be up our nose here."

192

David bit his bottom lip. "He's giving us rope. That's fine. I need more, that's all."

"Soon as they get that team over here, that be all you get."

David scratched his chin. "Do this. Assign Walker, Ash, and Thinker to assist this team Ogden's sending. Any luck, that'll keep everybody confused."

"The Elaki-Three? They'll pitch a fit, David. They're already moaning about being kept on the fringes of the investigation. Been complaining to Halliday every other day."

David smiled. "See, Della, they'll go along with it because *they* want the files."

"Yeah, but, David, that Thinker is no dumb bellybrain; he'll go through a stack of manuals, pick everything up, and probably redesign the whole program. And he's *already* studying manuals. I've seen him."

"He is really?"

"Get with the program, Silver." Della rubbed her eyes. "It's my ass on the line."

"Mine too." David put his arm around her shoulders and eased her down into his chair. He rummaged in Mel's desk till he found what he wanted. "Hold out your hand."

"What *is* that? M&M's?"

"Yeah."

"What's with you, Silver? You tired? Short on sleep?" Della shook her head sadly. "Pressure's getting to you, right? I mean, you can't seriously think this is going to help keep me from getting fired. Or do you want me to give Ogden some M&M's?" She stood up and smiled at the chair, nodding her head pleasantly. "Sit *down*, Commander. Coffee? M&M's? Nondairy creamer?" She slid a handful of candy in her mouth, then held out her hand for more.

David poured M&M's into her palm. He sat on the edge of his desk and leaned close. "Pay attention." He pitched his voice low. "The Elaki-Three want into the files, right? So you assign them to the team that also wants into the files. Now *everybody's happy*. Including us, 'cause we fucked up the files."

"Yeah, but—"

David held up a hand. "Ogden isn't in any big hurry for us to get to the bottom of this. You know why?"

Della shook her head. David poured more M&M's into her palm.

"Because he thinks the Izicho did it."

"So does Walker."

"True. But while Walker wants it made public, Ogden knows it's going to land him in a shitload. Because the powers that be aren't going to want to create Elaki diplomatic problems. See? So he's got to disengage, but not cover up. He'll either disassociate, or find a sacrifice. Right now, I'm not sure which way he'll fly. But now Walker, see. Long as Walker knows Ogden's team is an FBI deep-six operation—and you'll make sure she knows that, right, Della? So she's going to get in their way. She may actually be useful."

Della grinned. "I was just thinking. About Walker and the FBI, going head to head."

David smiled. "They have their agenda, Walker has her agenda."

"And this way we give them what they want, and still meet our agenda." She swiped the box of M&M's out of his hand. "David?"

"Yeah?"

"Good boy."

FORTY-FOUR

DAVID SAT BEHIND THE WHEEL OF THE CAR, GRINDING HIS TEETH. He looked at his watch.

"Ten after nine, David," Mel said. "And we ain't moved since eight-thirty."

"Have the priority switch?" String asked. He was folded into the back seat and his voice was muffled.

"Did that twenty minutes ago," Mel said.

"In the van," String told them. "We would be high on a clear view."

"Whatever works for you."

"What time is it?" David asked the car.

"Nine-twelve."

David looked back at his watch.

"She'll be there," Mel said. "And in case you want to know what I think, she's been in on it from the start."

"The Angel will know," String said wisely.

"Suppose—"

"Come on, David. Her bodyguard is in it to his eye stalks."

"She's retired," David said. "Just listen. Consider her past. Maybe she's given up. Maybe she's burned out, she's just been going through the motions the last years. At the restaurant—"

"Yeah, what about the restaurant?" Mel said. "You never talked much about that."

"She said she was afraid," David said. "Tell me what could scare a revolutionary leader who's been tortured, whose children have been murdered? What could scare her now?"

"The bill at the Café Pierre."

"Maybe she's afraid because she's just beginning to suspect the problems come from within. From her group."

"My point exactly."

"She does not fear," String said softly.

"Yeah, yeah, we don't know till we see her." Mel opened the

window and stuck his head out. "There's cops up there. Something's up. Hang on."

David glanced into the rearview mirror at a sea of deadlocked headlights. "Sure, Mel. We'll stay right here."

Drizzle collected on the windshield, and every few minutes the wipers slid across the glass. David found the irregular rhythm annoying.

Mel came back wet. He slid into the car, bringing the smell of damp streets.

"What's up?" David asked.

"Stink bomb in the Philharmonic."

"What?"

"You heard me. Broke it up, they got a bomb squad in there, but looks like nothing more dangerous than a seriously disgusting smell."

"Donovan and Dreamer," David said.

"Those two kids you talked to?" Mel said. "They stink bombed the dorm, didn't they?"

"My money says so."

"Maybe that is practice run," String said. "Rehearse for this. Dreamer and Donovan new baby Guardians."

"Looks like they broke their cherry tonight."

"What is this cherry?"

The radio crackled, emitting their signal.

"Thank God," Mel said. He punched the radio. *"What."*

"Code A100," dispatch said. "Dr. Stephen Arnold, location Bonaduce."

"Arnold. Shit."

"What is it?" String asked. "I cannot hear this."

"It's Arnold," David said. "Homicide."

"We go?"

"Yeah," Mel said. " 'Less somebody wants to call a cop."

David accelerated, guiding the car up on the sidewalk and turning around.

"Detective Silver," the car said. "Bad driving procedure, causing unnecessary wear on my tires, and risking the undercarriage."

"Shut up."

Bonaduce Road was a narrow country lane with no track to guide the car. The drizzle of rain jittered in the headlights, and the tires made swishing noises on the broken pavement.

The road climbed, twisting left and right, a sheer drop to one side. David glanced at the guardrail. Too flimsy to stop a car moving at speed.

He rubbed his eyes. A car rounded the corner in the oncoming lane, crowding David toward the dropoff. Headlights glared off the wet pavement. David squinted and leaned forward.

"You want me to drive?" Mel asked.

"I'm okay."

The car dipped and smacked into a pothole. String hissed loudly.

"Sorry," David said.

Both sides of the road had been sprayed in the highway defoliant push years ago, and the ground was brown and burned. David rounded a corner, and was hit with the brilliance of flashing red and blue lights.

Mel whistled. The guardrail had caved and broken, leaving a jagged six-foot gap. Mel leaned out the window, looking at the sheer drop.

"I got an idea what killed him."

The homicide van, dirty white, was half into the road. The tires were caked with mud. David parked next to a grey Citro. Miriam's car. There was another van. David saw Thinker cross in front of the headlights.

The rain was negligible now, fine and chilly. The wind was blowing, but not hard. David examined the guardrail, then looked down the brown, slippery slope. Mel and String headed down the hillside, holding on to the rope that had been strung like a rail.

The scene was familiar enough to feel like memory. The spotlights lit the cliff side, illuminating the scene in harsh yellow angles. Uniforms tramped up and down the slope.

Arnold had been dead awhile. Even from the top of the hill, David could smell him. He checked his pockets for nose filters, found nothing but a wad of thread and lint, a folded piece of paper, and a half-finished roll of breath mints.

David opened the paper.

Hi! Daddy! Miss you.
Yours sincerely, Kendra.

David smiled and refolded the note, tucking it back in his pocket. Yours sincerely?

He went through the break in the guardrail, hanging on to the rope. The ground was wet, muddy, slick. Farther down the hill it was easier going. The ground had recovered from defoliation, and weeds and grass gave traction. But it was still a seventy-degree angle, and David's left knee began to ache.

The car was right side up, angled sideways, the roof smashed and the windshield broken out. David figured it had turned over at least twice, probably more. He glanced over his shoulder. This was a remote spot. He wondered who'd called it in.

The passenger door gaped open. The driver's door had been wrenched off. David pictured the killer walking alongside the car, steering it over the edge.

The trunk lid was up, the center of activity. Mel and String were looking in and Miriam was there, holding a splash meter. She looked up and saw him.

"There you are." Her hands were encased in thin rubber gloves, and her fingers were bloody. She pushed rain-damp hair off her neck. "Come on over, so I don't have to answer everything twice."

David held a handkerchief over his nose.

Arnold was curled sideways. From the looks of it, he'd bled to death in the trunk.

Mel grinned at Miriam. "So what you know, condom fingers?"

"I know you're wasting your time asking my sister out."

"Ain't you girls got better things to talk about than me?"

Miriam leaned over the trunk, rolling the body till it rested on its back.

Arnold's eyes were open. His features were thick and swollen, and his skin was going brownish-black. The contents of his stomach had been forced through his mouth, and had mixed with the hardened moon of blood that coated his shirtfront where his vocal cords had been cut. His shirt had ridden up and there were gas blisters forming on his belly.

"How long?" David said.

"Three or four days. It's been rainy. And hot in that trunk. Get me the vitals of where he was last seen and all, soon as you can."

David nodded.

Miriam held up Arnold's hands. The fingers had been slashed, just as they connected to the palm. She flipped the hand over, showing a gash on the forearm.

"Fought them," Miriam said.

David nodded. Defense wounds always hit him hardest. The cut to the vocal cords had been vicious and finally fatal, but it would be the deep gashes in the palm of the hand that stayed in his mind.

A fly buzzed his ear. David waved it away.

"I put the laser meter in," Miriam said. "Just to get a preliminary look. His prints are all over the place." She looked at David, making sure he caught her meaning. "He was pretty deliberate about it. He wanted you to know he was here."

"Hard to miss," Mel muttered.

"He didn't know where they were taking him. Or if they'd leave him. And." Miriam held up the splash meter and flicked the switch. Blood drips, drops, and pools were recorded, conclusions drawn. "My friendly meter here tells me he was cut somewhere else, but bled to death in the car."

"Missing a piece of a pie?" Mel asked.

Miriam nodded.

"What is this pie?" String asked.

"Blood splats," Mel said. "Certain velocity, the blood makes a pie shape when it hits. Part of the pie will be at the crime scene."

"Or on the killer," Miriam said.

"Surely he will not have the clothes," String said.

Mel shrugged. "Be surprised. David, you member that—"

"Scales," Miriam said. "He was killed by an Elaki."

"Cho killing," David said.

Mel put a stick of gum in his mouth, then offered the box around. "Anybody?" He worked his jaws over the large wad of gum. "We knew they'd get him sooner or later."

String took a piece of gum.

"Don't swallow it this time," Mel said.

"The car belongs to Arnold," Miriam said. "But the trunk was forced open when they put him in."

"Arnold wouldn't give them the combination, huh?" Mel shrugged.

"He couldn't," David said. "His vocal cords were cut."

"Yeah, the killer miscalculated on that," Miriam said.

Mel shrugged. "Easy enough to force. Cutting him keeps him from yelling for help. Most he could do would be gurgle."

Walker came crashing down the hill toward them. She waved a fin at the trunk.

"Is cho killing," she said.

Mel popped his gum. "What was your first clue?"

Miriam showed David striations on the lid of the trunk. "Whoever it was used a crowbar, something like that. From the angle, they'd have to be at least seven feet tall. I expect to find scales or scale fragments. Could be Elaki secretions on the lock, or the steering wheel of the car. But nothing I can pick up now—all our equipment is geared to the human perp, so, like always, I need time. And, of course, we have no central Elaki typing system. So good luck in court. It would help if somebody *saw* something. Hustling him into the car maybe."

"Yeah," said Mel, turning away. "Except it likely happened after dark. And all Elaki look alike anyway. If you want the impossible, hope for a signed confession."

"Don't go," Miriam said. "You know I said he was trying to leave us evidence and stuff?"

"Yeah," David said.

"What do you make of this?" She flashed a penlight on the inside lid of the trunk. "It's sure not there by accident. Blood doesn't go *up* for no reason."

David stuck his hands in his pocket. Two round smears and a line. "I have absolutely no idea."

"He knew many languages," String said. "Does this look like an alphabet?"

"We could ask at the university," Mel said.

David reached into his pocket for his daughter's note. He turned it over. "Anybody got a pen?"

Mel fished in his jacket and came up with a black ballpoint. David sketched the blood smears, frowned, and handed Mel the pen.

"Get me a photo as soon as possible."

Miriam nodded.

"Who called this in?" Mel asked.

Miriam jerked her head toward the top of the hill. "Guy named Oscar. He runs a garage in town."

"What? He out trolling for business? Out here?"

"The car called in," Miriam said. "No specifics or urgency. Just come when possible. This guy, this mechanic, was backed up—"

"So what else is new."

"The order got stuck at the bottom of the list, and he just now got to it."

"He open the trunk?" David asked.

Miriam rolled her eyes. "Yeah. But swears he didn't touch anything."

Mel looked into the truck. He waved a fly away. "*I* wouldn't. Come on, Gumby. Let's go see what the poor sucker has to say."

David looked at his watch. It was getting late.

Should he let the McCallums sleep in what passed for peace in their lives just one more night? He glanced sideways at Walker, knowing full well the Elaki would call Enid West at the earliest opportunity, and see that the latest cho killing wasn't kept under wraps.

And Wendy McCallum might not be sleeping. She might be sitting up late, listening to the hum of appliances, listening to silence. Best she didn't catch this on the news.

Walker pushed past him to stare at Stephen Arnold. "Game over, dude."

FORTY-FIVE

THEY FOUND THE MISSING PIE IN ARNOLD'S OFFICE. DAVID STOOD on the thick beige carpet, looking at the bloodstain on the front desk drawer. The desk chair had been turned sideways. Books had been torn off the bookshelves, the desk lamp knocked over.

He had fought them, likely been pinned down near the window, considering the amount of blood smeared on the floor and the wall, then he'd broken free to go for the phone on the desk.

The computer screen, still lit, glowed white and grey.

IRRECOVERABLE MEDIA FAILURE
SYSTEM HAS STOPPED

Arnold's storage crystal had cracked. Or he had split it himself.

The killers had tacked a note on the door. FAMILY EMERGENCY. CLASSES CANCELED. Then they'd locked up.

No one had gone inside. No one had noticed the dried brown stains—not big, any of them—that spotted the hall floor, the staircase, and the walls outside. Arnold's prints were everywhere, and easy to pick up. God knows he'd been perspiring. They'd found them on the blood-smeared stair rail, along baseboards where he'd fallen and flattened his hands full on the wall. And there was a lamppost in the parking lot, among the prime spots reserved for full professors, that had a nearly complete set. So they even knew where he'd been parked.

And no one had seen a thing.

All the calling cards of a cho killing. Bold. Killers striking not in a dark alley in a bad section of town, but in the midst of safety— your bedroom, your home, your Elaki meditation grounds.

Nobody ever saw anything.

Whoever they were, they did their research. They'd gotten on and off campus, no witnesses, streetlights and appliances jammed.

202

Just like the pros who'd snatched Dahmi.

David left the office to the nano technician. He met Mel on the staircase.

"Where's String?"

"He's got a picture of those bloodstains we found on the trunk lid of Arnold's car. He's trying to run that down. And the Elaki-Three, there, are looking for witnesses, like everybody else." Mel pointed to a student who sat, dazed and tearful, in a swivel chair. "Norman Blackmun. He may be the last one to have seen Arnold alive. Says Arnold was working late."

"What was Blackmun doing?"

"Computer jock."

"When was this?"

"Wednesday night."

"Wednesday?" David frowned. The night of Angel's lecture. The night they'd had dinner at the Café Pierre. Was Arnold killed while they were eating?

"Arnold's storage crystal split," David said. "We may be able to get something from that. Time maybe."

Mel nodded. "Let's see what this Blackmun knows."

David shook his head. "I'm going to talk to Angel. See if she's heard the news. Find out where Weid hangs out, see if she saw him Wednesday after dinner."

"You arresting him?"

David bit his lip. Arresting Elaki meant a snarl of paperwork and trouble, none of which had been done yet. "I'll try to get him to come in on his own."

Mel scratched his chin. "Don't bring him in till I catch up with you."

"You and a couple of uniforms. Let's just hope he hasn't gotten another dog."

"Think you can sweet-talk this Angel, huh?"

David shrugged.

"More like she'll be sweet-talking you. Make sure you wait for me before you go after that Weid."

"Don't think he'll come along peacefully?"

"Yeah, him and the tooth fairy."

David headed down the stairs, skirting bloodstains.

"David?" Mel peered over the stair rail. "You want to talk to her yourself, make up your own mind, okay. But watch yourself, partner. She knows."

David kept going, dodging a technician and walking past a knot of students and teachers who watched him curiously from behind crime scene tapes.

In his mind, he pictured Arnold leaving fingerprints to mark his trail, leaving a bloody clue in the lid of the trunk. Arnold knew he was dead and he left them a trail.

Hell of a guy, David thought.

FORTY-SIX

DAVID STOPPED TO GET HIS BEARINGS, THINKING THAT PEOPLE who gave directions to places they were overly familiar with were the worst for leaving out chunks of pertinent information. Edmund University was big, old, and, like most conglomerations added onto in fits and starts, very confusing.

Angel was not in her office. David had gotten directions and information from a graduate assistant who had worked through the night in a badly lit, cramped cubicle. David checked his watch. Just after eight, and Angel's first class wasn't until ten.

He followed the brick wall until it ran out. The ground was still moist from yesterday's rain, and it was humid out. He kept going until he found the hedge he'd been told to look for—thick green leaves on tough gnarly vines, covering a rusting chain-link fence. The hedge was too high for David to see over, though an Elaki might get a look if it stretched.

The gate dragged when David tugged it open, scarring the grass.

As a visiting professor of rank and celebrity status, Angel Eyes had been housed in the small but historical residence of Annabelle Tilford, the university's first president. The house was nearly two hundred years old, red brick with black trim, interesting and ugly.

The landscaping was mature and lush. Huge old tulip trees had shed their pink and lavender flowers, and soft, fragrant petals were thick on the lawn. The sidewalk was dark grey and pebbled, and the generous network of trees and shrubs had brass plaques giving their names, genus, and botanical history.

David could not help comparing the opulent lushness to the tangle of brush, scrub, and overgrown meadow grass that populated his own seven acres.

The windows at the back of the house were tightly shuttered. Utility poles, useless now, bordered the property line. Something small and brown moved in the grass. David frowned. Lawn ani-

mal? It ran up a tree and David smiled faintly. Squirrel. A real
one.

The house had a door on the side, and concrete stairs with
an ugly black railing. A paved drive circled from front to back.
Another flight of stairs led down a well in the ground—probably
to a basement.

David's heels were noisy on the driveway. A rolled-up newspaper lay on the front porch, next to a ramp that had been newly
built over the top of the stairs. The ramp was too narrow for
wheelchairs. David picked up the morning edition of the *Saigo
City Times* and waited for the door sensor to ask his business.

Nothing happened.

He pushed an old-fashioned brass doorbell, charmed to hear
the metallic chime through the solid wood door. He rang the
bell again.

There was noise and movement behind lace-curtained glass
panes that framed the front door.

"David?" Angel focused on the rolled-up newspaper. "You
come to deliver this paper?"

David smiled, then wondered if Elaki understood smiles.

"Must come in." Angel did not lean forward, as he would
have had to. Her fin stretched and folded, and she pushed the
door wide.

David caught the warm, sweet smell of Elaki coffee.

"You have the coffee obsession?"

"Well put," David said. "And yes, I do."

"You take the cream."

"Please." She remembered, he thought.

The house felt good. The living room had impressively high
ceilings, three windows, and a tall fireplace. The walls were newly painted, beige, with white molding and trim. The floor was
polished wood, and the oriental rug was threadbare, intensely valuable, and had likely been there from Annabelle Tidford's time.

The only furniture was a small Victorian love seat and a marble-
topped mahogany side table. Overfurnished for an Elaki. Oddly
furnished for an Elaki.

His mother would have loved this room, David thought. He had
the feeling she would get along well with Elaki, had she lived long
enough.

"Come along in," Angel said. "The kitchen makes good hearth
room."

The kitchen cabinets were painted bright yellow, and there was a red braided rug, oval-shaped, in the center of the floor. A table was jammed against the wall, the chairs stacked on top.

"Please," Angel said. "Take down chairs and will sit."

She was moving stiffly, David noticed. Slower than usual, her back almost rigid. Was this the Elaki version of early morning sleepiness? David yawned.

Angel handed him a slender white mug. She'd put the cream in herself. David took a small sip of coffee and burned his tongue. He set the newspaper down on the table.

"How long have you known Weid?" he asked softly.

Angel backed up to the counter, and her left eye prong twitched. "So long I cannot count it. Why the question?"

David sipped coffee, wondering if Elaki, like people, could not bear silence.

"I know him from beginning, when I am the young political. He is some older. Dedicated and had the experience. And taught me much. He is something of the strongman. He teach us to fight and protect—there was much need for that, in the bad old days. After a time he became my own protector. He is as a shadow to me, a part to me. He and myself the last of my own chemaki. You know of chemaki?"

"I know." Mel was right, then. If Weid was involved, how could it be that Angel would not know?

He was married to Rose. There were times he didn't think he knew anything about her.

"I guess the Izicho harass you, even now," David said gently.

"I am to be retired. Those days be gone for me."

"But the other night," David said. "At the restaurant. You said you were afraid."

She moved to one side. "It is a stir of the old fears. The cho killings. I do not want the oppression to be starting up."

"What do you think should be done?"

The Elaki raised and lowered a fin. "These questions seem odd to me, David. Your own law does not tolerate the killing. Were there not years when the human societies put such criminals to the punishment death?"

"Yes," David said.

"And do not some wish to go back to those penalties?"

My wife, for example. "Yes."

"What about you, David Silver? Do you think such a thing is justified?"

"Honestly?"

"What other?"

"Some days, yes. Some days, no." He was lying. He wanted to tell her what he really thought. "I think the killing has to stop somewhere. Somebody has to finally say enough."

"Ah," said Angel.

"What about you? What do you think? Should the cho killers be put to death?"

She slid across the floor to the table. "More of the coffee?"

"No."

She went back to stand before the counter. "Yes, David, I think the cho killers should find death. But only by the law authorized and administered. I have seen these things get bad. Out of the whack? The authorized is the only way it can work. And even that will be abused in best systems."

"Systems are frustrating when you know someone is guilty. Aren't they, Angel?"

"These questions have a personal feel, David. Meanings behind meanings. I feel I know you enough to ask what is behind this. To ask what it is that you really wish to know."

David chewed his lip. "I need to talk to Weid. And to you. It might be better to do it down at the precinct."

Angel Eyes went rigid beneath her scales. "Are you *arresting* me, David? What this be about?"

"It's about Elaki Izicho who come through the Elaki Documentation Center and wind up dead in Little Saigo."

"Izicho? They are murdered, then? You think they are murdered by me?"

"I think you can help us in our investigation."

"To be how? You think I have done these things, do you not? Hurt these Izicho." She stayed very still, with none of the sideways skittering he saw in other Elaki. Her voice dropped, subdued. "If it would help you, my David, I will come to the headquarters. But I have the teaching today. Could it wait or . . . could we not talk here and now?"

She didn't know about Arnold, David thought.

"You heard from Stephen Arnold lately?"

"No," Angel said. "I am hearing Stephen has left without notice, some family thing."

"Is that usual? To leave and not arrange for someone to take over?"

"Most professor do cancel. But Arnold, no, he disapproves. Before when he go away quick, he make arrangements. This time he does not. But he is having the trouble time."

"You took his classes before, didn't you? For the conference, when his daughter was killed?"

"Yes. So sad."

"So you were one of the only people who knew he'd be gone."

"Yes? I am best qualified. He most careful of the students and—"

The sound of tires on pavement was loud, followed by the groan of brakes, the grind of a van door sliding open. Angel moved across the kitchen to look out the window of the side door.

"Weid has come," she said. "How odd, this."

Angel unlocked the door. David set his coffee cup down too hard, and it wobbled sideways and fell. Coffee pooled onto the table.

"Sorry," David said. "Is there a towel—"

Angel moved across the kitchen and opened a drawer. The back door opened, blocking David's view.

"They have find him." An Elaki voice.

Angel turned swiftly and raised a fin. "Find who?"

The kitchen became very quiet. There were none of the appliance noises David was used to.

"Come in, Weid," Angel said. "Detective Silver to meet."

The back door closed.

FORTY-SEVEN

THE NOISE OF THE DEADBOLT DRIVING HOME BROKE THE SILENCE.
Weid, at last.

He was different. There was a tension about him. He had none
of the aura of repressed formality David had become used to. His
stillness reminded David of Angel—no nerve-wracking skittering
from side to side.

David wondered if Mel would be coming along soon. They
hadn't exactly arranged to meet.

"Weid some coffee?" Angel moved against the counter.

Weid moved toward the coffeepot and helped himself. His
movements were confident, measured. He was thickly built for
an Elaki, covered by raw patches. Like Angel, his midsection
was scarred, the old wounds branching like shattered glass to his
upper torso.

"You know the Detective Silver?"

Weid sipped coffee, then turned to David. Still silent. Measur-
ing.

"Detective Silver is of the concern. There be Izicho who disappear after come through EDC." Angel turned sideways between
them. "They seem to be murdered. Bodies found . . . I am sorry,
David, but where?"

"Little Saigo," David said.

"Little Saigo," Angel parroted.

Weid's hostility was palpable. He turned to Angel, fluid, graceful. "I come to say to you that the Stephen Arnold be dead."

"Stephen?" Angel scooted backward, then raised up on her
bottom fringe. "David, you did not know this?"

"He know," Weid said. "Arnold killed cho killing."

"Still another?" Angel said, sweeping toward David. "And you
come to me for questions of Izicho?"

David stood up and edged toward the back door. "Let's go."

"Is this an arrest?" Weid asked.

"No." David unbolted the lock. "But it could be. If that's what it takes."

"We will come, of course."

"No," Weid said.

"Weid, is not like bad old days." Angel turned to David. "We be safe with you?"

Neither of them was afraid. David wasn't sure how he knew, but he knew.

"I have nothing to say to hot dog police."

"No?" David said. "The hot dog police have questions for you." He cocked his head sideways. "Tell me, Weid. Have you ever owned, or had in your possession, a Glock six semiautomatic pistol?"

David was not expecting the attack. The Elaki ran straight at him, hitting hard, smashing him into the door.

David tried to remember everything he knew about fighting Elaki, but it was like trying to wrestle an octopus. The Elaki's fins extruded into ridges like long, steely-strong fingers, latching on to David's temples, neck, the soft center of his throat. David fell, raking his back on the doorknob before he hit the floor.

The pressure on his throat increased and David's vision blurred. He grabbed handfuls of velvety Elaki fin, scales coming loose in his fingers. The pressure eased, but there were lights in his eyes. He couldn't breathe.

David brought his knees up and smashed them into the Elaki's midsection. Weid sagged, and David rolled sideways. He reached under his jacket, wrapping his fingers on the butt of the gun. Out of the corner of his eye he saw Angel leaning sideways, heard her talking urgently to Weid. He couldn't understand what she said, but she sounded frantic, angry.

David pulled himself up, palms flat on the kitchen table, then turned, gun ready, to face Weid.

Weid was not there.

David felt the smack against his back, but could not react before the Elaki wrapped itself around him and squeezed. David's fingers slid off the gun and it clattered on the floor.

His vision blacked and his knees buckled. He heard a drawer open and close, heard Angel calling to him, then to Weid. He opened his eyes, saw sunlight on her scales, beautiful, reflective, but no, his eyes were closed and he still saw the glint of light. Then he was falling sideways, against the counter, sliding to the floor.

He could breathe. He coughed, hurting his chest, his ribs. There was weight on his back, pinning him down. Something wet trickled onto his neck and pooled at the collar of his shirt. David put a hand to the back of his neck, then brought his fingers around.

He was expecting blood, bright red blood, but his hand was coated with runny yellow egg-yolk stickiness. Elaki blood. David squirmed sideways, and the weight eased.

Someone was crying. David wiped his hand on the side of his jacket, then rubbed his eyes with the back of his wrist. His vision blurred, then focused, and he grabbed the edge of the counter and pulled himself to his feet.

Angel was crying. Like a woman, like a child, like a human. She arched over the jerking body of Weid, whispering something that David could not catch.

She had used a bread knife, blade serrated up the side. Weid had been hacked and nearly sawed in half, in the midsection that housed the brain.

His eye prongs were knowing, he was still alive and aware. One of the prongs had twisted in the fight. His fins jerked, and his bottom fringe quivered and jumped, and yellow fluid flowed thick on the floor.

"He's not dead," David said. His voice sounded odd.

"But soon," Angel said softly.

David moved slowly, feet sliding. He touched her gently. She cringed, then twisted backward, leaning into him, and he pulled her up off the floor.

FORTY-EIGHT

ONE OF THE MEDS DROPPED HIS END OF THE STRETCHER, MAN-
euvering Weid's body down the back stairs. Angel hissed.

"Come out of the kitchen." David took her fin. "Come in here."

Her movements were slow and jerky. She would not look at
him.

"There will be jail term," she said. "For killing him?"

"No. He would have killed me." David rubbed a thick swelling
on the back of his head. "You saved me."

"He would kill you, yes," Angel said. "But this other. Of the
Izicho. It makes no sense to me, unless—"

"Unless what?"

"It is the old fears." Angel focused on David's face. "That must
explain. He reacts because of what has gone before."

"I don't think so," David said.

Angel slid across the floor until they were close enough to
touch. "He is close to me. He is good, in his way. But in his
life, the struggles. It makes for the reaction."

"It makes for a killer. He killed those Izicho."

"No."

"I have witnesses, Angel."

Angel stilled. "So. So, in truth, this is the fact."

"Yes."

"That would clear certain matters."

"Such as?"

"He not be around when I think him to. You understand the cho
killing has the Guardians to be most . . . most feared of becoming
victim. And Weid, he say I am to be the logical target. But wc
argue. My thought is I am too much target. You understand? Too
much backlash, too much publicity—I feel I am safe."

David nodded.

"Weid not agree. And when he is to be here, watches me most
careful. But there are times when he do not watch, he do not

come, I not know why. Or where he be. And if I ask, he say things that ring the funny bells. And are other things I notice. Is hard explain."

David's head hurt and he wanted to sit down. He moved to the stiff Victorian couch. It was like sitting on a rock.

"What about the gun?" David asked.

"I do not understand this question you ask of a gun." Angel settled close beside him. "I do not have gun. I do not see Weid with gun. What is the significance? Are these Izicho killed by guns?"

"Did Weid have a dog?"

"A dog? No dog."

The front door opened suddenly, and David winced and put a hand to the back of his neck. Mel walked into the living room, frowning. He looked at David and Angel, together on the couch.

"Professor." He nodded politely at Angel before he turned to David. "Didn't I tell you to wait?"

David leaned up against a column of the front porch and closed his eyes. Mel folded his arms.

"Get your bell rung a little?"

David shrugged. "No concussion. Just a lump from where I hit the floor. Or the table, or something."

"You have more accidents than your kids. Which is saying something." Mel scratched his left armpit. "So, you believe her?"

"I don't know."

"In itself an amazing feat of ignorance." Mel looked over David's shoulder while he said it.

"She's had a hell of a time," David said. He thought of Angel's pouchlings. He thought of Dahmi. "She's been through a lot."

"Yeah. Which gives her a motive."

"She killed him. She killed Weid to save my life."

"It's a point." Mel leaned up against a support post. "Whyn't you go home and get a shower, David. Couple hours sleep. Let me and Gumby give her a talk."

David frowned.

"You ain't deserting her. You're doing your job."

"Can you talk to her here?"

"Long as the captain don't mind," Mel said. "You go on home. And shave. I'm sending everybody home tonight. Time we all got some sleep."

David stepped off the porch.

"And when your head clears up," Mel said, "I want you to think about something. Like don't it tie up just a little too neat for her? Weid did it. Weid's guilty. Weid's dead. Funny thing about dead people. They always taking the blame."

"Prove it."

Mel rubbed his eyebrow. "Yeah. That's a problem."

"The DA has yet to bring an Elaki down in a human courtroom. We've never done better than those back-room deportation deals. We go to court, we got to be more than solid."

"It's still way too sweet, David. She's got to be dirty. She and her sweetheart bodyguard have been offing those Izicho. You know it. I know it. You just better get used to it."

"If she is guilty," David said. "Can you blame her?"

FORTY-NINE

DAVID COULD NOT REMEMBER NOTICING WHEN THE LEAVES BEGAN to turn. The air was cooling, the sky overcast—that dreary fall grey he hated. He thought of hot cider and bright kitchens, and steered the car onto the gravel drive. The farm looked good.

He put the car in the barn—for once he was staying. The barn, dark and cool, smelled like old hay. Motes of dust filtered through the dull bars of light that came in through the cracks in the weathered wood-plank walls. David slammed the car door.

Mel was right. Weid's death tied everything up very neatly.

The back door was open to the breeze, the windows wide, curtains billowing. David opened the screen door.

The breakfast dishes had been cleared and the dishwasher was running. David smelled coffee and the leftover tang of bacon. Alex meowed at him and rubbed against him, leaving a coat of grey and white cat hair at the bottom of his trouser leg. David squatted and ran a hand up and down the cat's back. Alex rippled, then flopped to his side, purring loudly. The house was quiet.

David checked every room—girls' bedroom, so cluttered with toys and discarded clothing he had trouble shutting the door. His bedroom. He stopped to make up the bed, tucking the sheets and blankets so tightly under the mattress that he knew Rose would complain. His mind flooded with ways he and Rose could loosen things back up.

David heard a shriek, and looked out the bedroom window. Rose, coming across the field, grass grown past her knees, waist high on Kendra and Lisa. He scanned the field, looking for Mattie. The calf, brown and amazingly puppylike, loped toward the house, Mattie running behind. The grass came to her chest, so that she had to tear her way through. Hilde barked and circled them, keeping the calf on the run.

"Wait!" Mattie yelled. "Wait, cow baby!"

216

The cow scurried ahead, past Kendra and Lisa. Mattie stopped and folded her arms. David recognized that stubborn stance.

Rose turned and opened her arms and Mattie ran to her. Rose lifted her in the air and settled her on one hip, never breaking stride.

"Hey!" David yelled and waved. "Hey!"

Rose spotted him first. "David!" He was glad to hear the pleasure in her voice. "See girls. There's *Daddy*."

Daddy was a novelty.

Mattie scrambled out of Rose's arms and ran to the house behind her sisters. "Wait! Wait for me."

Kendra stopped and took her hand.

David had the urge for fall pleasures. Fire in the fireplace, house locked up tight, bedtime stories—then the girls in bed, and long quiet evenings with Rose. In his fantasy the phone didn't ring, Mattie didn't wake up at awkward moments with nightmares, and Lisa didn't start in with a cough that wouldn't quiet.

David met them at the kitchen door. "You shouldn't go off and leave the house open like this."

Rose smiled lazily. "You're off duty, cop. You're in my precinct now." She stood on her tiptoes and kissed him. "It's still daylight, or didn't you know. What you doing home?"

"Having a very late night." The girls were chattering and hugging his legs. It was hard to make out the zigzag of their conversation.

"You haven't had any sleep? I figured you'd curled up at the office or stayed in at Mel's."

"I wish."

She frowned, but it was a sympathy frown. He knew it would be.

"*Did* you?" Kendra was pulling on his jacket.

He peeled a grasshopper off her shoulder, flicking it into the grass.

"Aw, Daddy," Mattie said. "Shouldn't let him go. Alex eats them."

Kendra was still yanking his jacket. He remembered the sticky yellow blood, dried now, and he reached down and peeled her hand away.

"What, sweet?"

"My note. Did you get it?"

"Note?" David had a flash of memory—standing on the edge of the hill overlooking Stephen Arnold's car, the smell of death, finding the note from Kendra in his pocket. "Yes, sweetheart, I got it. Thank you."

"You're welcome."

"See, I even kept it." He dipped his hand in his pocket.

Kendra smiled hugely, tossing her head.

"Earrings?" David said. "You get your ears pierced?"

"Ages ago, Daddy. What is that? Did you draw on it?"

Hilde was snuffling his knee and jumping. David patted the dog's head and pushed her nose away.

"Draw on it?" David turned the note over, focusing on the sketch he'd made of Stephen Arnold's death message.

"What is it?" Lisa asked.

David hesitated, then held it up. He caught Rose's eye. "What does it look like to you?"

Rose cocked her head sideways and frowned.

"It looks like a lollipop with a halo," Kendra said. She opened the screen door and ran outside, followed by Lisa, Mattie, and the dog. The calf kept his distance and bawled.

Mattie pressed her face into the screen. "He wants to come in. He likes it in the house. He wants candy."

"Cows don't eat candy," Lisa said.

"He wants candy."

Rose glanced over her shoulder at the calf. "Sometimes I think Mattie hears animal minds. David?"

David glanced down at his wife. His head was hurting again, pounding.

"With a halo," he said softly.

"Sit down," Rose said. She nudged him, pushing him onto a chair at the table. "Kids, out."

David stared at the sketch.

"David, you don't look too good."

He turned the picture one way, then another. And then he had it. Stephen Arnold had been bleeding, passing out, dying. He hadn't finished. This was not some esoteric alphabet, some complicated clue. He'd been hurting and afraid, mind working simple and direct. David pictured him crammed into the hot, dark trunk, reaching up with fingers wet with his own blood, enduring the bumps of the car as it latched on to the road grid taking him God knew where.

It was a simple drawing that he hadn't been able to finish. A stick figure with a halo, a rough sort of saint. Or an angel.

FIFTY

DAVID SAT IN THE KITCHEN WHILE HIS DAUGHTERS ATE HOT DOGS. They laughed and giggled and spilled food, happy to ignore him, but comforted by his presence.

"Aren't you hungry, Daddy?" Lisa was coughing too much and there were circles under her eyes.

David was suddenly worried. He wanted to ask how things were going at school, but she seemed happy and he didn't want to upset her.

"Yeah, Daddy, have a hot dog. Want a bite of mine?"

He was tempted to make up a story about having had a large breakfast, but it went against the grain.

"My job is worrying me," he told them. "I'm not hungry."

"Don't worry, Daddy." Kendra patted his arm. "You'll catch those killers."

"You're the best on the force," Lisa said.

Mattie nodded, and catsup slid from her hot dog bun to her lap.

He smiled at them, and fixed them ice cream cones to eat in the backyard.

A hot shower and a few aspirin dimmed the headache. David put on a pair of faded jeans with a hole in the back pocket, the waistband of the jeans loose and comfortable. He slipped on a clean white T-shirt and went barefoot into the mud room where he had his office.

"Code Shalom," he said to the computer.

"Good afternoon, David."

"Bring up the Arnold file. Stephen Arnold."

"No such file."

David chewed his lip, wondering what the hell they'd named this one. "Do a search. New file starting yesterday, and scan for the name Stephen Arnold. But don't bring the McCallum file."

"Scanning. Arnold, Stephen, found in file name Trunk Skunk."

219

David sighed. "Scan for estimated time of death."

"Scanning . . . time of death, estimated between ten P.M. and two A.M."

David scratched his cheek. He hadn't shaved and the growth of beard was heavy and dark.

He would proceed on the premise that Arnold had been identifying his killer. Angel Eyes. He would ignore the question of why, ignore the alternate possibilities—that Arnold was warning Angel of danger, telling her good-bye, sounding the Guardian alert.

David leaned back in his chair and narrowed his eyes. He had tucked Angel into the van outside the Café Pierre sometime after ten. Had that business with her back been trumped up? A way to leave suddenly, an alibi of sorts, where she could claim she'd been in too much pain to kill Arnold? The pain seemed genuine.

David picked up the phone. He got through to Bellmini General and asked for Aslanti, medical.

"Yes, Detective Silver. How is my patient?"

"Biachi? Doing fine, so I hear. Rose has him stashed with Haas right now. Too noisy around here."

"Ah." Her voice sounded disapproving.

"I need to know if someone treated an Elaki professor last Wednesday night. Sometime between ten-thirty and eleven."

"Elaki professor? You mean the Angel?"

"Yes."

"But yes, there is much talk of that. A big buzz, as you say."

"Who treated her?"

"I was the duty medical, Detective."

"Don't they ever let you go home?"

"It suits me, Detective. We have not the family pressure."

David thought of String. No family pressure, no chemaki. He rubbed the back of his neck. He was getting as bad as Mel, projecting human urges on Elaki. Like Mattie, thinking the calf wanted candy.

"I need you to tell me what you found when you examined her."

Aslanti was silent for a long moment. "I understand humans keep such information confidential. There are many privacy rules to learn. But the human habit is to use such information against patients, do I understand?"

"Elaki don't have privacy rules," David said.

"No. However—"

"However?" He could get a court order. Quickly. But Angel would be notified, and he didn't want her in on things just yet.

"No rules for Elaki, true. It is not correct to ask such questions unless knowledge necessary. So the rules not necessary."

"I'm conducting a murder investigation," David said. "The information is critical and timely."

"For Izicho."

David rubbed his chin. "I work with String and String is Izicho. You've spent enough time with him to judge his integrity."

Silence.

"Point taken," Aslanti said. "Let me—yes, please excuse, but desire terminal. Thank. Detective Silver?"

"I'm here."

"Angel Eyes has degenerative spinal injuries—a vertebra problem where the . . . the normal padding has worn through, causing swelling and pain. Let me call up . . . yes. Most severe. Does this answer the need of knowledge?"

"Is this a long-standing condition?"

"Months to years, depending upon her physical activities."

"Was it particularly bad that Wednesday? Any reason for her to come in that night?"

"But yes. Swelling and spasms, most severe, requiring medication and manipulation. It would have been best to administer electrical current, but she refused this treatment."

"Why?"

"She did not say."

"Your opinion?"

"Such treatment is a time consumption."

"I see." David heard the click of a keyboard as Aslanti manipulated her terminal. Evidently the hospital computers had no better luck with Elaki voice patterns that the PD computers.

"Is new condition, relatively," Aslanti said, sounding preoccupied. "Earth phenomenon. Not seen at home except among badly formed Elaki. Rare that, most such aborted."

"An Earth phenomenon? What causes it?"

"Unusual physical activities. For which Elaki physique unsuitable."

David chewed his knuckles. "Give me some examples."

"Say sitting."

"Sitting?"

"Elaki not made to curve in such bizarre fashion. Or. Riding in car with no Elaki adaptation. Spinal is curved and bumped on bad pavement or track. Much of this will cause the injury."

David closed his eyes. Angel was always sitting, riding in cars, blending in with people. Angel, the good diplomat.

"Thank you, Dr. Aslanti. You've been a help."

"Yes, have I not?"

David hung up. He called up Arnold's file and browsed. Mel had yet to file his report. Things were summarized in odd ways, and information that was supposed to be there wasn't.

David leaned back in his chair and closed his eyes. His fault. This was what he'd ordered. David thought of Ogden and smiled.

"More stuff here, David," the computer said softly.

Thinker's file came up on the screen. He had, as Della warned, constructed his own software, bypassing the old glitchy system Della had implemented.

Thinker had interviewed the security guard, Boyd Watkins. Watkins was a long-time friend of Arnold's. He'd been off duty the night Arnold was killed, but he said Arnold was being extra careful, and no stranger could have made it into his office without Arnold calling for help. The maintenance man had backed this up. One of the cleaning bots had needed work, but Arnold hadn't given him clearance to come in and tinker with it. He'd had to wait till morning—which was his off time, a point he harped on.

In Thinker's opinion, Arnold had been killed or lured to his death by someone he knew.

Angel. Why?

Stephen Arnold had been studying the relationship between the Izicho and the Guardians. By his own estimate, his work was crucial. What was it he'd said that night at the lecture? Pretty much that it was done.

Had he kept on it? Or gone to the next study, maybe, moving from past relations to the here and now? Had he stumbled across the missing Izicho?

His storage crystal cracked the night he died. If anybody could retrieve it, Della could. Della and Thinker. The key to Stephen Arnold's death was in his work. David pulled up Della's E-mail code.

She was logged on. Mel hadn't sent everybody home.

"Code name chocolate," he said.

An answer appeared rapidly across the screen.

YOU MIND, SHALOM? I GOT PEOPLE LOOKING OVER MY SHOULDER HERE.

David felt a chill. "Classified communication, eyes only."

HANG ON.

David rubbed his finger on the arm of his chair. The door creaked open, and Alex slid in through the small gap. The cat meowed, padded close, and leaped. David braced himself for the sudden weight. Alex stood on David's knees and purred. David scratched the cat's ears. Alex kneaded his thighs, claws pricking the jeans.

"Settle," David said.

An answer flashed on the screen.

JUST HANG ON.

David scratched his neck, thinking that there were certain advantages to the old keyboard system.

OKAY, SILVER. CLEAR. WHAT'S THIS EYES ONLY CRAP?

"Who's that looking over your shoulder?" David asked. "Ogden's guys?"

FBI. HANDPICKED BY OGDEN. LOOKING FOR WHERE WE SCREWED UP.

"Finding an embarrassment of riches," David said. "They got any interest in figuring who did it?"

NONE I CAN SEE.

"Good."

YOU WORKING TOO HARD?

"Ogden's going to disassociate," David said. "You hide and watch."

THIS HELPS US?

"Yeah, because we're going to get it figured out and he's going to look like shit."

YOU ON TO SOMETHING?"

"Pay attention, sugar."

The screen beeped. A warning about terms of endearment and sexual harassment slid across the bottom of the screen.

OKAY, SUGAR.

The computer beeped shrilly.

"Stop playing with the computer, Della, and pay attention. The night Arnold died, his storage crystal cracked. It may have happened right as he was murdered."

BY THE KILLER?

"Could be."

THEN WE'RE SHIT OUT OF LUCK, IF PERP'S GOT ANY BRAINS.

"The appliances may remember something from before they jammed. A vid, maybe, where we can see the screen. Who knows? Just see what you can do. Get Thinker to help if you want, but get on it. Whatever Arnold was working on the night he died could be the key to this whole thing."

WHAT ABOUT THESE DICKHEADS OGDEN'S GOT ON MY BACK?

"Throw them out. Tell them you got real work to do."

THAT SHOULD GO OVER.

"Walker there?"

YEAH. INFLAMMATORY BEHAVIOR, I THINK THEY CALL IT. AND SHE DON'T LIKE MY SCALE BRACELET.

"Let her run them off."

BRILLIANT, SILVER. GOOD BOY.

FIFTY-ONE

THE LIGHT IN THE STAIRWELL WAS HARSH. DAVID RAN UP THE steps to the bullpen, thinking that the office felt more like home than home did. Two cups of old coffee, brown with white streaks, sat on the edge of his desk. He ought to have dumped those.

Captain Halliday's door opened. The ancient female Elaki came slowly out. David felt guilty. He'd forgotten her.

Halliday's shirt had come untucked, and a suspender sagged off his shoulder. He saw David and nodded his head. "Good. Just the man we need."

Yahray had deteriorated, her palsy more pronounced. Her mid-section sagged, compressing the web work of white torture scars. David frowned at Halliday. If he'd come in just fifteen minutes later, he'd have missed all of this.

"You told her?" he asked.

"Yeah, she knows." Halliday glanced back in his office. "Look, David, we got trouble." He looked up at Yahray. "Excuse me, just one minute." He pulled David to one side and leaned close. "We got bomb threats being phoned in all over the city."

"More stink bombs?"

"No, supposed to be the real thing. The initial word is they're all fake, but we have to follow up. Every available officer is on it."

"Is it the Guardians?"

"We think so. I may snag you any minute. But first—" He glanced at Yahray. "Get her wrapped up and cleared out."

Yahray was watching them. "I must please have remains for death watch."

"Take care of this." Halliday disappeared back in his office.

"Please to discuss arrangements." Her voice had thinned. The commanding presence was gone.

David moved close to Yahray, but did not touch her. "Come over to my desk. Can I get you something? Some . . . some cream?"

225

"Nothing." Yahray skittered and slid, her body lurching sideways until her head hung over his desk.

"You understand what Captain Halliday told you?"

"I am old and slow, Detective Sssilver, I am not stupid. My Calii is most hideously dead. A homicide."

"I'm sorry."

"And so I please to perform death watch for my pouchling."

"There's no body."

"No body?"

"No remains. Likely, Calii has been dead since you first missed him."

"All this time, already dead?"

"Yes," David said.

"I not know . . . not feel this. Who kills my pouchling?"

David hesitated. "I don't know yet."

"You know."

"I can't say until I'm sure."

"This I not like, but understand. Details of death I would have." She looked like a gentle push would send her tumbling backward. "Now, please. Obey."

The words were there, but the steel resonance was gone. David pretended otherwise. He straightened his back.

"Here's what I think happened. Your son came through the EDC—the Elaki Documentation Center. Probably, he hadn't gotten your message. He was funneled into the market area. In this market—you saw it when you came through? In this market, there is a kind of conspiracy to pressure Elaki to spend credits. But in this conspiracy, there is another, nastier conspiracy. To kill Izicho, as they come in."

"Why do so this killing?"

"Your son came here because of the cho killings. The Izicho called him here."

"He would no do such things."

"No. Not to commit the crimes. To solve them."

"Not—"

"This is what I *think* happened. Your son was killed. And his body was taken to an underground place called Little Saigo. His remains were . . . disposed of."

"Specifics please."

David looked at his feet. "His body was thrown down a sump pump sewage operation."

"Sump and sewage. Sewage is human waste?"

David took a deep breath. "Yes."

He expected her to collapse. She stayed put, unmoving, one eye prong clouded, the other fixed on him.

"When you know ones responsible, I would know please."

David nodded, then remembered that meant nothing to her. "Yes."

She turned away.

"Wait," David said. "I . . . are you all right? Is there anyone I can call? Another Elaki?"

"I am not known here, Detective Sssilver. What I need cannot be helped. I need remains of Calii for death watch. Cannot be done. I will follow the rituals—the remains are preferred, but there is allowance for other ways. Then I will die. And there will be no Calii for my death watch. But again, you cannot help me."

He thought of Painter. "I know an Elaki who's done a death watch for a neighbor. I could talk to her—"

"What is neighbor?"

"Someone who lives near you. Next house. Same street."

"Neighbor does not do death watch."

"But—"

"Detective, do not be ashamed that you be ignorant, but respect what me say. Death watch is done in the close—would you say kinship? Among chemaki, or long-term closeness. Pouchling. Pouch-sib."

David frowned. Painter had said she barely knew Dahmi, that as Mother-Ones they had little time for friendship. And yet she had done the death watch for Dahmi's pouchlings.

"Are you sure?" David said.

"Rephrase or withdraw this question."

"But is it always like that? Even on Earth?"

"In such matters variation most improper. Better none of the watch than not properly done."

Why hadn't String said anything? And then he remembered. String had not been there. Why would Painter lie about being close to Dahmi? They had been very close. So close that she was afraid of the association? So close that she knew more than she admitted?

"Good of the night, Detective."

David looked at her. "Did your son have any dealings with Angel Eyes?"

Yahray quaked with palsy. "Why must you know?"

"Tell me," David said.

Yahray moved from side to side. She looked away from David and was silent for a long moment. Then she slid close. "The time ago is hard for me to count in human terms. My pouchling younger than Angel pouchlings. Her two. Angel of course know Calii. Angel play the pouchling games with Calii. She can be most charm with the young ones, if it suits."

David let his breath out slowly between his teeth. "Angel wouldn't hurt him, then."

Yahray emitted a long and guttural hiss and moved in close, too close. Her lime scent had a bitter whang. Her scales were a breath from his shirt.

"You do not know," she said.

He had the oddest urge to turn away. He had felt it before, most often when he came face-to-face with a killer who was going to confess to crimes that would sober the most hardened detective.

He said what he always did. "Tell me."

"You know about her baby ones? You know the pouchlings killed most terrible?"

"Yes," David said. "I know."

"It was bad, that. They suffered, the little ones. Suffered and died. These things happen then. To many."

David swallowed.

"This incident most important the effect. This you must be understand. It is what you would call the major moment, the—"

"Turning point?"

"Ah. Nicety of expression. It was the turnpoint. We Guardians go from presence, but truly fringe status, to martyr, much known. All on this incident. Other pouchlings, many innocents, had suffer, but this is one catch the . . . catch the wave. Angel calculates this well, make none of the mistake. She uses deaths of pouchlings."

David folded his arms. It was cold, but made sense.

The old Elaki canted sideways, her voice regaining, suddenly, the old hint of steel.

"Izicho not kill Angel pouchlings."

David sat slowly down in his chair. He was aware of the room's small noises. It was late, but people were working. The bomb scares were bringing them in. He heard the soft murmur as they talked to their terminals, the clack of keyboards from the old-fashioned. A knot of men in the corner laughed, a dirty, knowing laugh that meant the conversation concerned women. And always the hum of ventilation and light fixtures.

It seemed to David that he and the old Elaki were wrapped in a cocoon of impenetrable stillness.

"Who killed the pouchlings?"

"She order it," Yahray told him. "Angel."

And so it fell into place. One moment, chaos. The next, order. He closed his eyes, seeing the lecture hall, Stephen Arnold. Angel, Angel, the center of attention, drawing them all, Weid a shadow at her back. There had been another Elaki, moving purposely across the room. The other Elaki had looked at David and turned away, and David had been distracted—by Angel, always Angel—and he had not pursued it.

Painter. Painter had been there that night. Painter, who had been close to Dahmi, and afraid of police. Dahmi had trusted Angel. Had Painter trusted Angel?

The gun. Did Painter know where Dahmi had gotten it?

Dahmi had been warned of danger by someone she trusted— trusted enough to kill her pouchlings on their word alone. Weid had attacked as soon as David had mentioned the gun. It all centered on the gun. That was the point of vulnerability.

Painter knew where Dahmi had gotten the gun. David did too. But Painter could prove it.

David picked up the phone and tried to reach the Elaki Mother-One. Disconnected. Had she turned it off, or had someone turned it off for her? He glanced around the bullpen. Della, just Della, hunched over the computer.

"Della."

"David?"

"Listen up, babe." It was the tone of voice. The bullpen became quiet. People were listening.

"Get Thinker—he lives out near where Dahmi/Packer was killed."

"Yeah, but—"

"Tell him to get to Painter's house now, and warn him to be careful."

"What, David?"

"I don't know." He could be wrong. "She could be in trouble. I think there may be a cho hit team on the way."

"Jesus God."

"Get me uniforms, whatever you can throw out there—"

"Everybody's out on these bomb things. I'll come with you," Della said.

"I need you here, first. Get Mel and String, and then come."

"David—"

"If you move your ass you won't be more than ten minutes behind me."

David looked up, remembering Yahray. She was gone.

FIFTY-TWO

THE NEIGHBORHOOD WAS QUIET. DARK, TOO, NO STREETLIGHTS. Elaki choice.

"Off lights," David told the car softly.

"Traveling without proper illumination—"

"Shut up."

David checked his rearview mirror. Still early for Della or anybody else.

Trouble reports were rolling in over the radio. The Guardians had issued a formal protest over the supposed cho killing of Stephen Arnold. A bomb had gone off in a grid terminal, locking traffic in its tracks for miles. So much for Halliday's assumption that the bombs were duds.

David slowed to a crawl and squinted through the windshield. He had homed to Dahmi's house. The plastic that covered the windows was sagging and peeling from the edges.

He got out of the car, leaving the door ajar, checking his jeans pocket for quick loads. Painter's house was well lit, and he moved quickly but carefully in the dark. He grabbed the butt of his gun, registering fingerprints, leaving it at the ready.

He had the feeling he might be in a hurry.

He saw movement in the darkness, around the sides of the house, then heard a gun go off and the sputter of an automatic rifle. The lights in the house went dark. Sweat, sudden and rank, ran under his arms and down his back. He looked down the dark street for any sign of backup. Nothing.

The ground crunched under his shoes, noisy. Something moved, several yards ahead, and instinct made him dive, twisting to the right and going down hard. His teeth came down on his tongue and he knew he'd hit hard, but he didn't feel anything, not yet. The ground was warm, radiating the heat of the day.

Gunfire again, this time he saw flashes. It was all he could see. God, where were Mel, String, the uniforms?

He crawled, the ground gritty, scraping his belly, and dust clouded, getting up his nose and in his eyes. He was breathing too hard, too fast, and he coughed, and tried to choke it down.

Elbows and knees—what they called John Wayneing across the compound when he'd been in PD training. He had never figured out who John Wayne was, though he'd looked for him once, in a scan of contemporary and historical war heroes.

His elbows were raw, and blood welled, sticking his skin to his shirt.

Something, some noise, alerted him. They were rushing the house, a knot of them. More gunfire—this time coming from the house. Useless, he thought, trying to hit moving figures in the dark.

Elaki with guns.

David raised his own gun, then lowered it. Too much distance for him to hit anything, and no point giving himself away. And shooting without identifying himself would fry his ass with IAD no matter how justified. In the back of his mind, he felt their presence, second-guessing.

There was movement in the darkness. David squinted, counting five tall figures. They moved like Elaki. Two of them split off, heading around opposite sides of the house. The other three moved like a dark streak to the front door.

David went quickly, keeping his head down.

Painter must have barricaded the door. The three Elaki were having trouble. The door bowed inward suddenly, amid a clatter of gunfire. David heard a high-pitched whistle and a sobbing shriek that made the hair stand up on the back of his neck. The door cracked and broke open.

God.

He saw shadows moving, going through the door. David was right behind them. He braced his legs.

"Police." He zigged sideways immediately, going down. Gunfire, bullets over his head. Someone called out, then nothing.

It was pitch-dark inside the house. He stood up, tripping on a large, splintered piece of wood. His hair was wet and curly with sweat, his knees felt weak, the left one achy. Must have twisted it going down, he thought.

Yeah, yeah, big fucking deal.

He moved slowly, sideways, trying to see something in the darkness. It was cool suddenly, he was near the open door, the light was different here.

David smelled death in the room. His foot slid in something wet, and his leg went out from under him, stretching his thigh muscles to the limit. He went down hard.

Gunfire sounded from the back of the house.

There was something sticky all over the floor. Why did these things never happen in broad daylight? He grimaced, crawled, hand closing on solid mass. He heard a moan, his own. No light. He had to have light. He swallowed heavily, breathing hard, knowing the sound gave him away, knowing there was nothing he could do about it.

He kept crawling, out of the sticky wetness, away from the smells, careful, cautious. He thought about gunfire and tiny Elaki pouchlings.

It was the shatter of glass that broke him, hit him with the panic jolt that brought him to his feet, brought him running, stupid in the darkness, down the dark, twisted hallway to the back of the house.

"Police," he shouted, maniacal, running into walls. "Hang on, Painter; hang on, babies; it's Silver, Detective Silver. Where are you, sweetheart? Where are you?"

Odd noises, unrecognizable, hissing and high-pitched whistles and clatter. He ran full tilt into the damp velvet mass of an Elaki, and they both went down.

The Elaki sagged under him. It was too dark to see, only feel. The Elaki wrapped fins around David, squeezing.

"Painter?" He wanted to yell, but he could barely choke the word out.

Hissing, groans. Something like gravel under his back. The Elaki squeezed harder. David brought the gun up between his belly and the Elaki's midsection and pulled the trigger. The Elaki splattered like a water balloon dropped from a two-story window.

Silence settled. Nothing but the hoarse sound of his own breath. He was trembling, coated with Elaki blood and chunks of tissue. The room was resonant with emotion—he could not be alone. He strained his eyes—it was dark, so damn dark.

Something he heard—what? A rustle, like rocks and gravel. A plaintive whistle and wail. A pouchling?

Movement across the room. David brought his gun up, palm wet on the butt, his finger slick on the trigger. The gravel sound again, digging, and David remembered the borders, the strips of dirt and gravel that had lined the sides of the room like raised bed gardens.

The wails got louder.

"Painter?" David said softly.

The digging stopped.

"It's Detective Silver. Don't be afraid. Stay where you are, sweetheart. Ask your lights to come up."

"Lights?" Painter's voice was faint and shaky. But it was hers. "Lights *up.*"

Light, blessed light. David squinted and blinked. Painter was crouched over a gravel pit, digging with one fin. Her entire left wing had been severed, and hung like a broken kite. She had lost enormous amounts of scales, and her skin was raw and pinkish.

"Help for me," she said. "My little ones. Here beneath."

She had buried them, David realized. Hidden them away. David went up on his knees, scooting toward her, aware, from the corner of his eyes, of silent, crumpled Elaki. He bent down beside Painter and scrabbled in the rocks, scattering gravel. Could the pouchlings breathe? How long had they been buried?

They were buried no more than three inches deep. Dirt clumped and stuck in the yellow Elaki blood, blood that coated the gravel like batter.

An Elaki shot at close range splattered. David looked up every few seconds, trying for a body count. There had been five hunters. The carnage seemed a few shy.

Something moved beneath his hands. Something warm. He brushed gravel away and uncovered the black dusty back of a pouchling.

"Here," he said to Painter. "Get him. Here's one."

Painter was making odd noises, whistling clicks.

"Other one more that way," she told him, pulling the pouchling free.

David's fingers were sore, bloody. He scattered gravel, saw an eye prong, then moved gently to free the second baby-one.

FIFTY-THREE

DAVID COUNTED BODIES. THERE HAD BEEN TWO IN THE BACK room—one Painter had shot, one his own victim. There were two bodies here, too. Only one was a cho killer. The other was Thinker.

The Elaki had tied himself across the door, holding it closed with his body, even after he'd been shot. They'd torn him in half to get inside.

David wondered if he'd been dead by then. He remembered the loud, whistling shriek. He closed his eyes tight, shuddered.

He hadn't wanted them on the team—Thinker, Walker, and Ash. They were inexperienced, no street eyes. His objections had all centered around their inability to do the job. Never once had he mentioned that they'd be a danger to themselves, something that was always a consideration with rookies. Why hadn't that come up this time?

He knew why. It hadn't come up because they weren't human.

"He try to give me time," Painter said. "Hide the pouchlings."

She was sagging. The pouchlings were silent, awed. Both of them wore Boy Scout shirts. David touched the neckerchief of the smallest Elaki, finding it dusty and stained.

"Elaki scouts?" David said softly.

"First meet tonight," the little one said. "New troop."

David glanced at Painter. She was swaying, leaking yellow blood from the damaged fin. He moved up beside her, and put an arm around her midsection.

She went tense.

"*Lean* on me."

She did, lightly.

"Bodies only three," Painter told him. Her eye prongs were losing their focus.

"There were at least five of them," David said.

"The others run away?" The littlest pouchling skittered back and forth.

235

"Stay close to me," David said. "Yes, kidlet, they probably ran away." He moved toward the front door. "But I'm not leaving you here alone. And your mama-one could use some help."

"No one to go to," Painter said. "Would spread danger."

"You're going with me. We should be getting backup anytime now. Nothing to worry about."

David felt the tug on his belt as the pouchlings latched on with their fins. He moved awkwardly, dragging them along, supporting Painter and leading them into the night.

If the others were waiting outside, they'd make a hell of a target.

It was a long walk, across the bare dirt lawn to the street, then down to the car. He should have parked closer. David kept them moving, and he looked from side to side, watching. The other houses were quiet, dark.

The car was a haven in a night that had turned chilly. David opened the back door, scooting the pouchlings inside, shutting the door softly. He tucked Painter into the front from the driver's side, propping her head on the passenger door, trying to keep her from folding. He lifted her bottom fringe and slid into the driver's seat, letting her fringe rest in his lap. He locked the doors and scanned the street. No cho killers. No backup.

He picked up the radio. "Dispatch. Where the hell is everybody?"

"Who is this?"

"Silver, goddammit, where's my backup? Where's Detective Martinas? She was right behind me—is she okay, has she called in? Where's Burnett and String? I've been by myself in World War Five, for God's sake—"

"Okay, Silver, okay. Sit down and take a breath. You hurt? You—"

David took a deep breath. "I'm not hurt."

"Good. Good. Look, your people are tied up in traffic gridlocks—"

"How far away?"

"Martinas is a half hour out. Burnett and String about forty-five minutes."

"Uniforms?"

"Every available officer is out. There are two cars coming your way, Silver, we're putting avoidance routes into the computer that will keep anybody else from getting snagged in the gridlocks, but—"

"What in hell is going down?"

"Bomb scares. Six new warnings in the last hour. Another one went off fifteen minutes ago. We got people to evacuate."

"God," David said.

"We're getting off-duty people, but it's going to take time. Are you all right? Can you hold on?"

"I'm all right," David said. "Cancel the backup. We got . . . we got dead Elaki, but they're not going anywhere."

"You sure you're all right?"

David nodded to himself and shut the radio down. He glanced in the back seat. "You guys best stick with me."

FIFTY-FOUR

DAVID WAS DRIVING TOO FAST.

"Where you take us?" Painter asked.

"Bellmini General." The lights on the car flashed. Emergency. He glanced in the rearview mirror at the pouchlings. They sat close together, watching the pulse of light.

Painter sagged against the car door. The yellow blood had stopped flowing and was forming a crust.

"You okay?" he asked.

"Is gun that hurts me. I shoot, and it sends me backward and off rip the fin. Did not know so dangerous to shoot."

"Where'd you get the gun?"

"This place I find. I drive and look for bad spots. Find Little Saigo. Trade scales to make jewelry in exchange gun."

"They wanted your scales?" That explained the bald patches. David felt queasy.

"Not take money credit."

"You got your scales worth. Jesus, whatever happened to those old Saturday night specials? A Geld Brown is too damn much firepower for an Elaki. For anybody."

"This you tell me now?"

"You could have come to me."

"I would. But."

"But what?"

"I see you there with her. The Angel."

David clutched the steering wheel. It was hot in the car. He would have liked to open a window and let the night air in, but he didn't want to chill Painter or the little ones. Headlights flashed by in the opposite lanes.

"You mean the night at the university?" he asked flatly.

"But yes. And you work with this Izicho. Detective String. Do not know who to trust."

"So you went to Angel."

The Elaki stayed quiet.

"Where'd Dahmi get the gun, Painter?" He spoke softly, glancing sideways. "She got it from Angel. Didn't she?"

Packer hissed. "Such treachery."

David took a breath. The pouchlings were quiet, quiet in the back seat.

"You must catch and punish."

"Soon as I can. Soon as I drop you off."

"Now. I will be well. This is not the fatality. And Angel could come for me at the Bellmini. You take Dahmi there. She does not come back. Where she?"

David thought of the Little Saigo sump pump.

"We not find her evermore," Painter said. "Not ever, think I. Do not take me to hospital. We my babies stay in car. You catch the Angel."

"When did she give Dahmi the gun?"

Packer hissed. "Dahmi some wary. All of us wary after number two cho killing. Dahmi think she will get out of Guardian lecture. She considering—one way, then another. She tell Angel this. She, Dahmi, has heard the bad stories, from old days, when students meet for snacks social." Painter shifted sideways. "Humans do this snack social always." She sounded petulant. "Too much eating."

She was wandering off the point. David glanced at her, wondered if she was getting shocky. Would she be safe at the hospital? Should he take her home to Rose?

Painter hissed. "Angel come to her. Tell her she, Dahmi, is name on list have found. A list of maybe be victim."

"Why would she be a target? All she did was go to lectures."

The car veered suddenly, turning off onto a side street David did not recognize. Avoiding gridlock?

"Other victims have the small involvement," Painter said. "This makes fear for everyone."

David nodded.

"Dahmi decides no more lecture. But it be too late. She is on list. Angel tells of her own pouchlings, die the long slow death. Dahmi outrage worry. Angel give Dahmi the gun."

"Didn't she ask Angel for help?"

"Angel *offer* help. But say many name on list. Do best, see, but many name. And Dahmi tell me other victims were looked after when found on list. And still be killed. So not to be counted on."

"So Dahmi killed her pouchlings. Rather than have them killed."

"She call me. Say they on way. Not sure why she think this, but convinced—"

David nodded. "They did something. Something to put her in a panic."

"I try to go to her, but she not let me in. Say too dangerous. No more for me involved. I ask to take baby ones, she not let me close. I not know what to do. Who to call. Who to trust." Painter was quiet a long moment. "So I call hot dog police and I call news source and I call Guardian. I call all," Painter said. "I am the one. But this was too late. Because when she call me . . . it is after."

The Elaki was going rigid.

"Please, David Detective, do not take me where you take Dahmi. Do not make my pouchlings separate."

"I'll take you home," David said. "My home."

"You know where the Angel is?" Painter asked.

David cocked his head sideways. Would she be at the Café Pierre, just like she was the night Arnold was killed? Her favorite alibi hangout.

"I have an idea," David said.

"Go there. I will not have the safety till you bring her up. Because I go to her. The night I see you? I go to her first, to ask for gun, like she give to Dahmi. She does not know Dahmi tells me where she got gun, until I ask this. And we arrange the meet, for her to give me gun also."

David frowned. "What happened?"

"I do not know how I know, but when I speak to the Angel of the gun . . . I feel the danger. So we arrange the meet, but I do not go." Packer shifted her weight. "Go *now*. Get the Angel."

"She can't hurt you now, Painter."

"She can."

FIFTY-FIVE

DAVID SHOWED PAINTER HOW TO USE THE RADIO, THEN LOCKED her into the car with the pouchlings. He felt shaky. He knew he should wait for backup. But if he did, String would be there, telling everyone how dangerous Angel was. They'd send out a SWAT team like they always did to Little Saigo. They would escalate. They would kill her.

She might bow to the inevitable and come in with him. He promised himself that he would not approach her unless she was alone.

David went through the back door into the kitchen of the Café Pierre. It was poorly lit inside, dingy, but warm and fragrant. Pierre was leaning over an ancient, white, chipped enamel stove. He took the lid off a cast-iron stew pot and inhaled deeply, eyes closed, face showing enraptured concentration.

David snapped his badge open. Pierre gave it a cursory glance, and shrugged. He scooped up a handful of freshly chopped shallots and dropped them into the pot.

So much for that, David thought.

A white swing door, well smudged with grease and fingerprints, led into the dining room. No window. David pushed the door gently and peeped through the crack.

She was there. Angel. Sitting at a table in the back, eating what looked like a good meal. A nearly empty bottle of wine sat beside the bread board, next to a half-eaten baguette. David wondered what she'd eaten tonight. What was she thinking? About Painter? Did it remind her of her own pouchlings? Was she responsible for the bombings? Was she pleased?

A waitress, empty tray tucked under her arm, was speeding toward the swing door. David stepped back. The waitress hit the door hard, barely missing him, then stopped when she saw him. He put a finger to his lips, opening and closing the badge. Her eyes widened and she looked at Pierre. He shrugged.

David looked back out the door. Angel was sipping coffee. She

241

set the cup down hard, pushed it away, and rippled her muscles under the scales. She refolded the black cloth napkin and tucked it to one side of the plate.

David glanced over his shoulder. He had the feeling that Pierre was watching him, but when he looked, the man was stirring his sauce.

David wondered if any more bombs had gone off.

He moved quietly, the swing door closing gently behind. The restaurant wasn't crowded. Should he wait till she left? Someone might be picking her up or meeting her. He would have that many more Elaki to deal with.

People and Elaki were staring. He was aware, suddenly, that his jeans were torn and liberally laced with Elaki blood. Pretty much looked like he felt, David decided. Like hell. A wild man, exhausted, circles and shadows beneath his eyes.

There were two tables between Angel and the back wall of the restaurant. Both empty. David stopped between Angel and the rest of the patrons, gun on the ready in the back of his jeans. He knew as soon as she became aware. There was tension about her, a stiffening beneath the scales.

"Elaki don't cry," David said softly.

For a long moment she did not move. Then she turned and faced him.

She seemed different tonight, more alien than he'd ever seen her. Her mannerisms had changed. For once she was not aping humans. She was sleek, black, beautiful. There was still a part of him that did not want to believe what he knew was true. That was the part that could get him killed.

"You always stayed one step ahead," he said.

"Not difficult, David Silver." Even her voice was different. Flatter and older. Tired, even. He was tired too. "But Elaki do not *step*."

She was making fun of him.

"No," he agreed, "Elaki don't step, Elaki don't sit, Elaki don't cry."

"Elaki don't need others to be like themselves."

David cocked his head sideways. Behind him, the restaurant was hushed. No one moved. Everyone watched. Even the Elaki.

"Let me tell you what I know about Elaki," David said. "About Elaki revolutionaries. About you, Angel Eyes."

"You know nothing of me. A hot dog cannot know such as me."

Somehow he lost his words, the accusations he wanted to hurl at her in the hopes they'd be explained away.

"You killed them all," he said finally. "Your own followers, your own Guardians. To throw blame on the Izicho. You gave Dahmi the gun."

Angel was still. Watching him.

"There were no cho killings. They were Angel killings." He took a breath, wiped sweat off his temple. "How could it be so important?"

"Izicho must not be allowed stronghold here. Ever."

"I had it backward about Arnold, didn't I?" David said. "He wasn't a target, not at first anyway. You didn't want him killed."

"His work critical."

"So you made sure the killers hit when he was out of town. You were one of the only ones who knew he was going. You had the crime, the public sympathy, and you didn't lose a valuable player."

"I was genuinely fond."

"Were you? But I guess you loved your pouchlings, too. I hope to God you aren't fond of me."

Angel looked at him. "You lie then."

David looked away. "Why'd you kill him?"

She moved slightly to one side. "Stephen become suspicious of cho killings. Sees discrepancies. Really a most scholarly intellect. Excellent perception and top negotiator. Bad to let him go. Sacrifices must be made."

"Sacrifices? You've made all of them, haven't you? Your chemaki-mate, your *shadow*. Your children." David frowned. "One hundred percent ruthless revolutionary."

"I do what I must with one single-minded cause. It is my strength."

"You're under arrest. For conspiracy to commit homicide, multiple counts."

"You have not ability to prove. You are human cop, not Izicho. You must follow rules."

"Painter isn't dead," David said softly. "She knows you gave the gun to Dahmi. And we have forensic evidence placing Weid at the scene of two cho killings. The operative word is conspiracy."

He didn't know exactly what he expected. Not for her to come along quietly, but neither did he expect her to come straight at him, in blatant disregard of the gun.

"*Please*, no," she shouted, running at him. "*Izicho.*"

He fired, saw the piece of flesh tear from the top of her frame, and then she was on him.

She was a killer. He fell against a table, back smashing against a chair before he slid to the floor. She wrapped her body around his, enveloping him, squeezing tighter and tighter. He felt an odd, almost-electric shock as something sharp entered his ribs, something so sharp it went through bone without a hint of resistance. She pulled it away and he felt an odd relief, and the lukewarm wetness of blood.

He gasped when the stiletto went in again.

She hugged him tighter, jammed the blade in deeper. His fingers were oddly numb, and he squeezed his eyes shut, concentrating, bringing the gun to her back.

If he fired, the bullet would tear her to shreds and go through her into him. If he didn't, she'd kill him anyway.

He steadied the gun barrel and fired through her midsection. He felt her shatter just as the bullet entered his left lung, and took his breath away.

He did not expect to open his eyes again; he did not expect the face of Pierre peering into his. David coughed, felt the blood bubble up on his tongue. He wanted to move, or something. What, exactly?

"Ambulance," Pierre said roughly.

That on the menu? he thought.

He could not make the words come out. Too bad, it would have shown wit and panache, it would have finally impressed Pierre, who was pressing, pressing against his chest, his sides, stopping the flow of blood. So much blood too, getting downright impressive. Red blood, mixed with yellow blood, you could tell whose was whose.

One hard jab to the vena cava would have dropped him. Instead, she had stabbed through the rib cage, missing major veins, two, three times. Why hadn't she killed him?

People were staring. Elaki stared, then turned their backs. *Izicho.* He heard the whispers.

"They killed her," someone said. "That's Angel Eyes."

"After all this time. Now they get her."

David closed his eyes, thinking how it looked. She had been peacefully eating her dinner when he'd come through the door, clothes torn and bloody. He'd held the gun. And she'd died shouting Izicho.

She was still one step ahead.

David turned his head—an effort, that, an effort that made him sweat, and he looked at what was left of the one hundred percent Elaki revolutionary. His Angel.

He tried not to feel sorry. But he did.

BY THE CREATOR OF MARVEL COMICS' *X-MEN*®
AND DC COMICS' *SOVEREIGN 7*®

CHRIS CLAREMONT

__**SUNDOWNER**   0-441-00070-3/$4.99
Lt. Nicole Shea's been grounded for too long. Now she's got wings, a mission, and nowhere to go...but up. The controversial *Starswift* launching has divided the world. It's humankind's first team effort with aliens...and Lt. Shea's last chance to prove herself.

Don't miss any of CHRIS CLAREMONT'S
                    exhilarating Nicole Shea adventures

__**FIRSTFLIGHT**   0-441-23584-0/$4.99
"Breathless adventure...entertaining, thoughtful...excellent." —*Newsday*
"Fast-paced action." —*Science Fiction Chronicle*

__**GROUNDED!**   0-441-30416-8/$4.99
"One of the best pieces of action science fiction to appear in quite a while!"
                    —*Chicago Sun-Times*
"Reminiscent of early Heinlein...exceptional!"
                    —*OtherRealms*

Payable in U.S. funds. No cash orders accepted. Postage & handling: $1.75 for one book, 75¢ for each additional. Maximum postage $5.50. Prices, postage and handling charges may change without notice. Visa, Amex, MasterCard call 1-800-788-6262, ext. 1, refer to ad #501

Or, check above books Bill my: ☐ Visa ☐ MasterCard ☐ Amex	
and send this order form to:	(expires)
The Berkley Publishing Group Card#	
390 Murray Hill Pkwy., Dept. B	($15 minimum)
East Rutherford, NJ 07073 Signature	
Please allow 6 weeks for delivery. Or enclosed is my: ☐ check ☐ money order	
Name	Book Total $
Address	Postage & Handling $
City	Applicable Sales Tax $ (NY, NJ, PA, CA, GST Can.)
State/ZIP	Total Amount Due $

"When it comes to military SF, William Dietz can run with the best."
—Steve Perry

WILLIAM C. DIETZ

__BODYGUARD   0-441-00105-X/$5.50
In a future where violence, corruption, and murder
grow as rapidly as technology and corporations, there
is always room for the Bodyguard. He's hired muscle
for a wired future—and he's the best money can buy.

__LEGION OF THE DAMNED
                    0-441-48040-3/$5.50
*"A tough, moving novel of future
warfare."*—David Drake
When all hope is lost—for the terminally ill, for the
condemned criminal, for the victim who can't be saved—
there is one final choice. Life...as a cyborg soldier.

__DRIFTER'S WAR   0-441-16815-9/$4.99
"Entertaining, fast-paced adventure."
—<u>Locus</u>
A million credits' worth of technology on a high-tech
drift ship could leave smuggler Pik Lando set for
life—if he can live long enough to collect.

Payable in U.S. funds. No cash orders accepted. Postage & handling: $1.75 for one book, 75¢
for each additional. Maximum postage $5.50. Prices, postage and handling charges may
change without notice. Visa, Amex, MasterCard call 1-800-788-6262, ext. 1, refer to ad #519

Or, check above books	Bill my: □ Visa □ MasterCard □ Amex	
and send this order form to:		(expires)
The Berkley Publishing Group	Card#_____	
390 Murray Hill Pkwy., Dept. B		($15 minimum)
East Rutherford, NJ 07073	Signature_____	
Please allow 6 weeks for delivery.	Or enclosed is my: □ check □ money order	
Name_____	Book Total	$_____
Address_____	Postage & Handling	$_____
City_____	Applicable Sales Tax	$_____
	(NY, NJ, PA, CA, GST Can.)	
State/ZIP_____	Total Amount Due	$_____

Somewhere beyond the stars, the age of dinosaurs never ended...

ROBERT J. SAWYER

"He's already being compared to Heinlein, Clarke, and Pohl."—Quill and Quire

"Thoughtful and compelling!"—Library Journal

__FAR-SEER   0-441-22551-9/$4.99

Young Afsan the saurian is privileged, called to the distant Capital City to apprentice with Saleed the court astrologer. But Afsan's knowledge of his dinosaur nation's heavens will test his faith...and also may save his world from disaster.

__FOSSIL HUNTER
0-441-24884-5/$4.99

Toroca, son of Afsan the Far-Seer, is a geologist searching for the rare metals needed to take his species to the stars. But what he's discovered instead is an artifact that may reveal at last the true origin of a world of dinosaurs.

__FOREIGNER   0-441-00017-7/$4.99

A new age of discovery is being ushered into the saurian world. Novato, mate of Afsan, is mastering the technology of space travel, while Afsan, to overcome his blindness, is seeking the help of a new kind of doctor—one whose treatment does not center on the body...but the mind.

Payable in U.S. funds. No cash orders accepted. Postage & handling: $1.75 for one book, 75¢ for each additional. Maximum postage $5.50. Prices, postage and handling charges may change without notice. Visa, Amex, MasterCard call 1-800-788-6262, ext. 1, refer to ad # 483

Or, check above books	Bill my: ☐ Visa ☐ MasterCard ☐ Amex	
and send this order form to:		(expires)
The Berkley Publishing Group	Card#	
390 Murray Hill Pkwy., Dept. B		($15 minimum)
East Rutherford, NJ 07073	Signature	
Please allow 6 weeks for delivery.	Or enclosed is my: ☐ check ☐ money order	
Name	Book Total	$
Address	Postage & Handling	$
City	Applicable Sales Tax	$
	(NY, NJ, PA, CA, GST Can.)	
State/ZIP	Total Amount Due	$